1

# Missing

# in the

# Tropics

## By Valérie Lieko

Translated by Teia Laudouar

Editor, Valérie Lieko
Orient Bay Park
97 150 Saint-Martin
French West Indies

ISBN: 9798560669737
Cover image: (CC0) Pexels
Cover by Kouvertures.com

# Prologue

## On a deserted beach in the British Virgin Islands in the Caribbean, several years ago...

His hands were shaking, his breath so short he had to force the air up and down his knotted throat. He stopped for a second to get a hold on himself. The hole was big enough, but maybe it was safer to dig deeper. As he plowed into the sand, a flash of light ten or fifteen feet away caught his attention. It looked like moonlight reflecting on metal. He stared for a long minute but saw nothing more, only darkness, so he went back to digging and tossing, digging and tossing, glancing anxiously toward the spot every few seconds. He decided his fear must be making him see things.

His hands shook even more and his teeth started chattering when the hole was ready to be used. He had dug it where the bare sand of the beach met the trees of the coastal forest, mostly coconut palms so dizzyingly tall that some, having soared too high into the heavens, now bent back toward the ground to lie almost horizontal. Just a few nights ago, he'd amused himself by walking along one of them.

He looked around at the setting, so magnificent during the day, when the cove, carpeted with golden sand and filled with crystalline, fish-rich water reaching to the distant coral reef. No trace of human life, no dwelling to spoil its shores, not even the transient hut of a fisherman. Heaven on Earth. Never could he have imagined being here in the middle of the night doing what he was doing.

The Eden-like setting did not fit the sight of the oblong bundle wrapped in a blue tarp. The cords around it revealed the shape of a human body: the head, the trunk, the legs, the feet pointing upward. He had avoided looking at it since first driving his shovel deep into the sandy soil. Instead, he had concentrated relentlessly on his task, but now it was done, and he forced himself to turn to it. The sea occasionally caressed it with the tips of its wet fingers as he stared at it fixedly, horrified. But the minutes were ticking by – he had to go on to the next step.

He rammed the shovel into the dirt next to the makeshift grave and hurried over to the inert form, as if he were suddenly out of time. He dragged it to the edge of the hole, leaving a long trail in the sand, then he rolled and pushed it until it fell in. Although he'd never set foot in a church, he made the sign of the cross. A reflex or an instinct out of the blue. But the gesture prodded his conscience and brought tears to his eyes. He wept. He felt he should straighten the corpse, out of respect, even if the man's death was partly his own fault. But how could he have dared to molest her? He hesitated, then jumped into the hole and dignified the body by laying it flat, then he patted the head in a farewell gesture, repeating several times as if to convince himself, "It was an accident, it was an accident."

Life often hangs by a thread.

Climbing out of the grave proved difficult, and he started panicking, thinking he wasn't going to make it. How absurd to get stuck in there like an animal in a trap. When he finally managed to heave the top of his body out, he saw a pair of bare feet near his hands. He looked up, surprised but relieved.

"Oh, it's you. I thought you didn't want to help me."

"Sure I do!"

The barefooted man grabbed the shovel. He didn't like what he had to do, but there was no choice.

# Chapter One

"It is not up to the human being to save his brother from death. He can only love him."
Marie-Claire Blais, *The Day is Dark*

Yves Duchâteau looked annoyed as he filled in yet another form with the strong, sharp handwriting that mirrored his wounded childhood. He had received his share of blows before learning to avoid and then to land them. That was one of the reasons why, at twenty-seven, he had razor-sharp reflexes and the physique of a Thai boxer, slim but with supple, strong muscles.

He hated the administrative part of being a gendarme, but he conscientiously filled out each box on the form. Putting it off just made things worse; the papers piled up and made the task even more distasteful, especially since computerization here in St. Barts was at least a decade behind Paris.

He had just written the date "December 5, 2016," on a new form when his hand cramped up. He stopped writing and stretched, looking out the barred window, pushing his glasses higher on his nose to see every detail. The sea had taken on the color of anthracite, and the full moon was rippling its surface with silver stripes. The Fort Oscar brigade headquarters, where he worked, dominated Gustavia's small port, which was crowded with yachts all year round, but especially jammed now that high season had begun. The anchorage directly below, seaside of the red channel buoys, was the most popular on the island. Most of the boats were brightly lit, and he could make out the foreign flags on their mastheads: American, English, Russian, Belgian, French, Brazilian, Swedish. A broad sample from around the planet, except that the foreign nationals aboard these yachts were the richest of the rich in their own countries.

The flags were flapping harder now than in the morning. The rainy season was not quite over, and a storm was on the way. That didn't worry Yves – if it rained, he would still be warm, one of the advantages of living in the Caribbean. Even on December nights, the temperature usually stayed above sixty-eight degrees. This mild climate was what his wife Nadia appreciated most about moving to the island – she never had to worry about how to dress their two-year-old daughter, or even bother dressing her at all. She let Maya run around in her diapers or completely naked, free to move as she wished. So what if she had to mop the floor to sponge up what the little girl left behind? Freedom, a healthy environment and loving attention were the most important things they could give her.

Yves loved boats, especially sleeping aboard boats, and he envied all those yachties out there. But it was his turn to man the night shift, which promised to be as uneventful as always. Most of his friends had said "Lucky!" or "Cool!" when he announced his transfer from Normandy to Saint Barthélemy, aka St. Barts, considering it a nice secluded spot to raise their daughter without any fuss, without coats, without the colds and flus that constantly keep kids in bed in France's colder climate.

But he alone knew the reason he had battled and finagled his way into this post. Six years earlier, his half-brother François had disappeared from Tortola, an island just north of St. Barts, and Yves hoped he would reappear one day.

He and François had lived under the same roof only a few years before being separated and fostered out due to "maternal incompetence" and "paternal absence." Both of their respective fathers had abandoned them before they had blown out their second birthday candles. They stayed long enough to conceive, then they were off. Following the birth of a third child, their mother had suffered a nervous breakdown, and both boys had endured placements in one foster home after another. Neither were ever adopted.

Yves knew he might be deceiving himself, as it had been so long since François had given a sign of life. But an incident three years ago had sparked his hope.

8

His wife had accepted a dinner invitation from her friend Solange, a loquacious woman who lived for her Saturday-night parties, when a dozen guests gathered to eat Caribbean dishes and drink late into the night. Solange had excitedly narrated a story worthy of a novel. By pure coincidence, she had found the father she'd never known and had considered dead. His family hadn't heard of him since he abandoned them thirty years earlier. Forgotten by all, he was living on Terre-de-Bas Island in the Saintes archipelago in the Lesser Antilles, and Solange had chosen to visit that very island in that far-flung territory, oddly enough. A trivial detail had betrayed him – his accent. She had instantly recognized the peculiar accent, intonations, and idioms of her home town in Auvergne, traits that only another villager would possess. He turned out to be her father.

If this could happen to Solange, why not to him? His brother would resurface, or he would find him by design or by pure chance, and François would simply explain, "I wanted to put the past behind me, to be forgotten. I wanted to start from scratch."

In this crazy hope, Yves pushed his wife to take up sailing with him whenever they had a weekend free. Highly motivated, he easily obtained his boating license, and with the money they'd saved for a house in Normandy, they bought a small sailboat from an old island adventurer. They started taking off for a few days or a few weeks of sailing among the islands. During their getaways, Yves anchored wherever he had a feeling he should stop. He questioned the island residents, especially the older ones, who kept their eyes open and tended to eavesdrop. Eager to unearth a clue, he had learned to grill them, but with the innocence of a tourist fond of history and anecdotes.

Yves had kept his real motive secret even from Nadia, who figured he wanted a break from their relentlessly urban life to raise their daughter in the sunshine, to have more time together, to enjoy island life. This was partly true. He avoided telling her more because he thought she would worry. He knew that the search for truth did not always lead to happiness.

Either his brother was dead or had deliberately disappeared. But why would François want to disappear at age twenty-five? What could he have done so reprehensible as to make him run away? That still worried Yves. François was no altar boy, that was certain. Who would be after being shuffled from one foster home to another, never knowing the love of a mother and father? He'd ended up in a home for juveniles, and at fifteen, he'd made a terrible mistake, no matter how much the monitor had it coming. Fortunately, being a minor, the beating François had orchestrated with his buddies never appeared on his record. At eighteen, he moved on, but where, no one knew, and it wasn't until years later that Yves located him. But their reunion didn't last long, for François left for the Caribbean soon afterwards.

Yves would never accept that his brother had disappeared in Tortola, let alone died. How could he believe in the death of a young man who had set out on his own two feet, full of life and his dream to try his luck in the Caribbean? He had even found Love with a capital L, a woman named Sonia. He'd called her "the future woman of my life."

Yves had talked to Sonia a few weeks after his disappearance. She was still in a state of shock. She told him she had returned to their B&B early that night, leaving him in a bar with his friend Olivier Rousseau and a French tourist. She figured he would come back at dawn, as happened occasionally when they went out at night, but he didn't show up. Not that morning, or the next, or the day they were supposed to fly from Beef Island Airport to Puerto Rico, a hundred miles north. And yet, she had insisted he wanted to explore the possibilities in San Juan.

The Tortola Island authorities conducted maritime search and rescue operations, and interrogated customers at the bars he frequented, as well as some minor-league marijuana dealers. But nothing turned up; he had vanished. His brother wasn't

10

officially dead, but there was no evidence he was alive. Yves had conducted his own investigation a few weeks after the disappearance, but he was inexperienced then and may not have asked the right questions. Or maybe he hadn't wanted to find out the truth. As long as there was doubt, a person could go on hoping.

Cutting short his break, he forced his gaze back to his desk, and dove into the tedious paperwork. He'd just finished writing an 'A' in capital letters on the top of a form when his colleague Jérôme rushed in.

"Yves, listen. There's an American here, a real nutcase, goes by the name Harmony Flynt."

Jérôme pronounced "Flynt" like "Flighnt," which made him smile. He liked Jérôme Jourdan, even though he was terribly lazy. One of the negative side effects of "tropicalization." He was getting a roll around his waist and the start of a double chin, too.

"She's practically hysterical," Jourdan continued. "She claims her husband never showed up to take the last ferry, and she looked everywhere for him, but he disappeared, like magic."

Yves immediately stood up. Eight-thirty. Good timing – he welcomed a little action after hours of doing boring paperwork, and this might prove intriguing.

A disappearance...

He couldn't help feeling empathy towards the woman, and he decided her case couldn't be trusted to the gray matter between Jérôme's two ears. It couldn't possibly be a suspicious disappearance of course, since this was St. Barts. He'd probably hung around the bar too long and lay drunk somewhere. Sometimes, though, these things ended badly. A fall from a lonely trail or drowning through over-confidence were not uncommon.

# Chapter Two

"The journey is more interesting than the ending."
Peter Hamilton, *Pandora's Star*

The powerful catamaran *Voyager* linking the island of St. Martin to St. Barts abruptly reduced speed. The red buoy was in sight. The captain had cruised across the twenty-mile channel at full speed but the limit here was five knots.

It was ten in the morning, right on time. Harmony Flynt pulled away from the comfortable cocoon of her husband's broad chest and sheltering arms, then stuck her hand into her white duffel bag, far deeper than it was wide. It so perfectly fit her image of a Caribbean vacation that when she saw it the previous night at their hotel boutique, she impulsively bought it. The outlines of St. Martin and St. Barts were embroidered next to a couple of blue dolphins leaping under a yellow sun, represented by a circle with the kind of rays children draw. She hadn't been able to resist those details, clichéd as they were. They brought her completely under the spell of the tropics.

Getting exasperated, she dug through the bag, coming across hydrating cream, a new mist spray, a nearly empty bottle of Lancôme perfume, lip gloss, her American passport and a pouch of thick, flowered fabric. This old and worn-out pouch clashed with the rest of the items, so modern and in perfect shape. Trompe-l'oeil – in reality, it contained a hefty sum of money.

She shook the bag, tempted to dump it all out. What she needed was her iPhone, as she didn't want to miss a shot of their entry into the lovely port of Gustavia. On the starboard side rose the ruins of Fort Gustav III, a relic of St. Barts' remarkable past. The island had belonged to Sweden for a century before France had taken it back, and its name still paid homage to the Swedish king. She wanted to visit the historic monument perched up on the heights, rather than spend the whole day sunbathing.

Finally she found the phone, just in time to take some pictures. Despite her growing ecologist leanings, she vowed to get a flashier model the next time, maybe a yellow or pink one that would be easier to find in her purses, always so stuffed with odds and ends. Especially since it wouldn't cost her much, thanks to her cell phone subscription that provided for a brand-new model every year, even if the old one worked fine. A typical example of a consumer society: throw it away before it's worn out.

The entrance into the bay was as picturesque as a postcard – no need for Photoshop: blue skies with a few puffy white clouds, a smooth, turquoise sea, boats with multicolored sails gliding to their anchorages, low red-roofed buildings, painted white or pale colors, hugging the shores, lush green hillsides. The well-maintained shopfronts hinted at the cleanliness reigning over the island. In St. Barts, salubrity went hand-in-hand with luxury.

Harmony glanced at the young brunette woman next to her, slumped rather than seated on her metal chair. She was finally getting some color back. A reassuring pale pink was replacing the grayish-green, although drops of perspiration were still running down her thin neck. Her companion tenderly sponged them away. He looked like a golfer, with a white cap pressed down tightly on his head, orange polo shirt and cropped pants. He fanned her with a glossy magazine featuring the kind of high-end watches sold in the island's boutiques. The woman looked decidedly bedraggled. Mascara running, lipstick smeared, hair tussled. Everything meant to heighten her beauty was leagued against her, and no matter how outrageously the man pampered her, she would not disembark a starlet in this land of "People."

The crossing had been idyllic for Harmony, though. Only a short bout of mild queasiness, and once they'd passed Fourchue Island, the swell had dropped and her stomach had settled. Now

14

the sea was so silky it reminded her of Lake Michigan at certain moments. She loved to wander its banks, especially the most pristine ones far to the north. It was her home away from home, a place in the open air where her husband could accompany her. But when the weather was biting cold, she had to really push him. He preferred warm places.

Through love for her, Max Rousseau had left Florida, land of eternal sunshine, to live with her in Wisconsin, where the months of incessant cold far outnumbered the warm, a northern land where blizzards could ravage and rage. Another reason she loved him so much.

The weather here presented the opposite of what they'd just escaped from, and that made her happy. There was nowhere she'd rather be. She had combed through everything remotely interesting about these northerly islands, the French Antilles. Besides all the info she found on the internet, she'd also bought the latest Lonely Planet guide, and studied it from cover to cover. She'd also read every tourist brochure she could find in their hotel in Oyster Pond back in St. Martin.

For today's excursion, she chose a basic program: first visit some of the town's historical monuments, including the ruins of one of the forts, then have lunch at Le Côté Port restaurant. An Italian couple they'd met at the morning buffet had recommended it. The prices were a bit steep, especially for the wallets of middle-class people such as they, but on vacation, Harmony allowed herself an occasional splurge. After the meal, they planned to enjoy doing nothing at all on Shell Beach, the nicest swimming area that wasn't too far from the ferry jetty. Not knowing the island, she preferred remaining close to it.

If they had time left after the beach, they could stroll Gustavia's winding streets and do some shopping in the *Carré d'Or*, the "Golden Square," before catching the last ferry at a quarter to six. Finding a unique evening dress would be the cherry on top of the cake, and from the looks of the place as they entered Gustavia harbor, the cake was temptingly delicious!

Today, December 5, 2016, was going to be a day to remember, the kind of comfortable, leisurely day she appreciated. She'd never had the soul of an adventurer and that wasn't about to change at age thirty-two. Traveling the world with a heavy backpack or a taking a vacation full of challenging activities was not her style. The two-day sailboat cruise they were planning would be enough. If they could find a friendly skipper, that is. Maybe they would explore Fourchue Island, one of the morsels of land they'd passed between Oyster Pond and Gustavia. A private but uninhabited territory, if she remembered correctly.

She peered at her hands, then touched her face. A fine layer of salt had accumulated. She tried to clean it off with the finger wipes she'd kept from their New York-Sint-Maarten flight. She smiled, thinking of their long layover in the Big Apple. While waiting, a young, good-looking Englishman had sat next to her and complimented her on her outfit, a fuchsia pantsuit that gave her a vacation look. Flirtatious and clever, the English traveler had waited for Max to leave to search for a French newspaper before hitting on her, saying how beautiful she was. His eyes shone with desire. She had felt flattered, of course, and her ever shaky self-confidence got a boost, but she responded with cool indifference – she had Max, and needed no one else.

The salty taste went from her lips to her throat, and now she felt intensely thirsty. Where was that solicitous crewmember, now that she wanted him? The young man with coppery-brown skin had gone by several times with a full tray of tropical fruit juices. His method amazed her. Even when the boat rolled or pitched, he never let a drop spill. The perfect job for a high-wire performer or a clown in baggy clothes who pretends to be terribly clumsy and constantly trips but never spills the bucket of water he carries on his head.

Max had downed a cup of juice in one gulp, then carefully tossed the cup into a trashcan fixed to the deck. His day would have been ruined if it had ended up in the ocean. It seemed innate in him to want to protect the environment and recycle everything that could possibly be recycled. He took care of all back at home in Milwaukee. A Frenchman who had emigrated to the United States, he'd persuaded Harmony, the incarnation of an American city girl, to dig up some grass and put in a vegetable garden. And their vegetables were excellent, especially when he cooked them. A great chef, a French chef – who wouldn't dream of a husband who did all the cooking, grocery shopping, even the dishes? He liberated her from tasks she hated because, being the woman, it was generally expected she do them each and every day.

She admired his sense of organization, too. In fact, they were on this ferry right now thanks to him, as Max had checked ahead of time and learned they needed visas to cross from St. Martin to St. Barts. A Colombian couple hadn't been allowed to board the ferry in Oyster Pond because they didn't know about the visas. The ticket-seller had explained to the couple in impeccable Spanish that St. Barts was part of France, of course, but not quite French, as it was an "overseas collective territory."

Harmony had later described the uproarious scene to Max, who missed it because he'd gone ahead to find the best spot on the boat for them.

"They should have checked into all the details in order to anticipate the unexpected, like you do," Harmony had whispered in Max's ear before giving him a loud kiss on the cheek to thank him.

Harmony hadn't taken a glass of juice from the crewman. His constant passing and urging her to drink had made her uncomfortable, especially when, as happened several times, he placed himself right in front of her and gazed at her with his golden-brown eyes. She couldn't help noticing his hard torso, molded by the royal blue t-shirt with the ferry-line's logo, a white buoy circling a tiller, and the way he patted his forehead with a bandana taken from the pocket of his khaki bermudas, while looking her way. And his calves were worthy of a high-level athlete.

The young man's insistent stare had made her blush. She was wearing a light dress with a plunging neckline that attracted attention, and it was so tightly belted at the waist it flapped up with every gust of wind, showing the top of her thighs. She worried that the breeze would reveal her lacy, high-cut black panties, which she'd put on at the last minute, wanting to be sexy from head to foot. After all, she was on vacation! She didn't want to see or feel the lackluster underwear she wore to work.

But next time, she would opt for shorts, something more adapted to this kind of crossing. Had she also wanted to project the starlet look, unconsciously? Especially the wide-brimmed pink hat and red Michaël Kors sunglasses – glamorous but inappropriate. The hat had almost gone overboard in a gust of wind, but Max had caught it as it whirled away.

Her husband, her eternally devoted chevalier. So elegant in his white shirt and light-gray linen bermudas. She was nestled up close to him, with her back against the metal railing of the upper bridge. He'd chosen the ideal spot in the stern, the wind in their faces, and from there, they could see an incredible sight, huge banks of flying fish that seemed to be chasing them. On the horizon, they could make out the shapes of several islands, and because she didn't know their names, they were tinted with mystery, an invitation to new voyages and strange discoveries.

An idyllic crossing. They had laughed when some waves broke and sprayed the decks, accompanied by cries of alarm from some travelers. The spectacle had helped Harmony pretend not to notice the deckhand's keen glances. How old was he? No more than twenty-four or twenty-five. Was it the impertinence of youth or the sensuous tropical atmosphere that gave permission to men to dare any and all methods of seduction, even when a woman was cheek to cheek with her companion?

Harmony adored being in her husband's strong arms covered with black hair, as was much of his torso. A real male. The kind she'd always dreamed about: protective and virile, with a sturdy character but hopelessly in love with her. She'd had to wait a long time for him to enter her life. It wasn't until she was thirty, a sensitive number, a number that makes a woman get uneasy. A clock starts to tick in her head and in her womb. A time bomb. For Harmony, turning thirty had caused strange feelings. Every time a girlfriend started bubbling about getting engaged or pregnant, she reacted half-heartedly, forcing a smile, but inside, that uneasy feeling deepened. At every new announcement, blind jealousy mixed with her joy, because she didn't get to feel that same happiness for herself.

And then Max entered her life. A sunny spell began, with no shadow of a cloud. Or barely a shadow – there had been tiny doubts, a passing suspicion or two, but nothing serious or important. At least, that's what she hoped, and still believed. Many long weeks had passed since wondering about that one episode.

Why did her thoughts return to such bad memories when the place she found herself in was so perfect? She pulled her mind away from them. They had made the crossing safely, and the docks separating them from Gustavia were right in front of them.

Their vacation had only just begun.

# Chapter Three

"Being suspicious every second guarantees survival…"
Edward Bunker, *No Beast So Fierce*

Harmony seemed to be looking at the signs for the luxury stores you could glimpse beyond the docks. Max wanted her to pamper herself and buy something classy in one of them. He was such an ideal partner, even if now and then a cloud veiled his glow. One of those clouds was what she was thinking about…

It was a rainy day six months earlier.

Max went into the garden without his iPhone, which was highly unusual. Like many people in this high-tech, digital century, he was rarely without his smartphone. But heavy rains had fallen that night and he was anxious to check on the bird feeder and his flowerbeds, and see how his tomato plants were doing in the hothouse. Max loved his garden. She'd caught him talking to the plants more than once. He also loved animals and griped about their plight, to the point she would laughingly accuse him of loving them more than people, which he never denied. This tender side of his personality made her love him all the more.

He was out tending his tomato plants when his phone started vibrating then skidding around the coffee table like an animal searching for a way out of hostile territory. A number with the 305 Miami area code and the name "Sonia" appeared on the lit-up screen. Harmony was lying on the couch reading, but she grabbed the phone and ran out to the hothouse, which Max had built in the sunniest spot in the garden. Rainwater was still dripping off the big glass structure.

She handed him the still-ringing phone. When he saw the caller's name, his eyes narrowed in a frown. He didn't answer.

"Wrong number again," he said in an indifferent tone.

A strange response, so nonchalant, and Harmony knew a "wrong number" wouldn't show up on the screen with a name and number, like a contact. Her old fears of betrayal, infidelity and lies, had swept over her. She'd thought all that was behind her, but the fear and anguish became uncontrollable – her mind focused on nothing but that. So whenever he left his phone at home to go jogging, she went through its data, scrolled through all his contacts from A to Z and checked his incoming and outgoing calls.

One day, a cramp in his calf forced Max to cut short his run and come home early. Harmony didn't hear the kitchen door open and he caught her staring at the screen of his phone, her fingers navigating between apps. But Harmony had prepared for such a situation. With a neutral voice, she brought out her excuse: she was looking for the number of that plumber who'd fixed their shower without cheating them, and only Max had recorded his name and number. Harmony had an irritating tendency to throw away any and all commercial brochures in her mania to keep their place tidy, so she'd tossed out his flyer. And now she had to find his phone number to give it to her co-worker Dorothy, whose kitchen sink was stubbornly plugged. All of this was true, lending the excuse credibility.

As soon as his leg cramp eased up, Max took his phone and found the plumber's number, without ever – at least she hoped – discovering her maneuver.

By chance, or through her guardian angel's intercession, they decided to go to a nearby theater that evening to see the Ang Lee's *Life of Pi*, part of an Indian culture celebration around Milwaukee. They kept up the Indian theme by dining afterwards at the Maharaja restaurant. A marvellous, exotic evening out. The film was extremely moving, and their meal was delicious, serving to heighten all their feelings. They were serene, intimate, and in love, and from that evening on, her fears subsided. She felt safe again – he was the man of her life. Max had nothing to hide, and she felt ridiculous she had suspected him, especially since the name "Sonia" never resurfaced. His contacts consisted solely of useful connections: doctors, plumbers, pizza places, gyms, taxi services, and some neighbors who took care of their dog for them when they needed it.

She was glad to stop spying on him, as she had sensed it was becoming unhealthy. She owed it to him to give him her trust, completely. If not, what did their engagement and their marriage mean?

Marriage with Max was everything she'd ever dreamed of, and now here they were in the Caribbean! She looked at him and saw how happy he was. He loved her with passion and devotion. She felt so peaceful now they lived together, and she could count their quarrels on the fingers of one hand, and even those were minor disagreements, like on the choice of a restaurant or a hotel for a weekend getaway. No loud arguments, no violent language. Except once, she remembered, concerning her brother. Max had wanted to hear nothing more about him, but even though she knew he was right, it was painful to burn her bridges with her own brother.

They'd never gone to bed angry with each other. That was one of Max's notions, and the rule had helped keep their two-year relationship happy and balanced.

Sometimes, Harmony wished they invited friends over more often or accepted invitations to dinner with neighbors, but Max didn't much care for that. He was polite and helpful to people, but wanted nothing more from them. Simple happiness was what he appreciated – and for him, that meant living their lives oriented exclusively around each other.

# Chapter Four

"You find more certainty in the face than in the words."
Massa Makan Diabaté, *A Hungry Hyena*


Max looked forward to exploring Gustavia, and they would soon feel the ground under their feet again. He took Harmony's hand as they headed to the metal stairway to the lower bridge. He loved taking little pains with his wife. Hadn't he checked the weather report to make sure the weather would be fine today? The temperature had risen dramatically only an hour into the crossing, but at least it was sunny, and the sea was calm. The crossing only took forty-five minutes, even less on the return trip, but these waters could be choppy, especially in December. Harmony tended to get queasy in a car or bus and especially so on a boat. She'd already proved that on the ferry between Milwaukee and Muskegon on the eastern side of Lake Michigan. He would have been annoyed if the sea had been rough, as he preferred taking their excursion to St. Barts this day.

He'd also reserved their round-trip tickets the night before. After almost two years together, he knew his wife's little habits and vicissitudes. His Princess. She hated unexpected incidents that should have been expected, and she wouldn't have tolerated being told they couldn't embark, and have to return to the hotel like hapless children punished by staying in during recess.

Click, click, click, click, click…

With her iPhone in burst mode, Harmony continued taking photos of their arrival in Gustavia. This was one of their minor discords. Max preferred to live fully in the moment, seeing things with his own eyes rather than fussing with a camera or phone. Discovering St. Barts was one of his wife's top priorities and she wasn't going to lose a single crumb of it. They weren't going to spend the night, though. Any type of lodging there was far more expensive than in St. Martin, and at this time of year, it was astronomical, so sleeping in St. Barts would have been "a saber thrust to their budget" in his wife's exact words. He liked teasing her about being a little Scrooge. And they could console themselves with having a panoramic view of St. Barts from their hotel balcony back in St. Martin.

Harmony took a selfie, then cuddled up to Max with a brilliant smile to try and immortalize their faces, cheek to cheek. She might have a lot of hang-ups, but not about her teeth. She had a beautiful smile, with sound, perfectly aligned teeth, although she'd recently had recourse to whitening sessions because she drank too much coffee.

Pretty smile or not, Max didn't give her time to snap the picture. He pulled away, irritated.

"No, not my face! How many times do I have to remind you? Just take my lips, if you want. My lips are always kissable, but not the rest."

She didn't insist, and his aggravation quickly subsided. She knew he had a horror of having his face immortalized in a photo, but she'd tried it anyway to see if he'd changed his mind. He always had an excuse. His eyes were too tired, his nose too long or his hair was mussy, something or other. She sometimes laughed at him, saying he was like a coquettish girl who refused to be photographed without her makeup.

She would never frame his portrait and set it on her desk at work, not if he could help it. Max wasn't ashamed of his looks though. He had a strong face, square jaw and thick black hair with only a few gray strands around his temples, hardly noticeable. He might not have that striking beauty some men possessed, the kind that made women fall head over heels, but he had magnificent eyes. Eyes as blue as the skies of Florida, where it all had started. Eyes that had made his future wife take a second look, in that hotel in Miami, the city that had become their fetish place, the departure point of their idyll. As soon as they heard that name, their eyes lit up. Miami served as the founding myth all couples needed – a story to which the lovers could always come back to if they wavered.

She'd been so alone in Miami, or almost. Her brother was there, but that didn't count. He no longer counted. Max had been right to get her to stop all that – it was her brother who had made her spiral down into depression, or that's what he thought.

The boat started to maneuver toward the dock, then tied up. They kissed to mark the event.

# Chapter Five

"The fantasy fulfilled, the dream is lost."
Elisabeth Carli

Halfway down the metal staircase, Max suddenly felt anxious, and tightened his hold on his wife's hand. It was so important that nothing went wrong on this trip he'd planned so carefully three months ago…

After figuring out the dates and reserving the flights, he printed the e-tickets and a map of the Antilles with arrows in black marker pen pointing to St. Barts and St. Martin. He slipped the papers into an envelope, then put that into a mauve box. His wife loved every shade of violet, a color that featured in the décor of their home – dishware, paintings, towels – and especially in their bedroom, whose walls were painted entirely in lilac. Harmony was such a romantic.

He'd always had a penchant for fragile, sensitive women like her. His dream of having a fusional relationship was coming true, and too bad if the shrinks thought it was pathological. Always on the ready to shield her, to surround her with love, he thought that any neglect on his part could make her wilt away, and it was in fact in this state he'd found her in the Miami hotel. A fading flower, a woman on the edge of severe depression. He was proud to be able to protect her, and loved her all the more for it. He hadn't been able to protect his mother from his stepfather's cruelty, so he was grateful he could defend his wife and shower her with generosity.

He set the table for breakfast on the veranda at the back of the house. Here, they could prolong their summer habits, and it was warm even now, early morning in mid-September. She liked to look at the flower garden before going to work. To mark the occasion, he'd brought out the porcelain service they had bought as their sole wedding gift. The table was too splendid for a weekday, but he wanted to surprise her.

When she woke up, she discovered pancakes and grilled toast, fruit salad and scrambled eggs. To heighten the mystery, the mauve box sat on her plate. Harmony opened it impatiently, without a clue what it could hold. On her birthday a month earlier, he'd taken her out to dinner at Carnevor, a restaurant on Milwaukee's east side, and given her a gold necklace with a topaz, so she guessed it wasn't jewelry, especially since their income had shrunk when he decided to take a career break after their whirlwind romance and marriage.

Inside the box, Harmony discovered the envelope, and with unusual eagerness, she ripped it open, even though Max had put a letter opener on the table for her. He knew her mania for opening her mail carefully – she was an accountant to the tips of her fingers.

He was delighted when her eyes widened and she cried out, "A trip to the Caribbean – how crazy!"

Filled with emotion, he said, "That's how crazy I am about you."

Forgetting the pancakes and the time, they started kissing, and ended up making love in their living room. Much later, she drove to her office in her glass tower downtown. That evening, she told him how, before getting out of her car, she had smoothed her blond hair into a tight bun, thinking that a more severe hairdo would hide any trace of their lovemaking. She also told him how her colleagues had commented on how strangely radiant she was for someone who'd gotten to work so late.

She never told them about their incredible trip, explaining that she didn't want to make them jealous. He'd never met any of them. That didn't bother him, as he preferred keeping their life private. His wife's work relationships remained purely professional in her job at Miller Brewing Company, Milwaukee's oldest brewery. She had no attachments yet, having only recently moved to this city in southeast Michigan after getting fired from her job in Chicago. So they could easily go live somewhere else. Max had never even heard of Milwaukee before setting down his bags there to be with her. They had both wanted to radically change their lives, and he never regretted leaving everything behind.

Like in Chicago, Harmony had no intimate friends in Milwaukee. Not at work, not in the neighborhood, not at her fitness club. From things she said about the feminine sex, Max had come to realize she didn't trust women friends. The only close friendship she had was with Shirley Connors, whom she'd known from adolescence, but they saw each other only once a year. Shirley had moved to the West Coast, and their last meeting had been cancelled because Max was just recovering from a bad bout of the flu and wasn't well enough to go with her. Harmony had felt obligated to stay with him. Shirley was disappointed, of course. She wanted to meet her friend's new husband.

There had been a silver lining to missing out on that visit. Harmony hadn't been sick even one day in 2016, so she had accrued a lot of paid sick days to add to her annual two-week vacation. A tropical retreat in mid-winter was the perfect opportunity. Max thought it was essential for his wife to recharge her batteries. He didn't really need it, with this break from the stressful restaurant work. After having spent six years as head chef in the same hotel in Miami, he could now realize an ambition he had nursed since he was a teenager: writing a novel. He had started it over a year ago, but he didn't want to show it to anyone until it was complete. Harmony was thrilled with his project. Plus, he was very present in her daily life, and she needed that.

Harmony had made a fuss about the cost of an exotic Caribbean vacation. Numbers, accounts, balancing the budget – an occupational hazard that entered her daily life too often. She had to forget all that. So he reassured her by repeatedly saying they had enough savings to last several months without either of them working. At the worst, he would go back to the pots and

31

pans a little earlier than planned. With his brilliant resume – solid experience and a diploma from L'école Ferrandi, a top culinary school in France – he had no worries about getting hired.

They reached the bottom of the ferry's metal gangway. Many of the passengers had already taken the short, narrow passage to the dock, and it was Harmony's turn now. The boat tipped as she was about to step off, and without thinking, she grabbed a hand held out to help her. It was the deckhand who had handed out drinks during the crossing. Max noticed that when their eyes met, she immediately looked away and let his hand drop, and when she looked back at him, her cheeks were on fire. Curious.

Another line awaited them for the identity check, more of a formality than anything. No questioning or going through their luggage. They weren't border police, as was usually the case; several French police were there instead, looking over people's passports with a rather bored air. Harmony and Max went through the checkpoint, then joined the crowd pushing its way into the ferry terminal's narrow parking area, jammed with tourists ready to charge the island and its myths.

They eyed each other with a wink and smile. They'd officially touched ground in St. Barts, a first for both of them. Max knew she was bursting with impatience, as this foreign territory stimulated all her fantasies. How would she feel once they were fulfilled? Ecstatic, merely satisfied, or disappointed?

# Chapter Six

"Between young, amiable women, friendship is but a truce."

Nicolas Massias, *Relationship Between Nature and Man (Rapport de la nature à l'homme)*

Tires screeching, a taxi pulled up in front of Harmony and Max. The driver, a young redhead, peered at the crowd from behind the wheel of his white Renault Clio. He was hoping to make several runs in record time. People started pressing around them, eager to grab the taxi if they showed the slightest hesitation. They hadn't expected such commotion, even in the capital – so many passengers suddenly flooding in all at once challenged the infrastructure of this tiny French territory.

The taxi-driver gave them a tight smile, lit up a cigarette and told them to hurry and decide, then shouted to the rest of the crowd that he'd be right back. He had to keep up a fast pace in the high season to make ends meet the rest of the year. The more rides, the more riches, and ferry arrivals were the ripest opportunities of all.

For fear of being left without a ride, Harmony and Max jumped into the back seat.

"To the Fort, please," Max told the driver.

A few minutes later, the driver charged up a steep road then came to a halt at the fort's main entrance.

"That'll be twenty dollars, please."

"That's certainly a high rate!" Max exclaimed, but he dug into his pocket to get his wallet.

"You're in St. Barts, sir," the driver said with a grin, pocketing the bill. "Life is expensive here, and we have to eat and pay for a roof, too."

Harmony sat and stared at the driver before getting out, slamming the door behind her to show her discontent. She suspected a scam of some kind, and she was fuming. It was ridiculous – they could have easily walked that distance.

Wasting time with complainers seemed to irritate the taxi-driver, who lit another cigarette and put the car in gear, grumbling, "Cheapskates have no business coming to *Sen Bart*. They should stick to Santo Domingo, and their 'All-Inclusive' hotels with the plastic ID bracelets."

Max laughed at first, but took pity and stifled it at the sight of his wife's baffled look. Spending money that way enraged her, given her sense of economy. But she ended up laughing too – they'd just been had, like in the TV reports. Tourists get fleeced the minute they get out of their buses, and they're an easy mark with their shorts and sneakers, cameras and water bottles and sunburned noses. All the same, she hadn't figured they would fall victim that easily. Lesson learned: always ask the price of a trip before climbing into a taxi, even if a restless crowd is pushing at you from behind.

But they weren't at the end of their surprises. A white electric gate barred the entrance to the fort, and an official sign of the French Republic indicated a gendarmerie. Max turned around to go back to town, but out of curiosity Harmony tried the speaker phone, and after a few seconds, a deep-voiced man started talking in French, confirming the fort also housed the gendarmes' station. He said it was open at certain times – not during lunch or siesta time of course – and one of the lower-grade officers even acted as guide, but unfortunately for them, that wasn't the case today. Perhaps Madame had intended to visit the Fort Karl ruins, and not Fort Oscar? Or Fort Gustav, by the Light House, which has interesting ramparts, a wood-burning oven and so on?

Harmony suspected that the reason the gendarmes checking IDs at the port looked so bored was because part of their job was to act as tourist guide. She was disappointed, but took some photos through the bars of the gate anyway. The modern military building had an austere look that contrasted with the island's laid-back ambiance.

"Can we get going?" Max said.

She took out the map of St. Barts she'd bought before taking the ferry at Oyster Pond. In looking at the blown-up plan of Gustavia, she started to get her bearings and a sense of the town's size and layout. Gustavia was built around the port, which adopted the contours of a natural inlet. The urban area covered no more than a square mile or so. She saw they could have avoided the useless taxi ride. Oh well, they were on vacation, and she should welcome any little adventures they could talk and joke about later.

"Honey, there's a spot close by where we can work our neurons a bit – the Town Hall, where supposedly there's also a museum. Assuming they didn't install a school or hospital in its place this time."

The descent was steep, and she could see why the taxi driver had started up it with such speed. A monstrous green iguana startled her when some hens chased it out of the hibiscus bushes bordering the lane. It scuttled under a garden fence so fast she didn't have time to immortalize it in a photo.

She took Max's arm to help her down the lane. Her platform heels weren't easy to walk in, and she started regretting that she hadn't worn more sensible shoes. They made it down to the harbor and strolled along the waterfront toward the point, reaching an imposing building buttressed with columns. Flags of Saint Barthelemy, France, Sweden and the European Union waved softly in the breeze. Harmony liked the gardens surrounding the museum and Town Hall. Children were laughing and playing around some highly original statues there – a leaping frog, an elephant balancing on a ball. The whole place attracted her, but she sensed that Max was uninterested, and it was only when she read the explanatory signs planted in front of the iron statues that he came around.

The museum visit was enriching but short. Harmony recognized the young couple who had sat next to them on the crossing. The man's arm around the woman, they were contemplating a replica of a Spanish galleon, the same awed expression on both their faces. The pretty brunette had gotten her color back, revealing a bronze tint. She'd also redone her makeup and disciplined her wavy hair. With an unusual rush of sociability, Harmony surprised herself by going up and asking if she was feeling better, and hoping that all trace of seasickness had passed. She added that she had suffered through the unhappy experience of its lasting many long hours, even after getting back on terra firma.

The woman responded with a polite but cold "yes" and "thanks," then immediately looked away, and still encircled by her husband's arm, wandered over to a glass case holding antique navigation instruments. It was obvious she didn't want anyone bringing up her discomfiture, or taking advantage of a chance opening to get acquainted. And yet holiday trips, especially in the tropics, usually encouraged that very thing.

Harmony was vexed by their attitude. That type of reaction always hurt her, and she knew the scene would play over and over in her head for hours, and she would feel like the victim of a concerted attack. She would question her personality – did she repel people? She couldn't help feeling humiliated when that kind of thing happened, no matter how much Max tried to reason with her, explaining with his characteristic frankness that a lot of people were jerks by nature, and they were the ones who had the problem. For a long time, she had felt she was different from everyone else. As a teenager, her sensitivity was so exaggerated she had a hard time making friends. She would observe the other girls from the shelter of her protective bubble, listening to them without taking part in their conversations, which she considered pointless. And after high school, she had kept no contact with her old schoolmates.

The only friendship that had survived from those days was with Shirley Connors, but they hadn't been classmates. The way they'd met was far more dramatic: Harmony was in the hospital emergency room. Blood stained her pink turtleneck sweater, which a nurse had cut open so she could examine her wounds. Mute, Harmony lay on a bed looking at her hands, covered with dried blood, wondering where it came from. Shirley lay in the bed next to hers, suffering through a bad attack of asthma. She was inhaling a bronchodilator from inside a head mask, and her face was enveloped in artificial fog. She stared at Harmony with her black eyes, terrorized by the sight of the blood, but then their eyes met, and her fear melted. A friendship was born, a true one.

Not like the one Harmony had with her college friend Megan Sutton, a woman who betrayed her.

Megan died about ten years ago, but she didn't feel any sadness or even remorse for having wished her dead not long before it had actually happened.

But that was long ago; today she would forget the past, refuse feeling responsible for that odious woman's rebuff, and simply enjoy a perfect day with her husband Max. She grabbed his hand to connect to the present, the only time that counted.

# Chapter Seven

"Avoid serious subjects at the beginning of a meal. They can stagnate and cause clouds of uneasiness to settle, clouds that are very difficult to chase away." *Yves Beauchemin*


Max wasn't interested in prolonging their museum visit. Like a spoiled child, he pointed at his flat stomach and made circles with his hand over it – his way of letting her know he was dying of hunger. Despite their copious breakfast buffet, including bacon, eggs and sausages, his stomach was already crying famine. They had gotten up at six to be among the first served; that way, they had time to digest before taking the boat. But it was almost noon, time to have lunch.

"Okay, darling, I get it," Harmony said. "We'll go eat, but this time we're walking. Someone recommended a place called Restaurant Côté Port, and it isn't far. You can see it on the map. if you want."

"At your orders, Princess! We're off."

Max was irritable when he was hungry, so to avoid being disagreeable, he didn't talk much. They left the La Pointe neighborhood without exploring any more, even though she wanted to hunt up some post cards for her mother, Shirley, and the Clarks. She could do it after lunch. Church bells started ringing, and kept up for a long time. There must have been a funeral nearby. Bells always made Harmony think of the green countryside where her mother used to bring her and her brother to escape the city, images contrasting with what was now around them: yachts, luxury cars, turquoise seas.

With the sun at its zenith and shadows reduced to a minimum, the sun's rays hit them like invisible burning arrows. The tradewinds, usually blowing at this time of year, had decided to pause at the worst moment, and Harmony said she was glad she had her wide-brimmed hat. Her starlet look was actually serving a purpose.

Max suddenly stopped. His phone was vibrating against his thigh. He pulled it from his deep pocket, the one that closed with Velcro. Fashion had glommed onto this kind of useful military gadget, which Max liked because he could dispense with wearing a fanny pack, or worse, one of those French "manbags," which they both considered too girlish. But like her purse, his pockets could become major catchalls. She always checked them before washing his clothes, except that one time this summer, when his passport went through the wash cycle. Max had flown into a rage – the first time Harmony had seen him like that. But he was angry at himself, not at her. He'd gone to the bank to close an account that day, and he'd forgotten to take it out of his pocket before throwing the pants in the laundry before going to bed. She was so upset she had cried about it. He'd gone through a lot of rigmarole to renew it, even making a trip to the French embassy.

Max read a text message, then immediately erased it. As he did every time he received a message, he took care to tell her what it was about. Since he'd started doing that, there had been no more misunderstandings, no suspicions on her side. Harmony wasn't jealous, but cell phones were a means to create worry, and the day he surprised her going through his, he only pretended to believe her excuse about the plumber's number.

"It's the local telephone operator welcoming me to St. Barts," he told her in a detached voice, hoping to avoid any ambiguity. "We're really getting policed with our cell phones. They always know where to find us!"

He looked directly into her eyes and was reassured to see her relaxed, without a hint of any particular emotion. In any case, he was sure she would never find anything compromising. He loved her and he wanted her to never again doubt him, at least not his love.

Harmony also got out her iPhone, which she miraculously found in the first pocket she searched in her purse. Its main purpose for her while on vacation was to take photos or videos, and she now tried to film a cattle egret on the emerald green hillside they were walking past, but the white bird with the long, narrow feet flew off before she could click on "film."

She looked disappointed, but consoled herself by declaring, "The bird's right – it's better to distrust humans, even a pretty blond with an angelic expression."

She smiled at her joke, and looked back at him. He was still standing in the same spot, staring at her without really seeing her. He tried to smile. Microscopic faucets seemed to suddenly open under his skin and pearls of sweat collected on his forehead.

"What's wrong? Your face is so pale."

"I don't feel well. Too hot, too hungry."

She tried to help him by taking the beach bag, but he refused. Even when feeling extremely ill, it wasn't his habit to let her carry anything. He would remain a gentleman in all circumstances and too bad if he suffered. He'd just lied to her, but it was only a half-lie. Of course he was hot and hungry, but it was the message causing the problem. It hadn't come from a local provider. One like it had been sent to him at Oyster Pond when he got on the ferry. St. Martin was odd in how it had both French and Dutch providers, so as you moved around, even from one side of the street to another, you switched operators, and they sent you welcome messages. This text had nothing to do with that, though. It was an acronym of four letters and four periods: "M.I.T.T."

Having reached Rue Jeanne d'Arc, they heard a woman behind them calling to someone named Arthur. The second time they heard it, she turned around by reflex. She made out the figure of a rather short woman, who dove into a lane perpendicular to the one they were on, and disappeared. No one was following them. Probably a mother running after her kid.

Although he was feeling worse and worse, Max kept walking. When he was a teenager, he'd endured dozens of these dizzy spells, which doctors diagnosed as vasovagal syncope. At the sight of blood, or after sustained effort in high heat, or intense emotions, his vision suddenly blurred, his mind went blank, his legs got shaky and he collapsed, his face chalky white. Sometimes, his lips turned blue. People who didn't know him would panic and call an ambulance. But his friends knew what to do, as did the guards in juvenile hall: splash cool water on his head and elevate his legs until they were vertical. He would gradually come back to normal, encircled by worried faces.

Around the age of twenty-one, the fits seemed to disappear, most likely because he'd reached an end to growth spurts. But by then it was too late. One of these attacks had prevented him from realizing a dream – the stress of striving after it had been too much. He hadn't been able to suppress a fainting attack at a crucial moment, and that failure had set off a series of events, a prime example of the domino effect. His life would have probably turned out very differently otherwise.

He thought he'd finally found stability with his wife, but he always feared everything was going to unravel, and that he was living on borrowed time. He knew that time was running out.

Harmony fished her water-mister out of her purse. She'd bought it at the airport in New York, saying it might come in handy. She sprayed his face as if he were a wilted plant, and then tried to pull the beach bag from his hand again, but he obstinately refused, keeping an even tighter grip on the braided leather handles. He knew he was a hardhead, but she wouldn't be changing him any time soon.

They finally reached the Côté Port. Max felt completely exhausted, like he'd walked across a desert. A server stood under the awnings, an Asian woman with long black hair in a ponytail and a nametag displaying "Tania Charbonnier" above a smiley face. She came forward to greet them.

"Hi. You're here for lunch?"

"Yes, please," Harmony replied. "But can we be served quickly? My husband isn't feeling well."

"It's pretty quick if you order the daily special."

Out of the fog of his queasiness, Max noticed the server gazing at him as if trying to place him, but he dismissed it – his chalky face was enough to attract anyone's curiosity.

Despite her very short, very tight red skirt, the server quickly walked them through the restaurant over to the terrace, where a table had just been vacated. She whipped out a cloth and wiped it off before seating them. The terrace was part of the quay, and Harmony commented that it would take only one step to board a boat. At that moment, a luxury yacht gently bumped against the dock and tied up. Its hull was so shiny it was obvious someone spent long hours polishing it, day and night. All the crewmembers were male, and all handsome or rendered handsome by their deep tans, and seemingly chosen for the physical characteristic of having thick, silky light-brown hair. They wore black polo shirts with a golden line around the collar, with the name of the boat, "Evidencia," embroidered on the pocket, clearly showing this was a private crew.

"It makes me want to go aboard," Harmony said. "That boat deserves a post card of its own!"

Click, click, click.

Harmony took several pictures of the yacht. Max needed to find a skipper for their mini cruise, too. She could already see herself side by side with her darling, gazing at the ocean and the outlines of undiscovered islands. Milwaukee and the stress of her job was receding by leaps and bounds. She turned to Max, who was no better. Before even thinking of taking that boat trip, he would have to get over this. She thought the sunny terrace was splendid, facing the docks like this, but it wasn't having the same effect on him. The Jimmy Buffet song was too upbeat, the sun too glaring. There wasn't a breath of air and the heat was becoming unbearable.

"I feel like I'm in an oven, deprived of oxygen," he groaned.

Harmony got up and found the server, who set up a table for them inside with a high-speed fan above it. When she took off her hat, the cool air made her silky blonde hair blow into her face but Max started to breathe easier.

A few minutes later, Tania came back with a blackboard listing the menu items and set it against a wooden post. The specials were written in a round hand, like a French grade-school teacher's: Caesar Salad with Shrimp, Steak and Fries or Cheese Pizza. They both chose the salad. The mere thought of fries was sickening. The shrimp made Max hesitate, as he was apprehensive about seafood. He had helped reanimate a colleague one day, and besides…Sonia Marques had almost died from an allergy to shellfish, as even one bite could kill her. Maybe it would have better for him if she had died that day. Such hard words scared him. He thought about the domino effect again. If the paramedic hadn't managed to get the rubber tube into her trachea, his life would have been simple, smooth. Clear sailing. Nothing but him and Harmony.

"What do you want to drink?" she asked him.

"Plain water, Princess. But enjoy yourself – have a bottle of rosé."

"A bottle? Will you have a glass with me?" she said, surprised he would suggest that large a quantity.

"Yes, it's nice and cold. I hope this attack will pass after I have something to eat."

"You'll feel much better when we dive into the ocean, and this will all become a bad memory," she murmured, stroking his hand.

Tania came back with a champagne bucket. The sight of the bottle of wine plunged into the crushed ice instantly gave people a feeling of well-being. As she opened the bottle of rosé, Tania discreetly observed the couple. They'd awoken her curiosity as soon as they entered, especially the man. She wondered why. She was usually content to concentrate on serving, to be polite and efficient but to maintain a certain distance. She despised servers with too familiar a manner, who cracked stupid jokes to make people feel relaxed, or worse, servers who were so unctuous it was obvious they were merely laying it on thick to get a bigger tip.

It was after one, and the busiest part of the service was over. She never showed her fatigue to the clients, however. They saw only an energetic woman with a cheerful yet serious face. She was attached to her job and her life in the islands, especially this island.

As soon as she left the table, Max scooped out a handful of ice and rubbed his face and neck with it. The cold revived him. The server reminded him of someone; but to him, most all pretty Asian women resembled each other. Slender, firm bodies, long black hair, smooth golden-brown skin. And he figured that all blue-eyed blonde women must appear identical to Asian men.

Their salads were set on the table a few minutes later. Max remained mute, abstracted, a manner not at all normal for him, usually so talkative, who always had the right word or expression to make his wife laugh. Harmony didn't try to start a conversation, but let him eat in silence and have time to recover.

# Chapter Eight

"That famous 'love at first sight' we make such a big fuss about is but the shock of cymbals clanging together. The simple percussion of two urgent availabilities."
Alexandre Millon, *Mer calme à peu agitée*


His giddiness started to fade when he was halfway through his salad, which he ate but hardly tasted, too occupied looking back at his life, from infancy to childhood, adolescence and adulthood. The life of a nomad. Except that instead of moving around within a caravan or social group, he had been shifted from one foster family to another, from one 'less bad' to another, until ending up in an institution for juveniles. At eighteen, he reached the age of majority and left France.

His path became smoother after moving to Miami, but he was always on the alert. He dreaded having to abandon everything, to slam the door at any moment. And it seemed that Sonia Marques was always mixed up in it. Giving in, he worked every angle to snag a hotel receptionist position for her a year after he was hired as head chef. But her salary didn't suffice; she never had enough, and she often complained to him when things got tough. He soon understood he had to lie down and put up with it. If he gave her cash, she gave him peace. They were occasional lovers when neither of them had anyone else in their sights, but the initial passion had fizzled out. Back when Sonia believed he was ambitious, ready to grab any chance to succeed, she would use all her prowess in bed, leaving him dizzy with pleasure. But he had disappointed her, content to be a chef.

And then he married Harmony. He finally found stability, and he thought moving to Wisconsin would serve to turn the page once and for all on his past. But it had caught up with him. Harmony...the woman he considered the love of his life, his one true love. They could have spent so many happy days together until death finally parted them. Those words in their wedding ceremony suddenly took on all their sense. But was it only the Grim Reaper who could break the vicious cycle he was trapped in?

He meticulously chewed each lettuce leaf and crouton. His fainting attack was a good pretext for not being in a state to start talking with her. Instead, he recalled how they met.

Miami, November 2014. Harmony didn't remember what she had confided in him that first evening they met. It was a pity she had shared her secret, and even more of a pity that he repeated it to the wrong person afterwards.

Harmony was vacationing in Miami, and had been at the Kimpton EPIC Hotel for a week. She chose it for its unique architecture, featuring, among other things, a round tower straight out of a science fiction film, plus it was downtown, a more practical location to get to the beach and the city. This was the second time she'd visited Florida, but she had only bitter memories of the first time, when she had faked being sick to get paid time off. All that to please her brother. But she'd found herself face to face with Ellen Wiggins, the intractable HR director in her Chicago office. Immediate dismissal for willful misconduct.

But this second trip to Florida was a real vacation. One evening, she went back to the hotel kitchen to compliment the head chef. The excellent tiramisu she'd just devoured had been, in her opinion, prepared by the hands of a master. She had to wait a while to speak to him, as the kitchen staff was in the middle of "rush hour." Even so, Max caught a glimpse of her and noticed her delighted look. Maybe she'd had a glass or two too many?

Harmony ended up waiting until the kitchen closed. A few more glasses of wine had changed her mood, and when she came in to see him, she was laughing too much, too loudly, and lurched a bit when she got up from her bar stool. She planted herself in front of him and grabbed his shoulders to launch her

48

compliments. He was familiar with this kind of thing and he wasn't disturbed, more amused than otherwise, as he could recognize the difference between an occasional binge and the chronic alcoholic. Her skin was fresh, her eyes bright and intelligent. Her hair was cut in a simple mid-length bob, and her clothes were classic: a white polo with the famous green crocodile, and beige shorts, as if she'd just walked off the tennis court at Wimbledon.

When she lifted her hands off his shoulders, she nearly fell, so he insisted on seeing her to her room. Convinced she was a "nice" girl who had simply drank too much that night, he wanted to make sure she didn't attract too much attention. Staggering drunkenly through the hotel corridors could tarnish her image, even if she didn't live in Florida. People took photos of anything and anyone, and you were never exempt from going viral on Facebook and company. She also risked falling into the hands of some Don Juan who wouldn't hesitate to take advantage of her for a night.

They took the elevator to the thirtieth floor, stopping at almost every floor because she kept accidentally hitting the buttons. She got her room door open only after endless fumbling with the magnetic keycard, and he had to help her open the heavy security door. Then she pulled him inside by the hem of his t-shirt. He didn't put up much resistance.

Once in her room, she picked up an old teddy bear, dropped onto a chair by the window, and started crying, a real cascade of tears. The alcohol had made her spiral into melancholy.

In a choked voice, she shushed Max even though he wasn't talking, and pointed to one of the twin beds, saying, "My brother's sleeping."

Feeling uncomfortable, Max turned his eyes away and looked around the suite. It was ultramodern, sober, with bedding and pillows in beige and ivory, a mini-living room with a TV, and above the beds, abstract paintings in yellow tones to warm the place up a bit.

He was about to leave, but she got up and dragged him back, then she lapsed into confidentialities, including her difficulties with her brother, who followed her everywhere, guided her life and was the reason she'd gotten fired from her job. Above all, she talked about her broken engagement several years earlier, when she was only twenty-two. She related every last detail on how it had turned to tragedy, and she mentioned her sick mother, living in an institution.

Floored by all these revelations, Max couldn't tell if the wine had turned her into a pathological liar or if the wine had let the raw truth out. He listened attentively without interrupting. In general, it's the listener who falls asleep, but in this case, Harmony dozed off before he did. So he carried her to her bed, removed her blue ballerina shoes and covered her with a sheet. He even tucked the teddy bear next to her cheek. His face softened into tenderness as he looked at her sleeping peacefully. Noticing an open bottle of sleeping pills and a glass of water on the nightstand, he took the pills with him as a precaution.

As he closed the door behind him, he felt convinced this young woman was psychologically frail and that she was suffering. She stirred him, attaching him to her in some way.

But as luck would have it – bad luck in this case – Sonia Marques ran into him in the hall, tiptoeing out of a room, doubtless that of some ephemeral lover. Unlike Max, sleeping with hotel guests didn't bother her. Lost in his thoughts, he didn't recognize her at first, with her wet, tousled hair. It was she who accosted him.

"What are you doing here, Max?"

Over time, Sonia had become his confidant by default, as he had no real friends and didn't frequent anyone outside of work. So as they walked to the elevator and rode down to the lobby, he told her about how his encounter with a drunk vacationer. She laughed and teased him. He shared all the details Harmony had blurted out to him, never imagining the consequences. Harmony was simply a tourist he had gallantly accompanied to her room.

The next day, right before his shift, Harmony reappeared, hanging her head in shame. She embroiled herself in long excuses and insisted they see each other again in more "normal" conditions. So they met for coffee later that day.

He held out the bottle of sleeping pills he'd taken, but she refused to take them, and told him to throw them away. She said she'd caught herself staring at that little white container too intensely, and the idea of swallowing a handful and never having to wake up had wormed into her. It seemed the least painful method to end a life she no longer enjoyed.

Wanting to save her, to protect her, was perhaps a bad motive to fall in love. But that's what happened that morning, and he was still in love with her, still crazy about her. He wanted to be the one to bring meaning back to her life.

Over the next few days, they regularly met over coffee, creating an intimate bond without even being aware of it. And one evening, their love story truly commenced. The weather was blustery, and flashes of lightning revealed a threatening sky over Miami. They watched the storm from the thirtieth floor of the hotel, thunder rumbling and lightning forking down apocalyptically. Harmony instinctively took refuge in his arms. A warm kiss became a blaze. Love was born. Sizzling nights followed, one after another, and he found it harder and harder to wake up rested and ready for work.

She never again alluded to the broken engagement she had mentioned that drunken evening they first met. It was only by accident that Max knew about that slice of her life, the one she most wanted to keep secret if not outright forgotten.

He wanted to make a clean break in his life too, and not waste time stirring up the muck of their former lives. They began their relationship by resetting all the dials to zero.

Max once read in a psychology magazine that a couple forms the perfect criminal association. He had believed in the lyrics of Edith Piaf's song:

*Non, rien de rien,*
*Non, je ne regrette rien,*
*C'est payé, balayé,*
*Je m'en fous du passé.*

*No, absolutely nothing*
*No, I regret nothing*
*It's paid, swept away, forgotten*
*I don't care about the past!*

But a few months back, he learned those words were false. You can never reset your life back to zero; you always dragged the millstones of your past behind you. And Sonia was one of those millstones.

Max put his fork down, sat back, and kept his eyes closed for a moment, taking deep breaths and exhaling consciously to bring himself back to the present, back to sitting next to Harmony in the Côté Port restaurant. His attack had dissipated entirely. His wife looked radiant and glad to be there with him. These next few hours had to become a lasting, wonderful memory for her, for he'd made his decision: this time, the slate would be wiped clean for good. It was time to get to Shell Beach, as their day was timed down to the last minute.

"That was excellent. I feel much better, and you – did you have enough to eat, Princess?"

"Yes. Do you want coffee?"

"No, thanks," he said, shaking his head. "We should leave. Are you buying?"

"As usual," she said with a sly smile.

Harmony got up and headed to the bar, where she saw their server watching them. It wasn't the first time she'd caught her at it, but she figured the woman was merely making sure they didn't need anything. She paid cash from the money in her old coin purse, and because she felt relieved that Max had recovered his warm, brown tint, she tipped a generous ten dollars. She knew the tip was included in the bill in France and its territories. But Tania had been professional and friendly without faking her smile. Harmony was never stingy when it came to rewarding qualities like that. Tania thanked her warmly.

As they walked off, Tania stared at them with a persistence rare for her. The man was gazing lovingly at his wife, who looked happy to be loved by him. He reminded her of somebody, but who? So many people came and went.

She glanced at the clock on the shelf behind the bar. She still hadn't replaced the battery in her watch; she was always too tired to take care of it. She would have to go to the island across from St. Barts, to the Indian merchants in Marigot. Her watch was old and precious, and they would be sure to have something that would work, no matter what the model.

Her shift was almost over, and she looked forward to the evening. Her boyfriend Brandon was a crewmember on the ferry, and he had two more trips to make before quitting for the day. They made an odd couple: a francophone Asian with an anglophone Antillean. Her friends considered him too much of a charmer, and it was true he unabashedly flattered women, and wouldn't hesitate to turn around to stare at a pretty pair of legs or a nice butt. But that was all show. Tania ignored it – she knew how attached he was to her.

Their love had survived, and they had been a tight-knit couple for seven years now. Was it because of what they'd witnessed together, what they never should have seen that awful night in the past?

# Chapter Nine

"I so love you, you so love me, we sow our love."
*Maurice Chapelan*

Harmony and Max had walked over to the point on the left side of the cove, where scattered boulders dividing small stretches of beach lent a feeling of privacy. Harmony lay on a beach towel spread between two outcroppings, whose charcoal black color made the turquoise waters of the Caribbean look even more vivid.

"Four o'clock already!" Max said, as he spread coconut oil on Harmony's back. "We have to be at the docks in an hour and a half."

The oil was perfumed with Tahitian tiare flowers, which wafted up and mixed with the briny smell of the water. Max liked pampering her, and she didn't mind. He admired her finely chiseled muscles – she had always been assiduous about working out at the gym – and he loved to caress her firm skin. He said it was so soft it was like a baby's, without a blemish. Her meticulous skincare routine paid off. He said he'd noticed it the first time he'd touched her, and at this memory, a shiver of desire ran through her.

"Princess?"

She craned her head to look at him. He was staring at her strangely.

"Tell me, if you were forced to choose a place to live out the rest of your life, where would it be?" he asked.

"That's an odd question – I don't get it."

"I'll ask it differently. Have you noticed that old people, or someone who's seriously ill or close to death, they know the exact place they'd like to be? Where would it be for you?"

"Wherever you are!"

"I figured that, but that's not an answer."

"Sure it is," Harmony said. "Tell me what country, what town you'd want to be in, and it will be the same for me."

"In Sweden…"

"In the cold? I never would have guessed that. I thought you would opt for a place in the sun for your old age."

"Appearances are often misleading. Sometimes you have to imagine the other person in the exactly opposite situation. Will you remember that?"

"I guess."

"Harmony, I can't emphasize this point enough – you have to imagine me in exactly the opposite situation. Repeat it to make sure."

"Are you joking?"

"Do I look like I'm joking?"

Harmony had to admit that he looked serious.

Intrigued, she repeated what he wanted to hear, "I'll imagine you in exactly the opposite situation."

"Okay," he said, smiling. "But we should get going if you want to find a chic outfit for tonight."

"But we're so cozy here – let's stay put. I can make do with the clothes I have at the hotel. Why not my long red dress? After all, I've only worn it twice."

"No, you should treat yourself. You wanted it so badly – you might find a dress that Scarlett Johansson has touched with her very own hands!"

"Stop teasing me."

"Me? Never! Come on, I'll pack our stuff. You go ahead. I want to find a classy shirt, something my wallet can handle, if possible. If we lose each other, we'll meet at five-thirty at the wooden gate to the pier. The boat leaves at five forty-five. You know where it is?"

"Who do you take me for? The port is miniscule, so I can't miss it, let alone get lost. I'm not a complete idiot."

"An idiot, no. A little tipsy, yes. How many daiquiris did you have sent over here?"

"Only two. I won't get drunk from that."

"You're forgetting the three glasses of rosé at the restaurant."

Pretending to be irritated, she flipped over, revealing her apple-shaped breasts. This was the first time she'd ever sunbathed without her bikini top. Her delicate pink skin had absorbed too many tropical UV rays, and it was bright red. A sunburn in the worst possible spot. Sitting cross-legged, she tapped him lightly on the cheek as if to scold him, then she jumped up and pulled on her dress over her still-wet bikini bottoms, not bothering to hide behind him or look every which way to make sure no men were watching. At the worst, her dress would soak up a little seawater. In the islands, tolerance levels were high when it came to dressing carelessly. Especially at the end of the day, when it would be natural to suppose she had been swimming.

She grabbed her shoes. She had almost brought along her one pair of flip-flops but then left them at the hotel, and she sighed at the thought of having to walk in these high platform shoes. Not to mention the interminable lacing halfway up the calf, like Roman sandals. They were sexy, but not at all practical. Most of the people here wore shorts and t-shirts, even the ones who stepped out of hundred-thousand-dollar cars. She hadn't made any of the right choices for this daytrip, except for the hat, which had gotten a lot of use. She plopped it back on her head, even though the sun was now beginning to make its descent.

She strolled along the waterline, letting the waves caress her feet one last time, and went past the sole restaurant. Its architect had succeeded in tucking it into a wall of the cliffs, and it had several floors of terraces overlooking the beach. Beige canvas chairs were lined up in front of the tables nearest the sand, and most were filled with young people straight out of the pages of a fashion magazine, one more beautiful than the next, skimpily attired yet elegant. Lounge music floating out from the bar added to the impression of mingling with the "stars."

Max had asked one of the friendly beachboys to bring them their cocktails instead of paying for a chair. Back in their shelter between the rocks, they had enjoyed a more intimate, less urbane spot. Max would have added, "And less expensive, too." That point had its merits.

She suddenly halted and hurried back to Max. She had omitted the essential: a goodbye kiss. When he saw her coming, his face brightened, but he adopted the vexed look she knew so well, "the victim of injustice." He couldn't stand it when she left without kissing him, even if she was leaving for only a few minutes. Amused by his attitude, she gave him a kiss and took off.

The Rue de la Plage was paved, so walking was easier. She wanted to take advantage of that to accelerate her pace, but then realized her shoes weren't going to cooperate and slowed down. It would be ridiculous to twist an ankle that way. Avoiding an accident was primordial. So many people told stories about this kind of thing – sprains, a broken arm, lumbago, bumps and bruises – that ruined their vacations. She walked even more slowly, until she found herself following the slow-motion rhythm of a woman in front of her, who was herding two kids, and trying to carry their pails, shovels, rakes, molds and balls in a big sack that threatened to rip apart at every step. The tiny blond boy was about two, and the surprisingly black-haired boy about four, and both were fussing noisily.

As a child, Harmony had never had the chance to go to a seaside town, much less the West Coast. California… Her mother would often conjure images of it as an inaccessible dream, an expensive vacation spot they'd never have a right to visit. Instead, they made do with a camping trip to Silver Lake Resort on Lake Michigan every three years. But were they less happy for all that? She had sometimes envied their neighbors for the places they got to visit, but a tent and the great outdoors were every bit as fun as a hotel room for three in California, if not more.

She remembered the special treat of eating ice cream from a glass bowl, and the tiny paper umbrellas they came with. They loved to collect them. Her brother kept the blue, green and yellow ones, and she got the red, pink and purple ones. They were more girlish, he thought. She liked spinning them in her fingers, or using them as umbrellas for Ken and Barbie. At the resort's beach, they would spend entire days in their little territory, walled in by hills of sand they shaped and reshaped, an imaginary galaxy the size of a living room.

She was twelve the last time they had played there, building roads bordered with skyscrapers and shopping centers. Her mother, Rosanna Flynt, had noticed her daughter's budding breasts, and told her it would soon be time to put away games like that. True, but it wasn't the beginning of adolescence that had put an end to their innocent play.

Harmony swallowed hard and pushed away her memories of camping trips, of her poor mother and her brother.

The woman lugging all her kids' beach paraphernalia had just abandoned some of their toys at the foot of a tall coconut tree, sheared of nuts. She had read that deaths from falling coconuts were no joke. Ironically, that had made her laugh, and even now provoked a smile that pulled her from her nostalgia.

Her eyes met those of the harassed mother, who rolled her eyes and shrugged. Lifting the smallest boy to one hip, and pulling the other by the arm, the woman started to grumble about her husband, who it seems should have met them before four o'clock. Harmony hoped she would never find herself in this kind of situation with Max. He'd never left her in the lurch, and it was unimaginable he would act that way if she had a child or two in tow.

She sometimes came across mothers sitting on the bench in a public park, warning future moms about how the arrival of a baby shakes up a couple, too often transforming the man in the wrong way. Instead of taking on the role of head of a family, with pride and honor, they regress, and yearn for their old bachelor's life – some of them, to the point of returning to it.

The sweltering heat of mid-day had lifted, and a curtain of clouds veiled the sun. The tradewinds started to blow, and sand sifted down the beach. She had to keep grabbing her hat. They chose the right day to visit St. Barts, she thought, as the weather was sure to degrade that night. The forecast had announced gusty winds and a growing swell, with yellow- to orange-level storm warnings. Harmony was not about to step foot on a boat in rough seas, so if they found a skipper, they would have to choose their dates accordingly, and keep their fingers crossed for better weather in the next ten days. She just hoped the crossing back to St. Martin wouldn't make her get seasick.

On the Rue de la Place d'Armes, she was going to turn left, but held back, sensing a presence. She stopped and glanced over her shoulder. There was Max, not far behind, walking jauntily. He saw her, smiled and murmured a few words to her, and judging from his lips, his words were, "I love you." She could have sworn he spoke them more intensely than usual. It must have been because of the holidays coming up – they revived our feelings. If you loved, you loved even more deeply. The inverse was equally true, she knew. Her depression used to be far worse around the holidays.

She didn't want Max to catch up with her right now, however. She wanted to choose her dress without his input. In the beginning of their relationship, he accompanied her everywhere, thinking he was helping her by offering his opinion on every purchase. He thought he was doing good, but eventually, she didn't dare try anything on. A sort of auto-censorship set in, the fear he would consider her ugly or fat. The usual unjustified complexes of women, no matter how athletic, slim or pretty. She would hesitate endlessly, trying on dozens of outfits, and often, they would leave one boutique totally confused only to repeat the process in another. An inestimable waste of time for Harmony. As a highly organized person, she considered every hour precious, subject to accountability. As a result, she now did her shopping alone. That way, she could surprise him, and above all, choose things that fit her own taste. And he seemed to have finally learned that a woman finds herself beautiful only when she feels irresistible in her clothing.

She blew him a kiss, then disappeared from his view, and he from hers.

# Chapter Ten

"You can wash your clothing, not your conscience."
Persian proverb


She came out on a sidewalk of Rue Général de Gaulle. As chic and charming as a place could be. Shutters in carmine red, sky blue, or pale green cheered the white facades of wood or stone, maintained to perfection. The stone-paved road lent a romantic, antique cachet. It was fifteen hundred miles from home, but St. Barts felt like being on another planet. Calling Gustavia a "city" was a bit exaggerated, as Harmony saw nothing urban around her. Certainly, this was St. Barts' principal town, but it seemed more of a prosperous garden-like village for rich tourists. Or a place for the middle classes to come and break their piggybanks with glee. We can all afford to dream.

At the end of the road, she passed a café unlike all the others. The red bricks had been left natural, and the terrace, shaded by trees, was strewed with solid but rudimentary wood tables and plastic chairs. Rather like a Belgian bistro in a university town during summer, with a relaxed, simple ambiance. Its name was "Le Select," a bit tongue-in-cheek, seeing the décor, but it was nice to know the island was not all bling-bling.

A red Mini stopped to let her cross, and she entered the Rue de la République. Through its choice of street names, St. Barts wanted to show it was French, a miniature Paris even if it was well over four thousand miles from Paris. A poster stuck to a window attracted her curiosity. A real estate ad showing a house for sale near Saint-Jean bay, "only" a million six hundred thousand euros, not including fees. Harmony scoffed – the place was barely a thousand square feet! She had read that real estate prices here set new records every year. It was hard for the locals to resist the temptation to sell a piece of their heritage – land or a family home – when such astronomical sums were offered. But succumbing to the temptation meant taking the risk of disappearing as a people.

She could imagine daily life here. The idyllic views all around, views that even stormy weather couldn't ruin, the exemplary cleanliness, the sea a playground for water sports, the endless sunny terraces in chic or not-so-chic restaurants. A way of life some people considered paradise, but she couldn't imagine living here year-round; she needed the city and its art exhibits, concerts, plays, and simply its urban vibes pulsing through her. She could understand why it attracted celebrities, though. St. Barts was the perfect place to come and relax a few weeks out of the year, and if you became a resident, there were no income or property taxes. Her mother would have crowed about that.

She stopped to gape at a Christmas theme window display: a polar bear and its cubs surrounded by heaps of gifts wrapped in shiny red and gold paper. Like many of the stores here, the clothing and fashion accessories evidently didn't suit all budgets – no price tags were posted.

Even with duty-free advantages, Harmony wasn't ready to throw money out the window. Max teased her for being tight-fisted, but she considered herself thrifty, not stingy. She couldn't forget the many times throughout her childhood when money didn't stretch from one paycheck to the next. Soon after her brother's birth, her father had slammed the door on family life, the true prototype of a man who couldn't take on the role of father. She was barely five when he deserted them. Her memories of him were fuzzy, even though she'd seen him again briefly when she was twelve, to hear him confirm that he would never take care of her.

To make ends meet after he abandoned them, Rosanna Flynt had juggled her hours as server in a fast-food café in Chicago with her hours cleaning homes in the wealthy Gold Coast area. Every dollar counted, as she ceaselessly repeated to her kids. For all these reasons, Harmony avoided using her credit card as much as possible. Her guardian Jonathan Clark felt indebted to her and would never hesitate to help her if she needed it, but she wanted to take care of herself.

Paying cash let her visualize her money slipping away. She calculated a certain sum for each day, and put it in her worn-out, grubby old coin purse, which she liked because it didn't attract attention when she pulled it out of her purse. She forced herself to stick to that limit. That morning, she had tucked an unusually large roll of bills in her coin purse, for the exceptional purchase of an evening dress. The only spree she would allow herself during their vacation. She wasn't going to burn up money at the casino Max wanted to bring her to – the chance of winning was so infinitesimal it was a waste of effort and money to play with the hope luck would be on your side. All the same, she would willingly go to the casino to experience the "James Bond" ambiance and spend a little to please her husband. He was going to look so handsome tonight. She would ask him to put gel in his hair like when they got married in Las Vegas, and wear his Italian shirt and the heather-gray pants he set aside for big occasions.

She suddenly stopped. An outfit had finally caught her eye. Four hundred forty-nine dollars. She pushed open the door of the boutique, the idea of negotiating the price already in mind. A curly-haired saleswoman came forward, eyes shining.

"Hello, Madame. I'm Clémentine – how can I help you?"

It was disconcerting how quickly the shopkeepers could pinpoint her as an American, even before she had opened her mouth. But Harmony answered with the French she'd learned at the Lycée Français de Chicago, the international high school Jonathan Clark had enrolled her in. Always looking to her future, he'd sent her there to get the best education possible. She often spoke to Max in French. Despite his long years in the United States, he still spoke English like "Pepe le Pew" in the cartoons. The image of the Frenchy skunk made her smile. She promised herself she'd watch some reruns when they got home.

"Hello. I wanted to take a look at your evening dresses. I noticed the one in the window. Can I try it on?"

"The silvery one on the mannequin?"

"Exactly."

"Excellent choice. I'm sure it will fit you like a glove. It's a unique piece and it's just your size – thirty-eight, French size?"

"Right. You've got a good eye!"

Max had taught her the difference in sizes, whether French, American or even Italian. She thought the European norms should be unified to have one system for sizing, and that led her thoughts back to her job, and the accounts that were so complicated whenever they had to do with exports or imports.

For the first few months in her new job in Milwaukee, she had reluctantly dragged herself to the office every day. All her bearings had been left behind in Chicago. But that was only normal, after the way she'd lost her old job. Jonathan Clark had gotten her the new position thanks to his connections.

She looked around the boutique. Rustic wood furniture painted in cheerful yellow and blue gave it a warm ambiance, a look straight out of a Provençal flea market in. But the modern silvery metal lamps diffusing cold, white light created a striking contrast between antique and high-tech. The dresses took up an entire wall, and some of them were so sheer they looked unwearable. But maybe you could pull it off in St. Barts. Next to the counter was a replica of a French beach cabana, painted blue and white, that served as a dressing room. The door was purposely too short, and let show a large part of your legs. A shoplifting deterrent?

She looked over the dresses, grouped by color, but the one in the window remained her favorite. The saleswoman came back with a triumphant air. She'd managed to take the dress off the mannequin without crushing the jewelry and knickknacks displayed around it. Clémentine had a feeling this was a serious client, not another penniless tourist who tries on heaps of outfits and takes dozens of photos to post on Facebook, only to crack jokes at her expense. Savvy to selling techniques, she handed over the silvery dress as well as a shimmery black one with delicate straps crossing the deeply cut back.

Inside the dressing room, Harmony stood in front of the mirror looking at her reflection. The saleswoman had unintentionally awakened a painful memory. She had worn the same style dress several years earlier, before she met Max. She'd chosen it because she knew it would please her former fiancé Steven Reardon, a man she was obsessed with.

She'd never shared this part of her life with Max. She was only twenty-two then, and she had just gotten her diploma. Marriage seemed a logical outcome of the three-year relationship she and Steven had enjoyed, and when she introduced him to Jonathan Clark, who was usually skeptical of her boyfriends, he had immediately liked Steven, seeing in him a promising young man who could make her happy.

The future spouses planned to move into a duplex in Chicago's Near North Side. Harmony had just snagged her first job as an accountant there, so she wouldn't be far from Steven. His parents held "traditional Christian values," and they wanted the couple to be joined in marriage before living under the same roof. They were receptive to the idea. The ceremonial aspect of it was proof they were serious about each other.

On a day she would never forget, November 18, 2006, Steven had called her to cancel their dinner date at Kamehachi, a Japanese restaurant in the city. Steven was also an accountant, in his first job at a new law firm, and hadn't finished an important case report due the next day. He was truly sorry. Disappointed, Harmony had reluctantly taken off the black dress with the deeply cut back, which she had bought specially for the occasion.

They were seeing a lot less of each other because of their respective jobs, and Harmony thought it was time to get the wedding over and move in together. The date was fixed for the fifth of May, which suddenly appeared very far off.

She had trouble going to sleep, so she read some articles in her interior decorating magazines, trying to console herself by imagining how she would spruce up their new duplex. Finally, she fell asleep, but in the middle of the night a terrible dream startled her awake. In it, she was wearing her wedding dress, standing in a church crammed with people, waiting in vain for Steven to arrive. Then the sun set, and all the people left, leaving her alone with the two wedding rings in her hand.

She called Steven several times, but his voice mail kept kicking in with that irritatingly cheerful message of his. Some intuition pushed her to get dressed in the same sexy black dress, her back almost naked. She redid her makeup, but clumsily, and her lipstick smeared. She had to find him, no matter that the weather was glacial.

Before opening her car door, she noticed her neighbor Phil Peterson, an ambulance driver, staring at her out of his window. She wasn't surprised – he was an insomniac, probably due to his irregular working hours. The Peterson couple were friendly, and their teenagers made no trouble. She often parked in front of their place, as she had that evening, so she waved at him, got in and headed to Steven's.

She didn't think she was driving fast, but she was amazed to recognize the first houses in Jefferson Park only thirty minutes later. In the daytime, it could take up to an hour and a half to get ti his house from where she lived. Steven's car was in its usual place in front of his living room window. The blinds were drawn. His house was the last in a line of duplexes, then came a basketball court before the next series of houses started. The court area served as a parking place for his visitors, and she pulled in.

Another car was parked there, one she recognized. And she suddenly understood. Hadn't she always known, without being able to admit it? Her typical ostrich policy.

A few hours later, Harmony learned that God did sometimes punish the "bad guys." Steven and her best friend Megan had been killed in a tragic car accident.

But their betrayal left its marks, and after that experience, Harmony no longer wanted to make new friends. Never again would she dream of a wedding with hundreds of guests and an immense hall with a splendid banquet that would be talked about for years. She lost all confidence in men. Every now and then, she tried to find consolation through online dating sites, but they did nothing but increase her disgust of herself.

Then Max had come into her life, and with him, deep and lasting love.

The idea of a Las Vegas wedding had tickled her from the start. They said, "Yes" in the anonymity of a city dedicated to games of chance, without family, without friends, even without Shirley or the Clarks – just her and Max.

Harmony slid the long zipper up the front of the unashamedly glitzy dress. But this was her vacation, the ideal moment to dare it. She admired her flat stomach. That would soon change – they had decided to have a baby, their greatest project. A blend of Max and Harmony. She wondered what color his eyes would be, and his skin and his hair. Max had a Mediterranean look, with his easily tanned skin, thick black hair and blue eyes, while Harmony's skin was rosy, her fine hair blond, and her eyes blueish gray. They had immediately assumed it would be a boy, and couldn't imagine it being a girl. Too hard to manage, Max had joked, and if she were as pretty as her mother, he could already see himself kicking the butts of any aspiring beaux. Projecting into the future like this was balm to his heart. A happy future. A family with a father, a mother and children playing in the garden. Max would always love her, and she would always reciprocate.

Happiness could be so simple.

Clémentine was right. The silvery color set off her eyes, and the dress showed all the curves Max appreciated. He was going to drool, like Tex Avery's wolf. The comparison evoked a genuine smile this time. She changed into her street clothes and left the dressing room, pretending to be uninterested.

Clémentine, ignoring her indifference, pretended the sale was already made.

"A bit of advice for when you wear it: put your hair up in a high chignon. No need for a necklace, as it's flashy enough without it. Just earrings, but discreet ones. And of course, high heels."

"I have the heels and the earrings. But I'm not sure about the dress. I hadn't noticed the price before, so maybe I'll come back with my husband. Thanks, anyway."

Clémentine couldn't let her run off like that, so close to the goal. She knew most people never did return to make a purchase, but would buy something somewhere else. She worked on commission, so she always pampered her clients, even the most odious, bitchy whiners, swallowing her pride in the name of that damn commission. She had the gift of being able to flash a natural-looking smile even when deep down she wanted to strangle someone. And for that reason, when night fell, she often overdid it at the private parties so popular on this island. She had to evacuate all the hypocrisy out her system, and that was one way to do it.

She took a deep breath, rapidly calculated in her head, and lowered the price, without the smile ever leaving her face.

Harmony walked out with the dress, wrapped in fine tissue paper in a classy gift bag embossed with the shop's address in St. Barts. That made it extra chic. She wouldn't be throwing this sack away. Her maneuver had paid off. Rosanna Flynt had taught her this bit of acting and how to adapt it to certain businesses, along with her mantra, "A dollar saved is a dollar earned."

Max would smile and shake his head, rolling his eyes, when she recounted the ruse and how much of a discount she'd managed to get.

As for the memory provoked by the black dress, she relegated it back to the farthest reaches of her mind.

# Chapter Eleven

"We arrive early, on time, or late according to whether we love, still love, or no longer love." Diane de Beausacq

Five-fifteen already!

"Why does times fly so fast when I'm shopping?" Harmony wondered. She didn't feel like she'd dawdled. She saw the dress, tried it on, negotiated the price and bought it, all very quickly. But she headed straight to the waterfront without risking the least glance left or right at the tempting boutiques. Hermès, Chanel, Dior, Bijoux De La Mer...

A crowd was starting to form at the gate to the docks. Max wasn't there yet. She figured he was on one last errand. Maybe buying some post cards for her or still searching for a new shirt? A business on the other side of the road drew her attention. Its sign displayed a cornucopia of ice cream cones, arousing her sweet tooth. Without a second thought, she hurried across and went inside. It was so narrow there was barely enough room to hold the counter display. Three clients waited in line, including a man wearing a red cap she'd noticed on the ferry that morning. On a small island, encounters like this were inevitable.

When it was her turn, Harmony ordered her favorite combo: one scoop vanilla on top, one scoop strawberry underneath, so she could eat it last. A gentle nostalgia for her childhood, when the ice cream truck's tinny music announced its entrance into the Pilsen neighborhood and she and her brother would run outside for their weekly treat, cheering happily. She missed him all of a sudden. Almost two years had passed since she'd talked to him. Max, the love of her life, was responsible for this silence, but he'd convinced her it was for her own good.

At five twenty-five, she returned to the ferry gates, where double-parked cars now bottled up the passage. The driver of a flower-delivery truck was honking his horn impatiently, which didn't solve anything. He must have been new to the island, as everyone here knew that ferry arrivals and departures were the worst time of day for traffic in this part of town.

Harmony sat on a low wall next to the entry gate, licking her ice cream. She was starting to get disturbed that Max hadn't shown up. Back home, as soon as she left for work in the morning, her one desire was for the hours to spin by in fast motion so she could return to him, and in the evening, she loved turning off the ignition and running up the steps to the door, where he would greet her.

Where could he be? He didn't have another minute to spare. Why was he so late – was he hesitating in his choice of a shirt? That was one of his little weaknesses: having to decide between things. Besides, he had a terrific Italian shirt hanging in the hotel room closet, one that could make any man look handsome and elegant.

Five-thirty. The ferry from Oyster Pond that was to bring them back to St. Martin tied up, and at the sight, Harmony got annoyed. He'd missed their meeting time, even though he was the one who had insisted on it. She called him: voice mail. She tried again: same thing. The small crowd that had been calm up until now started to get restless and move into a vague line, like a herd of cattle who automatically form a line every day at a precise hour, anticipating the arrival of the farmer to make sure they wouldn't be forgotten.

Harmony stood up and tapped her feet, almost dancing in her anxiety. Should she join them or wait it out? This is where he'd said to meet, but she ended up doubting even that. She took out her passport and the return tickets from her bulging wallet. She needed to go through all the loyalty cards she'd accumulated, just like she'd gone through her friendships, discarding all but one, the most precious, that of Shirley Connors. She often found it hard to refuse a clerk's offer for one of these cards, with "all its advantages." She would accept, saying, "You never know. A dollar saved is a dollar earned."

Five-thirty-seven. The gate opened, the crowd quivered, then slowly filed through. No one pushed, but no one left an inch to the adversary behind them. Everyone held out their tickets like magic keys to the kingdom. Harmony put away her passport. Max had given her the tickets, but he'd held on to his own passport. Apparently, there was no identity check when traveling in this direction. Verifications were so strict when entering St. Barts, but anybody could go back to St. Martin.

Five-forty-five. She was the last person on the dock, and she felt ridiculous as she hopped from foot to foot, looking around for Max, scrutinizing every last masculine figure that might fit his, near or far. The ticket-taker pressed her to go aboard. He was a tall blond whose skin looked so pitifully scalded by the sun that she wanted to give him a spray with the mister. She settled for trying to buy some time. It would only be a few seconds, she insisted, then her husband would arrive; he was never late. Never! she repeated.

Five-forty-eight. The departure horn bellowed out, giving her a terrible pang of sadness. The sound was synonymous with good-bye.

"Madame, we can wait no longer," the ticket inspector said. "Please, embark immediately or we must leave without you."

"Wait just a little more, please."

Five-fifty. The crew lifted the gangway and pulled it aboard. The sunburned blond turned to her with a worried air.

"The next boat won't come until tomorrow morning. I suppose you have lodgings for tonight? Otherwise, you're going to spend a fortune!"

She watched the ferry pull away from the dock. She prayed that Max would show up, and imagined how she would make such desperate gestures toward the boat that it would turn around and come back. But it soon chugged out of sight, and her husband had still not reappeared.

# Chapter Twelve

"The disappearance of a loved one affects adults more than children,

for only the adult's pain feeds on the imagination."
Bertrand Godbille, *Los Montes*

She wandered Gustavia's winding lanes, which suddenly seemed too numerous, too long, all identical. She had the strange feeling everyone was staring at her, as if she were the one who was lost and not her husband. She came across Clémentine, the sales clerk, climbing onto a sporty moped. Harmony asked her if by chance she'd seen her husband, and since she had no photos of him, she described him in minute detail. No, Clémentine had seen no one like that.

Nearly an hour passed. Night had fallen, abruptly, as if someone in the heavens had switched off the light, and she hadn't even noticed. For the umpteenth time, she went back to the pier. No Max. Irritation had been replaced by anguish so intense it seemed to suffocate her. Her throat was in a knot and she felt a dull pain in her chest. Why wasn't he here? Did he think it was six-forty-five instead of five-forty-five? But if that was the case, it was already six-forty, so he should have been there.

Max had never been late for a rendezvous.

Harmony recalled how sick he'd been earlier, just before lunch. But he seemed fine that afternoon, so attentive, so loving, like when he'd rubbed the coconut oil on her back. Had he suddenly gotten another attack? She decided to return to Shell Beach and look for him.

The town was completely changed – from animated to deserted. The beach as well. Only a few employees were still there, stacking lounge chairs at the one restaurant on the waterfront. She asked them about Max, but none of them recalled seeing him.

A young guy with bulging muscles spoke up. "So many tourists come and go in the space of a few hours, they all start to look alike. I only remember big jerks or big tippers."

"Or girls with big boobs," added a much skinnier Indian man diligently wiping tables.

They all started laughing and joking, heedless of the gulf between their high spirits and the worry filling this tourist with the absent gaze.

Harmony saw the beachboy with the chocolate-colored skin who had brought their cocktails to the beach, so she went over and questioned him. Taken aback, he said he'd been on the run all day, but he remembered her vaguely. As for her husband – not at all. Max had been in the water when he'd come over with the drinks, and she had paid the bill.

Harmony gave up on Shell Beach and started to jog clumsily down the Rue de la Plage. Her platform heels kept tripping her, and when she ended up twisting an ankle, she reacted by venting her pain and anxiety by screaming, "Max, Max, Max!" A local couple out walking with their three children halted, surprised at seeing this blond woman on the verge of hysteria. Harmony started shouting louder, scaring the children, so the parents huddled them together, telling them to hurry in Creole, "Fè vit! Prese!" and they walked off without stopping to see what was wrong. She seemed drunk, and people in St. Barts disapproved of that kind of spectacle.

Other people noticed Harmony's outburst, too.

An elderly woman, Madame Questel, peered out of her window, hidden by the curtains she had crocheted herself. That type of high-pitched scream was so rare; sometimes you heard shouting from the festivals or from passing drunkards, but not that tone of distress. But instead of going out to help, she called the gendarmerie. Officer Jourdan listened to her amiably, mustering up as much seriousness as he could, if only out of respect for one of the island's doyens. But when he hung up, he shook his head and laughed. Her calls – at least once or twice a week – had become an amusing ritual, and the insignificant things she described didn't even warrant the attention they would accord to a lost dog report. He went to tell his fellow gendarme Yves Duchâteau. He could use a good laugh.

A young man noticed Harmony as he was plodding home, exhausted from working all day fixing a roof. Like many construction workers on the island, he was Portuguese, and his gray overalls spotted with paint attested to his livelihood. When he realized she was panicking, he ran over to her.

"Madame, is everything alright? Can I help you with something?"

"No! I mean yes, please," she said. "I'm looking for my husband. We were here late in the afternoon, but he didn't come to take the ferry back to St. Martin with me."

"To return to the French or the Dutch side?"

"Oyster Pond, on the French side."

"Are you sure he didn't accidentally take the boat going to Philipsburg?"

"Yes, I'm sure. And he couldn't have done that anyway, as I have the tickets."

"Have you asked at the hospital? Maybe he's there."

"I thought of that, but he was fine when we split up. But you're right; he must be there. I don't see any other possibility. Thank you so much, sir."

"Do you have a map of the town?"

"Yes, why?"

"I'll show you how to get there. Nothing is far away on this little island, but you can still get lost."

After listening to his directions, she limped away with one last grateful look at the Portuguese man. His face was tanned like leather, but his eyes were a stunning greenish blue, and extremely gentle. His expression reminded her of her brother. This island never stopped bringing out old memories and strange coincidences.

She tried Max's number but got his voice mail again, with the message she used to think was funny but now only frustrating: "Hey, hey, no problem, I'm not here, or maybe I'm taking a long nap, or maybe I just don't want to talk to you. Call me later if you dare."

Cold sweat up and down her body. She must resemble that American tourist on the ferry. She felt dizzy too, as if she was only now getting seasick. She couldn't find Max, and that was more and more disturbing. Maybe the Portuguese man was right – he could have had an attack and been taken to the hospital, and fear flooded her. Something serious had happened. Sometimes, driving back and forth work, she heard stories on the news about sudden, totally unexpected death, where a person apparently in fine health, even an athlete, died from some unsuspected malformation, or disorder of the cardiac conduction, that had decided to strike a mortal blow, stories that reminded the living that nothing was absolute, no instant of life was without value, and every day that dawned could be the last.

The road leading to the hospital got steeper, forcing her to lean far forward. She searched the sides of the road for a branch to use as a walking stick, but just as with litter, it seemed no untidy vegetation existed on this super-clean island. She reached De Bruyn Hospital gasping for air, with her ankle so swollen the inflamed flesh was puffing out between her sandal straps. The term "hospital" was an exaggeration. The place could easily be taken for a high-class tourist lodge, being an ensemble of small Creole-style villas with sky-blue walls and white doors and window moldings.

Ghassan Nasser, a young doctor from Lebanon, was leaning against the façade at the emergency room entrance, smoking a cigarillo. He was bored. Every day was like the next, and the absence of seasons didn't help. He was disenchanted with St. Barts, and feeling suffocated, so he smoked, which paradoxically helped him breathe. Tomorrow was his day off, and there was nothing to do but go to the beach or swim in his pool. Despite the crowds that daily filled the island, he always talked with the same people, his fellow doctors, health workers, the baker or grocer, and most often it was chatty gossip, never a serious discussion.

Next to him stood a curvy nurse from Martinique, Sandra, who was counting the minutes until the night shift arrived. She was delighted to see the pretty blond woman limp up to them. Ghassan wasn't very talkative – since their one-night stand a few months earlier he was practically mute every time they were alone together. And having nothing to do or say made the time pass so slowly.

"Hello, sorry for bothering you," Harmony said. "I'm looking for my husband Max Rousseau. He missed the last ferry and I can't find him, so I came to check if he's been admitted."

The two health workers immediately noticed the American accent even though her phrasing was perfect.

"No, sorry," the doctor replied, ungluing his back from the wall and putting out his cigarillo.

"Please, I insist – could you take a look at the register anyway?"

The doctor couldn't repress a grin, which made the nurse chuckle, her shoulders shaking up and down.

Getting hold of himself, Dr. Nasser said, "Our register? This is more a dispensary than a hospital. There isn't even an operating room. We have precisely five patients in our beds at the moment, and I know them all down to where they live and the name of their dog. And the people who came to the emergency room today were all old ladies or children, I don't know why. Not one man."

"I see why I made you laugh, then. Could he have been transported somewhere else? To St. Martin or another nearby island, Anguilla maybe?"

"No, impossible. All evacuations of sick patients go through our hospital, aside from the VIPs no one never sees, who fly directly to the States in their private jets. But you're

79

limping badly – you should show us that ankle. Looks like a sprain."

"I twisted my foot. I'll take care of it later. I have to find my husband. Excuse me again for bothering you."

Why did she say that? They certainly didn't look very busy. It was by habit, by fear of being a hassle to others. She always wanted to disappear from view. Her father had disappeared from her life without ever inquiring about her afterwards – was that why she sometimes felt so insignificant? Whenever she started brooding on this kind of dark thought, Max raised her spirits. He made her feel special, telling her how wonderful she was, using superlatives wherever possible: the most beautiful, the smartest.

But he wasn't there, and she felt completely at a loss. You can't just disappear like that. If you're not at the hospital, where are you, Max?

She turned her back on the nurse and doctor. But where should she go? She looked around, thinking.

"Hold on, you can't walk around like that," the doctor said, coming toward her. "Sit down on that bench, and we'll apply an ice pack for a few minutes, then wrap it. That should help with the pain. And you'll have to avoid walking, as much as possible."

Harmony let him persuade her, hoping to get rid of the stabbing pain. The nurse came back with an ice pack and applied it to her ankle. Harmony was astonished they would take care of her without making her pay upfront or show an insurance card. That was unimaginable in the United States. It comforted her to know small acts of kindness, free of charge, really did exist here and there. In the city, you had to prove yourself clean or harmless or somehow worthy before others would lift a finger to help you.

After they applied a wide compression bandage, her ankle seemed less painful, so she thanked them again, stuffed the shoe into her bag, and limped back down the hill. At the bottom, she looked at her watch: eight o'clock already! Going to the police was the only solution. The fort wasn't far, but she would have to hike that steep road to reach it. At least she could walk without grimacing too much, thanks to the doctor insisting they treat her ankle. It wasn't just the ankle hurting – everything hurt. Her head, her stomach, her shoulders. A generalized ache provoked by her fear and her imagination, because if he wasn't at the hospital, something other than a fainting attack had happened to him.

An assault?

# Chapter Thirteen

"He confided to me that he dreaded this interrogation, having what I believe he called a guilt complex." Julien Green, *Diary, 1943*

Out of breath, her heart pounding, she entered the gendarmerie, but this time, it wasn't to ask about a guided tour. Right then, a stocky man in his sixties burst in and tried to push in front of her, but Jérôme Jourdan, the officer on duty, detected his maneuver and signaled to him to wait on a bench. They all knew Philippe Barnabé, the boat mechanic. He grumbled as he took a seat, setting his green cap on his knees, and examined his nails, black as usual from motor oil. He'd had a rough day at work and he wanted to go home, take a shower and relax with his wife in front of a good American film, streamed rather than rented from a video store, where all St. Barts heard about what you were watching and you ended up stuck with a label reflecting your tastes. At least that's what Barnabé thought.

Harmony approached the desk, at a loss as to what to say.

"Bonsoir Madame, what is the problem?" the gendarme said.

"My husband... My husband disappeared. I'm afraid some gang of low-lifes might have hurt him."

Jourdan lifted an eyebrow. A Sean Connery mimicry most normally constituted people could not execute because physiologically, eyebrows synchronized their movements. His colleagues found it hilarious.

Known as JJ to his friends, he thought this Monday night shift would be nice and calm. Friday's had been busier than usual, with scooter accidents and the arrest of several drunken tourists. Nothing serious, but a lot of work, especially the paper-pushing. Yves Duchâteau was still stuck in his office filling out forms. Last night was typical for Sunday: quiet as a graveyard in Gustavia, and with most of the shops closed, the tourists weren't out in droves.

A busy weekend, but nothing compared to the island across from them. He pitied his colleagues on St. Martin, who spent their time in high-risk confrontations, break-ins, conjugal violence, all types of "settling of accounts," with never a respite, or if there was, it meant something especially bad was about to happen. Like the time the Goldfinger jewelry store was robbed in Marigot in plain daylight, followed by a chase on the waterfront, bullets flying between the authorities and a Venezuelan gang.

St. Barts was a paradise, without serious crime. So what was this American claiming in her excellent French? That in itself was unusual – most of them never made any effort to speak his language, as if it was a given that people around the world speak their language, and he was tired of having to trot out his broken English – why should the effort be all on his side? One more year and he would return to the real France; he just hoped her wouldn't be transferred too far north, where the cold would be a shock to his system.

Who was this woman? Was she a compulsive liar? Lots of psychos ended up here, like that New Yorker who insisted someone stole her wallet at the beach, only to find out she'd left it in her hotel room. Nothing serious, in general.

There were also the new arrivals who, confined to an island of only thirty square miles, ended up blowing a fuse. Their commandant could confirm it – his wife was approaching that point.

And there was the case of the husband who hadn't actually disappeared, but who had fled from his nagging wife for several hours. All wives got like that from time to time. Sometimes, he wanted to flee his wife too, like yesterday, when a quarrel erupted because he'd omitted the fruit from the kids' afternoon snack. He hadn't wanted to mess with cutting up melons, so he replaced them with chips. His wife had laid into him, and when all he did was shrug, she had gotten even crabbier. He had walked out of their apartment near the fort and motorcycled around the island. When he came back, she pretended to drop it, but that day, he'd made sure to peel apples and cut up bananas for their snack. She always won.

"Let us start from the beginning, calmly, from A to Z, Madame."

"I am calm, Monsieur, but extremely worried. I arrived this morning with my husband. We were supposed to leave on the five-forty-five ferry to St. Martin, but he didn't show up. I searched for him everywhere, but I can't find him. I even went to the hospital to see if he'd been admitted."

"Where was he the last time you saw him?"

"Shell Beach. Actually, no, it was in a little lane just after having left the beach. I went ahead of him because I was in a hurry."

"You were in a hurry?"

"I wanted to buy an evening dress. I saw him about fifty yards behind me before I turned into another road. I didn't want him to catch up though."

"You didn't want him to catch up?"

At that, she wondered why people got all confused as soon as they stepped through the door of a police station, or in this case, a gendarmerie, and blurted out things that sounded incoherent or even suspect in the eyes of the law. She could understand better now why Jonathan Clark had tried so hard to protect her after her fiancé's terrible accident. If the cops, or a life-insurance inspector had questioned her like this, what impression would she have made? Would they have discovered she wasn't telling the whole truth?

She forced herself to stand up straighter, and described everything she and Max had done since arriving in St. Barts. Another gendarme came up to listen, and several interrogatories commenced. Their repeated questions overlapped and intermeshed. If she were paranoid, she would have thought they were trying to destabilize her to make her crack. She didn't dare imagine the situation of people they held behind bars.

Jourdan left, reappearing a few minutes later with a colleague, Yves Duchâteau, who seemed more sympathetic. He even brought her a coffee and a brownie, not home-made, but it tasted alright – the only sweet thing about this evening. But it seemed strange their asking to confirm her spouse's identity, making her repeat "Rousseau, Max Rousseau" several times. She wasn't gaga, or upset enough to forget her husband's name, after all.

Then came a deluge of questions about whether they ever fought, or if he'd ever taken off from their home, then came counter-interrogatories and even a breathalyzer test, and finally, they came out with their conclusion, unexpected as it was.

"Your husband may have been swept out to sea by the strong currents."

At this point, their chief Thierry Roland came in, having been wrenched from his couch at home in the middle of his favorite police drama. But his presence changed nothing in the debate, and the events that followed were out of her control. She was no longer mistress of herself or anything. Everyone started scurrying around.

She caught snatches of their talk, though.

"…no admissions by that name in St. Martin or Sint-Maarten hospitals…not in Anguilla either, or Saba…"

"…Sea Rescue boat will be here in fifteen minutes…"

"…a helicopter isn't possible, too dark and the weather is getting worse…"

Everything was in motion now, as they prepared for a sea rescue. A hypocritical name for the mission, since they were actually setting out to search for a drowned man. The Maritime Gendarmerie was heading to Shell Beach with professional divers. Harmony followed them out of the gendarmerie like an automaton, and they seated her in an old, highly uncomfortable jeep for the drive to Shell Beach.

86

Back to the place they'd spent their last hours together. Happy hours. The coconut oil massage, the goodbye kiss, the anticipation of going out for an exhilarating evening at the casino. She wanted the officers to stop all this fuss, to stop this senseless expedition. They should be searching the roads and alleys of Gustavia, other parts of the island, every path and every trail. They should question everyone and announce on loudspeakers: "Who has seen Max Rousseau, a handsome man of thirty-one, with dark skin, blue eyes and medium build? The most handsome, loving and loyal of husbands. Dressed in gray safari bermudas and a short-sleeved, white linen shirt, carrying a wicker basket containing beach articles."

Instead, she was being helped out of the car and hustled to the middle of the beach, amidst the idlers and gawkers attracted to the scene like flies to a corpse.

She felt their gaze on her, judging her as guilty. The woman who let her husband drown.

# Chapter Fourteen

"All anguish is imaginary; reality is the antidote." Henry
Kissinger


Tuesday, December 6 – 2 A.M. The Sea Rescue patrol
boat, recognizable by its blue hull and orange cabin, sped
toward the port of Gustavia, leaving a broad zigzagging wake in
its path. The last diver had just clambered aboard, exhausted,
and the pilot, who knew the Northern islands like the back of
his hand, as well as all its passes and traps in the coral reefs,
shook his head at the gendarmerie commander as they went by.
They'd found nothing.

His feet planted in the sand like a solid post, Roland
watched the boat melt into the darkness. The sky had lost its
stars when a lid of clouds had suddenly covered it, and the boat
was soon no more than a light fading into an invisible horizon.

The commander, a man over six feet tall, was in his early
fifties, and shaved his head not because he was balding, but by
choice. With a step made heavy from fatigue, he headed back to
his service vehicle, an old Peugeot P4 that needed replacing, but
the State coffers were empty. It always started up, though, and
despite its age, it ran like a charm.

The next few hours were going to be even harder than the
ones he'd just gone through. And yet that evening, he'd been
lying on his sofa, bare feet up on a cushion, for once spending a
pleasant evening with his wife watching TV after dining on a
delectable Salade Niçoise. A glass of red wine at his elbow,
kids tucked in bed, his wife snuggled up with her head against
his shoulder. It looked to be a nice evening. Too nice to last. At
eight, a call from his men had torn him from the comfort of his
home.

How was he going to deal with the missing man's spouse?
He looked at her from the corner of his eye, still seated on the
same rock, immobile. She made him think of a lost migratory

bird. He fervently wished he could avoid this part of the job. It was so hard to find a way to inform the next-of-kin of bad news – he had to find the most humane way, and at the same time, preserve a certain distance. People reproached him sometimes, either for being too cold or for being too emotionally invested. But Mulhouse, a city in northeastern France where he was last posted, was not the same as St. Barts. He had considered himself sheltered from this kind of situation here. People here were supposed to be cut down only by old age or illness. The news of a death came from a doctor, or like in the good old days, a priest, but not by a gendarme. And yet, drownings weren't that uncommon. Just recently, they had fished out the body of a retired man on vacation, reported missing, in Gouverneur Bay. And there were always people who overestimated their state of health and started out on dangerous hikes that proved fatal.

His phone startled him out of his reverie, with its electronic ringing. All these useless apps on his smartphone, outpourings of a futurist world his brain did not yet comprehend, a world his ten-year-old manipulated as if he'd imbibed it with his first milk. Roland felt so out of touch sometimes. He was a child during the seventies, when you still drew on paper with crayons, played board games and marbles. He remembered the first touch telephones.

He was in no hurry to answer, but the ringing became more insistent. He firmly believed his phone rang differently according to the mood of his caller. The tone was soft when his sixteen-year-old daughter Julie called, or languid when it was his wife in one of her depressed moods, one she was falling into more and more often. It was her way of saying she did not to prolong his posting here. She came from Lille, and she missed her city and its folklore terribly. Her shoulders would slump, crushed by an invisible weight, a visceral need that neither boozy parties with new friends nor cigarettes could fill, and God alone knew how many cigarettes she chain-smoked throughout the day, especially here, where she could get them tax-free.

He picked up, trying to keep his irritation hidden. Fatigue was starting to overcome him, but if he wasn't mistaken, this must be the twentieth call he'd received. This was reaching the threshold of harassment. But when he heard the anxious voice on the line, he sat up straight.

"Yes, *Monsieur le Préfet*, that is correct. Yes, most likely a drowning, but we're halting the search for now. Of course, more prudent for the men."

Through innate respect toward the hierarchy, he forced himself to listen to a litany of caveats and counsel, and hung up only after delivering a final courteous phrase, "Yes, Monsieur. I will alert you instantly if anything new comes up."

The Prefect had been freshly promoted to the Northern Islands by no less than the *Président de la République*. Swelled with the pride and responsibility of his charge, he wanted this missing person case wound up as soon as possible, so he could sleep with a serene conscience. Case closed, and too bad if the drama had an unhappy ending.

Yves and his team had combed Shell Beach for five hours and still, no body, no clue as to where to direct their search next. The strong swell announced by the weather service had hit, and he'd had to send the two divers home. The commander didn't want to take any risks, especially to bring up a cadaver. The only wise decision possible, as his wife would say.

From her perch on one of the black rocks, Harmony watched the wake left by the patrol boat's departure. It was fading away, just like any hope of finding Max in the ocean was fading. With clammy hands, she held her knees folded against her chest. Even though her mind was filled with strange thoughts, and anguish mixed with mad rage, she retained an unfathomable, almost cold expression on her face. No one could guess what she was going through inside. She'd always had trouble matching her facial expressions with her real emotions.

Patricia, the island's only female rescue worker, had wrapped a gray blanket around her shoulders, making it look like she'd just survived a capsizing. The woman had maternal instincts, and had noticed Harmony shivering, slightly at first, but then so intensely that her teeth started chattering. A cool night breeze associated with extreme fear provoked reactions like that.

Coming out of her stupor, Harmony unfolded her stiff limbs like a contortionist exiting a narrow box, then got up and took off the blanket to give it back. Patricia gazed at her with pity in her eyes, trying to find comforting words, but none came. Sometimes it was better to choose silence rather than utter awkward phrases. Non-verbal communication could be more effective than empty or poorly chosen words. Patricia knew what Harmony was going through, because her vocation for this career had emerged after a similar unhappy experience – not the ocean, but fire had taken a person beloved to her.

Harmony nodded at her, then moved away with a "thank you" in her eyes. She couldn't speak either. She tried to ignore her aching body. How long had she been crouching on that rock? An atrocious, interminable length of time, gnawed by anguish. She hadn't moved a muscle aside from the involuntary clacking of her teeth, that made even her head shake, something that had never happened to her before. The weirdest thing was having it happen it here in the tropics rather than in her native city of Chicago or her city of exile, Milwaukee. Even during the most rigorous winters, even during long walks around the frozen lake, her teeth had never chattered like that.

*Max, where are you? What has happened to you?*

The thousands of shells carpeting the beach crunched under her feet. She needed to get away from here as fast as she could. Shell Beach, a dreamy paradise just hours ago, had changed into a nightmare setting. She carried her shoes in one hand, as there were some shallow cuts on the palm of the other hand. She didn't even know how she'd hurt herself – maybe climbing on the rocks. She dismissed it from her mind. It was unimportant compared to the drama she was caught up in. Her feet did hurt, though, as she walked on the broken shells, plus her ankle ached, in spite of the bandage. At least she knew she was alive, however much she wished she could awaken from this bad dream.

This rescue expedition had been decided on and organized in such a hurry. Naturally, time counted in disappearances at sea. The gendarme Yves Duchâteau, the only one who seemed to have some compassion, had told her several times that every minute lost was a minute too many.

Around ten o'clock, he had left with a younger colleague on another call, far less serious than the search for a drowned man. However, they had to pay attention, since it was a resident of St. Barts, Philippe Barnabé, who claimed a fisherman from Anguilla had let some tourists disembark at Chauvette Bay. It would have gone unnoticed except the man's Saintoise fishing boat broke down, and he'd been forced to come to Barnabé's repair shop in the Gouverneur quarter. Barnabé was a real watchdog, and he spied Captain Richardson from afar. He was closely followed by a Latino-looking couple carrying suitcases, who then took off like fugitives on the run toward the Lurin neighborhood east of Gustavia.

Barnabé had accompanied Richardson to his Saintoise. He saw two long parallel lines on the sand revealing suitcases had been aboard, then dragged up the beach. Now, it was strictly forbidden to let vacationers disembark in this way, and Barnabé wanted to preserve his island from any and all lawbreakers. What if people started hearing about tourists coming and going like that without any passport control whatsoever? He took it to heart to help the gendarmes, especially since the "real" St Barthians no longer considered him a "Maudit Corbeau," or "Damn Crow," the name given to newcomers who bought land on the island. After doing everything he possibly could to fit in, Barnabé had risen to the status of "Blanc-manger" or "Custard Pudding," a famous Caribbean coconut desert and the word for "local." He had become one of them.

He would have reported it a lot earlier, but it had been so busy that day he couldn't close his shop until eight o'clock. He'd reached the gendarmerie right after Harmony. Since then, he'd been waiting for a veteran officer to return to take his deposition, and his patience had reached its limits. He knew a search-and-rescue operation at sea was more important and more exciting, of course, and being curious to hear the news directly at headquarters, he didn't complain too much. It would be even better than television. But the new recruit, a woman at that, who was "holding down the fort," had nothing to tell him. Monsieur Barnabé wanted to discuss his information with an officer of more long-standing experience on the island.

After Duchâteau left, Harmony found herself without any solid support among the gendarmes, who were engaged in a search which, to her mind, was unaccountable, a sheer waste of time. Her husband couldn't have been swept out to sea by currents, and even less to have drowned. They didn't want to listen to her or believe her, because then they would have to consider a different hypothesis, that of a more sinister kind of disappearance.

Thierry Roland wished only to go home and climb in bed. He approached her with what he hoped were firm steps, for he'd decided to adopt a determined tone, and avoid an endless discussion with this woman who, he could tell, didn't want to imagine the worst.

"I'm sorry, Madame, but we'll have to halt the search for a short while, due to deteriorating weather conditions. We will continue at six in the morning with a helicopter, which will do some flyovers. I'm not sure how to help you face the next few hours, which will be difficult ones for you. I don't suppose you know anyone here?"

"Not a soul. It's the first time I've been here."

"We can find somewhere for you to sleep. If you want, we will requisition a room at the hospital. You've undergone such a shock that I'd feel more reassured knowing you were well looked after by medical professionals."

"A hospital room? No, anything but that! Don't worry about me, I'll take care of myself. And then, you're on the wrong track. I've repeated from the start he can't be drowned. If he'd gone back for a swim as you conjecture, why hasn't our beach gear or the basket been found here?"

"An insignificant detail. It may have been stolen, or some restaurant employees found them and put them away. They often do that with items left behind by tourists, who come asking for them in the morning. You're in a state of disbelief – I'd doubtless react the same way myself. It's difficult to accept this kind of tragedy. Hours ago, your husband was with you, and now, he's no longer to be found. It's normal, perfectly human. But you must prepare yourself for the worst, even if a miracle always remains a possibility. At Réunion island, a few years ago, a hiker was carried away when a flood rushed down a ravine, and found in the open ocean over a day later. He was saved because he had his inflatable mattress with him, regardless of the sharks that infest the zone. A fisherman rescued him. A miracle!"

"Please stop with your fairytales!"

"It's a true story," Roland said. "I merely wanted to end on a positive note."

"I know you think you're acting for the best, but I've heard enough, and borne all I can tonight. You're on the wrong track, and that's final."

# Chapter Fifteen

"Any and all water is the color of drowning."Emil Cioran

Harmony was too tired to try to convince this man, so full of condescension. Roland was stuck on an absurd path. The commander was obstinate, like all men who thought they held power and knowledge, men who rarely admitted their mistakes. A question of pride, of fearing to lose face. Yet her husband was certainly not out there in those turquoise waters, now black as the night.

A sea rescue was so much easier for them – just call the rescue unit, scan the waters, and examine the coasts, taking into account the direction the currents would have carried the person in trouble, or that person's body. At the worst, simply wait for the sea to disgorge it. Then, the last step: perform an autopsy to discover the cause of death. Drowned from exhaustion or from a sudden illness that had caused drowning?

Those were the two scenarios that Thomas, a young gendarme as handsome as he was vain, had recited to her without one ounce of tact. A peacock proud to fan out his smattering of legalistic medicine. He had come up to her around ten-thirty, when the rescue boat had started out on its mission, to explain the four phases of a typical drowning.

First came water distress, where the victim panics and bobs up and down in the water, holding to survival and seeking any help in the immediate area. Next came partial hypoxia, where the victim becomes exhausted, but is still at the surface and conscious, despite having swallowed a lot of water. This is when they see their life pass before their eyes.

The third stage is unconsciousness leading to convulsive hypoxia, where they have inhaled so much water the brain shuts down from lack of oxygen, and the body can go into convulsions. They must be saying their goodbyes to friends and families, saying they loved them.

Finally comes the last stage, where respiration and cardiac activity stop, cyanosis sets in, and the face turns blue because the blood, without enough oxygen, becomes darker.

To top it all off, Thomas explained how not all victims go through the four stages. For example, in the case of a sudden heart attack or hydrocution, those victims turn a waxy white color. And obviously, he added, murder victims, whose cadavers are thrown into the ocean to erase all trace of the crime, float on the surface and when found, autopsies easily rule out drowning as cause of death.

The young gendarme had spoken to her as if he were a coroner, adding psychological details about the drowning person's train of thought and the total experience they lived through, how they saw their lives flash by and the faces of the people they loved most. Chin up and chest out, proud of his knowledge, he had finally set his eyes on Harmony, and his satisfied smile drooped. This was the probable widow of a drowned man, and he hadn't at all considered how she would feel. A beginner's mistake. His mother's saying, "Think twice before opening your mouth" came to mind, but he'd developed this defect very early on and it only got worse the older he got.

Harmony had glared at him, and looked him up and down disdainfully. His regulation-razed head hanging, he had moved away, carrying the weight of his enormous blunder. Harmony then complained to the commander, who had excused the indiscreet gendarme as being "young, impulsive and unexperienced." That was when she had retreated to her rock, and only Patricia had come to break her solitude by wrapping her trembling shoulders with a blanket.

Drowned. A common occurrence at the seaside, especially since the island's swimming areas had no lifeguards. And the officers had no wish to launch into the investigation of a possibly criminal disappearance, which clashed with the idyllic image of their super-safe island where you could leave your keys in the ignition and your house unlocked with your wallet in plain view on your terrace table. Pilfering or petty larceny was more in line with St. Barts, and provided tidbits for local gossip wires, which treated banal incidents as if they were brutal serial murders.

An investigation into an abduction would change their cushy jobs, usually limited to handing out tickets for speeding, drunk driving or nocturnal disturbances. At least those were the only crimes Harmony could imagine taking place in St. Barts. What else could they do here? Oh, yeah, search for supposedly drowned people! They hadn't wanted to believe her when she insisted her husband had left the beach right after her.

Yes, she had been in a hurry to get her shopping done before the ferry left for St. Martin. But she couldn't walk fast because of those stupid platform shoes that threatened a sprain at every teetering step. Which had ended up happening.

No, he wasn't tired from their outing or their voyage. He'd had plenty of time to recuperate since their arrival, plus, there wasn't even a time difference to adjust to.

No, no, they hadn't been drinking too much. Why had they been so relentless concerning that question, hammering it at her again and again? All because she'd accepted Officer Jourdan's request to take a breathalyzer test. It had turned out .04 percent, supporting their theory Max drowned after drinking too much and taking one last dip, the "one too many" for this unmindful tourist. She could already imagine the headline in the local paper.

No, certainly not – he didn't take sleeping pills or heart medicine.

No, he didn't smoke.

No, he had no history of depression.

No, no, no, they hadn't argued before his disappearance. A marital dispute, they said. Furious, Max had gone back into the water after drinking a last cocktail, only to drink some saltwater...

Yes, her husband was an excellent swimmer and had incredible endurance. She'd repeated this information, but it hadn't seemed to interest them. They'd known many excellent swimmers to drown.

They seemed even less interested when she insisted he'd never go back in the water knowing they had to get back to the boat soon. And she'd seen him carefully brush the sand from all their belongings and put them back into the basket. He loved the sea, but he hated how sand got into everything. He always did that, and he always carried the basket, just like on their honeymoon in Malibu.

So where was their beach basket? It held their snorkeling gear and two huge blue and purple towels with their names embroidered on them. No one had found any of it. Supposedly it was in a restaurant or it had been stolen. A wicker basket containing nothing of value, no wallet, key or passport, a silly larceny on an island where hardly anything was ever stolen.

And finally, yes, yes, and yes. She was definitely certain she'd seen him for the last time less than a hundred feet behind her, a question they asked many times. She had indicated the exact spot on Rue de la place d'Armes on the detailed map of Gustavia that covered a good part of one wall in the station. That's why he couldn't have gone back for a swim on the spur of the moment. It didn't make any sense.

All their questions drove her crazy. They'd even managed to make her hesitate about the number of cocktails and glasses of wine they drank and what they ate for lunch; was it light or heavy? Two Caesar salads with shrimp, what could be lighter than that? They would have preferred she reply, "Steak and fries with Bearnaise sauce," to uphold their drowning theory, that he'd eaten and drunk too much, gone back in the water one last time and drowned!

Harmony would have to convince them later on; it was useless to try tonight.

Roland already had one foot in his jeep, but then turned back to her.

"Let me at least drop you off at a hotel. I'd like to be sure there's a room for you."

"No thank you, I want to be alone. Don't worry about me. I'll figure it out."

He was expecting this refusal – she'd been stubborn from the start. Denying reality. That was why he'd deliberately recounted the story of the rescued man in Réunion, to get her to adhere to the possibility her husband had gone back into the water, resulting in a tragic outcome, that he had drowned. This fit the concept of progressivity he'd learning during one of his obligatory police training sessions where, for the most part, he yawned from beginning to end.

He climbed into his very dirty jeep and ordered the driver to get going. He knew he would have trouble sleeping despite his fatigue. What a plague! A drowned man whose body couldn't be found, and a wife who would wander the town for the rest of the night, a homeless woman on an island dedicated to luxury tourism and its accompanying licentiousness.

# Chapter Sixteen

"Passports are only good for annoying honest folks, and aiding in the flight of rogues."
Jules Verne, *Around the World in Eighty Days*

Monday, December 5, 2016. It was three in the afternoon according to the microwave clock. Her watch battery had died, so she hoped the clock was right. Even though not much time was left, Sonia Marques felt a little release from the pressure. To have missed the boat because of a visa! They had organized every last thing, but missed this detail. To cross from St. Martin to St. Barts, the French authorities required a visa for certain non-Europeans. But she absolutely could not delay the crossing. They would have to start all over, and it would be more difficult. Putting off such a meticulous plan would risk ruining everything. She'd had to find a solution in a hurry, and at Marigot's maritime station she had found it. And now here she was, finally in St. Barts, in the famous villa. She could heave a sigh of relief.

Fernando Sanchez was with her, ever ready to lend a hand, especially if it was both useful and agreeable. Sonia had chosen the ideal drop point, nice and discreet, and she paid for the plane tickets, which got Fernando to wondering how all this money had come into her hands. He was no idiot. Her receptionist salary didn't cover all that. He did know this rich man's villa had come to them through an old acquaintance, a sucker she could easily cajole with a simple phone call and a few endearing phrases like, "I love you, darling. I miss you so much."

Fernando didn't understand the fascination she exercised on certain men. She could make them crazy. Fortunately, there was nothing more than platonic friendship between them, and each took advantage of the other as much as they could. If Sonia had confided in Fernando, it was because she needed his protection in case something went wrong, which was odd, since she had assured him everything would be easy. But she also needed his help to pass incognito on the island. Since their arrival in St. Martin, she had used his little sister's Columbian passport. So Sonia now went by the name Gloria Sanchez. They resembled each other: Latino women, five feet, two inches tall, identical figures, the same long black hair, round face and pouty lips. The only difference was that Sonia was a "made in France" Latino, descending from Spanish immigrants, while Gloria was a "made in Bogota" Latino who could cook *ajiaco* soup like Sonia would never be able to do.

Sonia hadn't told him much about their destination, however. The less he knew, the fewer faux pas he could make. But she had promised him five thousand euros in cash. A vacation in a heavenly spot and easy dough – what more could he ask? Therefore, Fernando kept his mouth shut.

How could he know you had to have a pass to travel between two French islands? And what a state she'd been in when they failed to board the ferry in Oyster Pond! They could have simply gotten their visas and taken the evening ferry, but no, Sonia was supposedly on a strict schedule, down to the minute, and had to reach the villa by three in the afternoon, at any price. Not a good start to his vacation. She'd found a quicker solution by hiring a boat, but the Saintoise had broken down three miles from the St. Barts coast. A little longer and Fernando had imagined paddling with his arms or being picked up by the coast guard in the middle of the Caribbean. The incognito she wanted to maintain was in danger of unraveling, but then the engine had finally started and gotten them safely to St. Barts.

They had landed on a beach, and lost their way getting to town, as the skipper had given them the wrong directions. But they'd had the bright idea of following the trajectory of planes descending into the airport, and they knew the Avis car rental agency was there. Sonia had reserved a car under the name Gloria Sanchez, so after filling out forms and paying the deposit, they had climbed into a Suzuki mini-SUV with heavily tinted windows. Not to stay cool, but to stay discreet. From outside, you couldn't tell what was happening inside, and that's what Sonia wanted: to see without being seen. She was lucky to find one. In many countries, windows that opaque were illegal because they led to an explosion of delinquency and attacks.

Fernando whistled as he looked all around the sparkling villa. Nothing to complain about here: the immense living room with French doors opening onto wood decks, a tennis court, an infinity pool whose water seemed to melt into the turquoise Caribbean Sea. He was dying to dive in. Then he would float around on the yellow air mattress, with the floating table in fluorescent pink that had little pockets to hold drinks. He envisioned a rum punch full of ice cubes. The rum, lemons and sugar cane syrup were in the fridge, and all he had to do was serve himself. That was the first thing he'd done: make sure the refrigerator was filled up, the survival reflex of a child raised in the favela with a large family.

Sonia had told him that her former lover, whose place they were squatting, would soon be there. The sucker Cédric Deruenne, whom she had dubbed "Cederico" to sound more Spanish. Another guest would also be showing up within the hour, but Fernando would hardly see him. A businessman, a certain Stéphane, who was not to be bothered under any pretext, and who would remain in his room for most of the time. Another of Sonia's machinations, as secret as ever. It had nothing to do with him – to each his own. As long as he got his five thousand euros, it was all fine with him.

Fernando planned to go out that night to see if the local girls here were shy or not. Or better yet, the tourists. Women who were far from home acted a lot looser than at home. After all, he was on vacation, too, and may as well enjoy it, even if he didn't have an official job the rest of the year. He was no millionaire, but he knew how to use his Latin charm. His eyes glowed like embers, his dark skin gave him the rugged look of someone who spent his time outdoors, and too bad if he lacked "culture," whatever that was. Once in the sack, he would show them what his culture was all about.

Sonia visited the six bedrooms, each with its own bathroom. All were tastefully decorated with white lacquered furniture and touches of sky blue on the chair-rails. She immediately chose the room with an ocean view, so she could watch the ferries coming in to Gustavia.

She wasn't sure if she should have asked Fernando to take part in her scheme, but on the whole, she thought it was a good idea. She needed his sister's passport to remain incognito, and if necessary, he could protect her from the mysterious guest. But Fernando constantly got things mixed up, which annoyed her. He couldn't manage to call her by his sister's name, and had used "Sonia" in the fisherman's boat and in the Avis office, and now he had to remember to call her Sonia in front of her old lover Cédric. It was too complicated for that poser's brain.

Cédric had gotten worried when he didn't see them arrive on the ten o'clock ferry, and tried to call her a thousand times. Too angry from their difficulties with visas and all the rest, she had answered only after they'd rented the car.

Cédric's impatience, the fisherman's engine troubles, Fernando confounding her name – it was getting hard to manage. Months of preparation risked going to the dogs. Luckily, it wouldn't be long now. In another ten days, she hoped it would all be over. She would have her money and her revenge. No one was going to get away with pulling a dirty trick on her, like Max Rousseau had tried. He was going to pay for it.

After getting fired from his head chef job, he abruptly left Miami. She called him repeatedly, and at first, he responded, only to trot out some nonsense or other. Like the one that he was taking jobs as an extra in Chicago. But he was lying from the get-go. Firstly, he hadn't been fired; he had quit. She learned that a few months ago, when she overheard two HR execs talking about how it was too bad Max had quit. She'd called him for an explanation, but it was all bunk. He hemmed and hawed, searching for something believable, and finally said he'd felt obligated to resign because clients had complained about the cuisine. It sounded lame, false. And then he stopped answering her calls, even when she hid her number.

He was a wary one, but she had found him. No one tosses her away like that! She carried out her research, learning that Max had been seen with the "poor, depressed" hotel guest many times, and one of the waiters surprised him leaving a suite on the thirtieth floor in the company of a pretty blond, a certain Harmony Flynt. With her keen intuition, Sonia had guessed the truth, and eventually found the address in Milwaukee where she lived with her new husband.

Sonia unpacked, then took off all her clothes, slathered her body with sunscreen, and put on a gold bikini. She looked at herself in the closet door mirror, not a little proud of her generous chest overfilling the bikini top, her wasp waist, her curvy buttocks. She even forgot the inferiority complex she sometimes felt because her Mediterranean genes had given her a short stature. But she hadn't had any kids, and she could still show off her hourglass figure. She wondered if she would be like her mother after having a child or two, and become a solid block of flesh. She swore it would never happen, not to her.

Their forced march along all those roads of St. Barts, dragging their suitcases, had made her perspire heavily. What a race against the clock that had been! And this day was timed down to the last minute. She had just enough time to take a dip. She got nervous again. After the pool, she had to go to Gustavia. She liked to be a bit early, rather than late. Otherwise, she would have to start all over.

Before heading to the terrace, she verified that her Gloria Sanchez passport was in her purse, and she hid her own passport in the suitcase.

# Chapter Seventeen

"We endlessly search for a shelter. A place where the wind doesn't blow so hard. A place to go to. And that shelter is a face, and that face is enough for us." Olivier Adam, *Cliffs*

December 6, 2016 – 2:50 A.M. Not a soul around, but Harmony felt relieved at that. She could clear her mind, and maybe this headache, like a metal band around her head, would go away. She wandered the lanes of Gustavia, retracing for the umpteenth time the path she'd followed earlier that day, until the place became almost familiar. The trendy night clubs, the hushed villas. She wished she could enjoy it all and forget the last few hours, or file them under the category of bad dreams. But this was all too real.

Rue de la place d'Armes. She recognized the exact spot where she turned around and saw Max, because of the graffiti standing out on an otherwise white wall. A heart drawn around two initials, an "N" then the plus sign then an "A" that someone had tried to erase. Her husband had smiled at her and mouthed the words "I love you." His expression and the way he said it had been so intense. Knowing him, she had figured he was glad to see her so cheerful, so excited to go find *the* dress. She had quickly walked away, so he wouldn't follow her or see which boutique she went into. And she had not seen him since.

She was no longer sure if he was carrying the straw basket or not. Sometimes, she pictured him with his hands in his pockets, nonchalant, but then saw him with one hand holding the basket handles. The brain often reconstructs memories into the version it wants. If he had his hands in his pockets, maybe he went back to the beach to get their forgotten beach gear and then been tempted to dive into those turquoise waters, as the gendarmes supposed. No. She discarded that hypothesis entirely.

The disagreeable sensation that she was being followed suddenly made her turn around. Nobody. She waited a few seconds to reassure herself, but there wasn't even a cat in sight, or rather there were two, a white one and an orange striped one, measuring each other and flexing their muscles. They circled each other, glaring, and broke out yowling their war cries. These little felines could be so impressive. Max didn't like them much, distrusting their fickleness. But there was no human in sight, so she limped down the street again. Darn ankle!

A few minutes later, she reached the boutique where she'd bought the silvery dress. The display window, illuminated by strings of Christmas lights, seemed surrealistic in this tropical clime. A mannequin was dressed in the sparkly black dress with the straps crossing the back, so similar to the one she wore the night of her surprise visit to Steven Reardon's. The resemblance was so striking that she staggered.

The past always comes back, like a boomerang, especially that moment she so wanted to forget. She wondered if she should have told Max about Steven's death, and that of her alleged best friend, Meg Sutton. Such a quiet girl, with a prudish manner. Harmony should have suspected that odd smile of hers, almost a smirk. But what good would it have done to tell Max? After all, the police had concluded it was an ordinary car accident. And now she'd finally met the love of her life – she'd done right by not saying anything. That would have only stirred up trouble and provoked questions and then suspicions. Nothing good.

Her former fiancé's insurance company had settled a large sum on her after his death, but the money was well-hidden and idle. She'd never touched that cursed money. She had considered giving it to a charity, perhaps one that helped car accident victims, but Jonathan Clark advised against it, saying no one could predict the future, that he wasn't immortal and that the money might come in handy one day.

She had wished she could bury it all: her engagement, that black dress, that freezing cold night. Those years altogether. To get married and start a new life "until death did them part." To make a clean break with the past.

And it had happened. They even planned to conceive a child, who would seal the indivisible bonds of their blood, of their love. Thinking of all this made her imagine the worst, and she had to force herself not to sob. Commander Roland and his whole band of gendarmes exasperated her. Max would reappear; he had to reappear.

She was still carrying the sack with the silver dress, a costly purchase that might never be of any use to her. It somehow made her responsible for all these misfortunes, like in the "domino effect" she'd often discussed with Max. That one action of hers had caused another, and another. If she hadn't been so bent on finding the "perfect dress" at any cost, maybe none of this would ever have come to pass. She would have been with him all this time, taking the same road, eating an ice cream together before boarding the ferry and returning to their hotel room in Oyster Pond. They would have dressed up like a royal couple to have fun at the casino, excited and laughing, drinking just enough, not too much, and then they would have returned to their room to fall on the bed and make love, no holds barred, no fear the neighbors might hear them. That was part of vacationing too: not caring what others thought. You didn't know them and would never see them again.

She yawned for the first time that night. The adrenaline that had kept her awake was fading, and she needed to rest. The search would continue in less than three hours, but they would end up halting it sooner or later, when they realized it was in vain. They would finally listen to her and admit their error. She could still hear mocking insinuations in their reaction when she mentioned the possibility of his having run into some criminals: "Why would someone kidnap your husband – you're not rich, are you? If you were, you would have arrived in a private jet, not on the ferry like ordinary people. And your careers don't exactly attract attention – you're an accountant and he's a chef taking time off to write a novel. You're not exactly rolling in dough, and then, this is St. Barts. There's hardly any crime here. You read too many detective stories or watch too many police dramas, Madame…"

Their pat speeches ran through her mind like a broken record until she entered the Rue de la République, by the pier. Light filtered out from a small hotel, the Sunset, which she had photographed from the upper bridge of the ferry. She was exhausted, and without further consideration, she walked in. On the right, a striped blue and white sofa invited her to lie down, and on the left, a young hotel clerk sat behind a stately colonial-era wood counter, ensconced in a leather armchair, his feet up on another chair. He was watching an English soccer match, Manchester versus Liverpool, and despite her entrance he seemed reluctant to unglue his eyes from the screen, as if hypnotized, and merely gave her a swift greeting. It wasn't until the referee blew his whistle to end the first half that he stood up and looked at the woman who'd just come in, noticing her tired blue eyes.

He ran a hand through his hair and said, "Bonjour, Madame, or rather good evening. Are you a client of the hotel?"

"No, I need a room for the rest of the night. Do you have anything available?"

"Well, it's really late, the middle of the night. It's weird---"

He broke off. If his boss had heard him speaking in such a familiar tone, he would have made a scene, at which he was quite an expert. The soccer match, even if it wasn't live, had made him forget he was at work. Saint-Barthélemy, Saint-Barth, St. Barts… Celebrities, riches, Russian oligarchs, highest-class service, big dollar signs, caviar, lobster, champagne. Words that made his head spin. He couldn't wait for the season to end, to go back to the French countryside, to the dairies, pastures and rivers, to where people were genuine. But his boss wasn't there, that's what counted. And the security camera had broken down the day before, so he could breathe again.

Harmony paused before answering, feeling somehow guilty for being caught roaming around in the middle of the night.

"I missed the last boat. It's too long to explain, but I just want to sleep, at least a few hours, in a bed."

"I'm truly sorry, Madame, but hotels here are limited to forty suites, and we're fully booked until the end of January."

"I was afraid of that. Thanks anyway."

Harmony already had her hand on the doorknob, thinking she'd have to find a park bench somewhere, when the clerk exclaimed, "Wait! Please have a seat on the sofa, and I'll check to see if there's a room nearby. I assume you're looking for something in the same price range as the Sunset?"

Harmony merely nodded. She wasn't too optimistic about finding a bed, and she didn't even know what price range he was referring to. She collapsed on the sofa. All remaining decorum fled. Usually so irreproachably dressed, she felt like a beggar in her wrinkled, dirty dress, with sandy feet, one shoe, and mussed-up hair, topped off by her anxious look, that of someone searching for a roof over her head. The only things she wished for at this point were a hot shower, clean clothes and a bed. And above all, for her husband to be found safe and sound.

Her eyelids felt heavy and the comfortable sofa was dragging her down into dreamland, but she had to resist, and wait for the clerk to finish his inquiries.

After calling the few lower-priced guesthouses and B&Bs, all of which were full, he decided to play his last card, and fished out a flyer from his wallet. It showed a sailboat and the interior of a carefully appointed cabin. He called the number, printed in large letters, and a asked about lodgings. He repeated his request several times, as if the person were deaf, but finally hung up, muttering, "I should have fixed it so I could've gone to that party, too…"

But his enthusiasm returned. Just in time, too: the players would soon hit the soccer field after the half-time break.

"I've got something for you, but it's not a room in a hotel," he said, sounding proud he'd found something to help her out. "It's a cabin on a yacht. It won't cost much, at least not for this island. Two hundred euros a night, including breakfast."

"Sleep on a sailboat?"

"Don't worry, the captain is a local, or almost. He's lived here a long time on his boat, and he rents the cabins. As a temporary solution, you won't do better than this. I could call other hotels, but – hold on to your seat – they'll set you back between eight hundred and two thousand euros a night."

"I guess I have no choice, then. It's either that or sleep under the stars, as I don't want to throw that much money out the window."

"I would offer to let you sleep on the sofa here, but my boss would be furious if he found out. And he's sure to be at six-thirty. Should I phone the guy to come pick you up?"

She sighed and said, "Alright."

"Don't worry, he'll be here right away. You're in luck, as he's at a party not far from here."

Harmony thanked him and went out to wait on the sidewalk. Three months earlier, when she was ripping open the envelope with their plane tickets, she could never have imagined being in this situation, standing on a sidewalk in Gustavia waiting for a total stranger to pick her up in the middle of the night. And her Max missing…

A few yards away, she thought she saw a movement, a furtive shadow that instantly disappeared. Was someone spying on her? She shook her head, thinking she was creating drama. Why would anyone follow her?

# Chapter Eighteen

"It reassures me to be haunted by my old obsessions. Better a tame nightmare than the raw wound of a recent memory."
Daniel Sernine, *Quand vient la nuit (As Night Falls)*

A gray Chevy station wagon pulled up in front of her. Surfboards were piled up in the back, and squeezed in among them an enormous black Newfoundland sat lolling its tongue, and gazing at the stoic woman on the sidewalk. A slender man in his mid-twenties immediately got out and stuck out his hand. He was mestizo, with dreadlocks and black eyes, and a virile look about him. A somewhat rare type here. Unlike most of the Caribbean islands, the majority of St. Barts' population was Caucasian, the ancestors of French settlers.

"So you're the absent-minded tourist who forgot to get back on the boat?"

He spoke French with a slight accent that stressed the "r," which meant he wasn't Antillean.

"I guess that's me, Harmony Flynt by name," she said, holding out her hand timidly. "And you?"

"Florent. And that's my dog Tempest."

"Florent...what?"

"Does it matter? You'll be on my boat for only a few hours. You'll never see me again after tomorrow, and you'll have forgotten it anyway."

"I like to know people's names, especially if they lodge me."

"Do you know the name of the owner of the hotel you're staying at?"

"You're being funny, I assume? In general, when I stay at someone's place, I know his or her name."

"I'll give it to you then. Florent Van Steerteghem."

"Van...what?"

"You see now why I don't give my whole name – for a lot of people, it's unpronounceable. But congratulations, it's rare for an American to speak French so well. Such a relief."

He gestured for her to take a seat in the old Chevrolet, and he climbed in behind the wheel. He took off so fast she had to grab the door handle. Maybe it would have been better to go find a park bench. Starlight and mosquitos suddenly seemed perfectly fine compared to Florent Van-whatever's driving. Too late though – she no longer had the nerve to order him to stop and let her out.

His racecar style made her relive some painful moments, like when she was twelve, going to the hospital in an ambulance without being able to move a muscle, being in shock. And the rollercoasters at the fairgrounds. Her brother had a fixation on them, and she'd finally caved in and brought him to the Promised Land of attraction parks in Florida. She'd climbed into one of those infernal cars, the kind that fly around on rails, and where in some spots, only empty space surrounds you. She kept her eyes closed, hid her feelings, tried to forget her fear. She did it for her brother.

But to give him that treat, she'd faked an illness and used her paid sick-leave days, and as she exited the rollercoaster, she encountered her human resources director. What was the probability of that? The same vacation dates, the same destination, the same ride at the exact same time? One mischance in a million. She should have bought a lottery ticket that day. The axe fell; she was summarily fired. Then followed the move from Chicago to Milwaukee, where Jonathan Clark's connections helped her land a job. She thought about the domino effect again, a theory Max held dear.

Florent drove without talking, concentrating, his foot moving constantly from accelerator to brake pedal. Changing gear every fifteen yards, hardly ever to fourth though. Uphill, downhill, curve after curve at the same wild speed. A real-life rollercoaster.

The memory of her brother, her anxiety at Max's disappearance, her pain and fatigue, and the ordeal of this muscular driving – it was all too much. The windows were open, but a hot flush made her scalp tingle, and her body felt imprisoned in an oven. Duchâteau's brownie and coffee, the ice cream; it all felt abnormally present, undigested. It was crazy how the stomach could hold on to food, churning it without letting it go on to the intestines. She threw up.

Florent instantly screeched on the brakes and came to a halt at the side of the road. "Oh, no. Goddammit! What did you do?"

He jumped out and opened her car door, grabbed her arm and pulled her out. He had her sit on the side of the road, where her weight flattened the tall weeds growing there, then he headed to the trunk. The dog had been calm until then, but now she started to jiggle and wave her huge tail, ready to come to his aid.

He came back with a jug of water, which he poured on the vomit before scrubbing the seat thoroughly with a rag and some disinfectant spray.

"Sorry I dragged you out of the car like that, but I had to clean it up right away. With the heat here, it gets encrusted and leaves a terrible smell. It takes days for the stink to wear off."

He handed her the jug, saying, "Here, rinse your face."

Harmony poured it over her head. Although tepid, it revived her. She took a sip, gargled, then spit it out.

"Is it still far?" she managed to say. "I can't handle many more of those curves or your driving. If you don't slow down, it'll probably happen again."

"Get in. I'll drive slower, and as soon as I drop off these boards at a friend's place, we'll go straight to the boat."

He kept his promise to drive more reasonably. To calm her nausea, Harmony kept her eyes fixed on a point far ahead and tried to keep still. They made a stop in the Grand Fond area, which was wrapped in sleep. He unloaded the boards with the help of a young man who looked European but had dreadlocks

117

half hidden under a cap of the colors of Jamaica. He'd come out of a small cabin wearing nothing but tight orange underwear, seemingly oblivious of how revealing they were. They said goodbye with a fist bump, so much more virile than a handshake.

It was only on the second try that the car started with a jolt. In the meanwhile, the enormous dog had hopped into the front seat and planted itself between the two of them, curious about the new occupant. Harmony now had to tolerate the smell of wet dog as well as its drooling. It seemed she was to be spared nothing.

The time seemed long, but within ten minutes they passed a sign announcing Corossol. Bordering a bay close to Gustavia, its houses could not be crammed closer together; not an inch of land was lost, understandable given its value per square foot. A thick cement wall seemed to serve as a dike, in front of which were lines of parking places. Definitely not the most idyllic spot on the island.

Florent's dinghy sat in the middle of the beach, flanked by small fishing boats. The sea was rough, as the weather reports had predicted, and every wave rushed right up to his inflatable. Florent appeared angry with himself for not having been more vigilant – it could have been swept out to sea. He muttered to himself as he pulled the bow around and untied it.

"I was lucky this time, but I won't make that mistake again."

Tempest ran around the boat a few times, then leaped in and curled up under the wood bench.

"Take off your shoes. I'll push the dinghy out a bit, then you jump in. No hesitating. And don't worry – you'll be better once you're on the boat. You really feel the swell here, but much less out there."

Despite his assurances, this was yet another ordeal for Harmony. But she managed to tumble into the dingy in a ridiculous manner. Her normal suppleness let her down completely, and her joints felt as stiff as an arthritic grandma's, not to mention her throbbing ankle. Both her bags got wet, as did her dress, right up to the waist. The last straw for her moral. She felt like crying, but a sense of shame kept them in check. Her host had already seen her throw up – that was enough, too much in fact.

The sailboat was anchored fairly close to the beach, among a multitude of other boats, a floating village across from a terrestrial village. His magnificent fifty-foot catamaran was named *Bísó na bísó*. She asked him about it.

"That means 'between us' in Lingala," Florent said. "My mother came from the Democratic Republic of Congo."

Africa! Harmony had often dreamed of a safari trip to Kenya, as clichéd as that may be for Western tourists. Some day, perhaps.

The boat, her substitute hotel, was swinging roughly from one side to the other, tugging at its anchor, and yet her nausea did not get worse. Her stomach had already emptied itself.

With the waves and wind, Florent had difficulty coming alongside to hitch to the catamaran, and he was so tired he couldn't handle the dinghy as well as usual. He definitely regretted accepting the invitation to that party. What a waste of time. And he dreaded the next day – the hangover, the pounding head. He'd limited his alcohol consumption, but skipped too many hours of sleep, something he didn't tolerate well. He had wanted some feminine company, and while the girls there had been pretty, they'd also proved superficial and empty-headed. They had turned his stomach with their stupid laughter. He wouldn't screw an idiot, even if she was hot and didn't ask for payment. He thought of his friend Carolina's sensual body, and smiled. He would be seeing her soon in St. Martin.

After a few attempts, Florent tied up to the port stern. Feeling relieved, Harmony extricated herself from the dinghy, which seemed too capricious to be safe, and stepped up to the deck, then into the cockpit, hoping this would be her final effort before resting. A woman in her forties was sitting there, her legs on the table, feet crossed, sipping a glass of rosé. She looked the unexpected guest up and down, grinned, and said "Hi" before hiccupping loudly. Harmony replied with a murmured "Hi." She didn't want to start a conversation, especially since the woman seemed ready to party despite the hour and the blustery weather.

Florent introduced them. "Madame Harmony Flynt, this is Brigitte Blondel, who's also staying with me. I'll serve you breakfast in the saloon tomorrow morning, or should I say in a few hours..."

Florent arranged the snorkeling gear and bodyboards strewn around the deck, and threw some beer bottles into a trash bag. Brigitte had evidently kept up her intake during his absence.

"Madame Flynt, there's the galley," he said, pointing down into the main cabin. "Cold drinks are in the fridge. They're free and you can have as many as you want. When do you want me to serve breakfast?"

"I'm not sure. When I wake up, and if the nausea is gone, which is unsure at this point."

"Don't you have to take the ferry tomorrow?"

"Yes. Well, not the morning boat, but maybe in the evening. Nothing is certain right now, and I may even have to stay here longer."

"No problem. The cabin's available for another ten days. Okay, let's not stay up any later. We have to get a little sleep, right? Follow me down the starboard hatchway, and I'll show you your cabin. I sleep on the port side."

Harmony followed him as he pointed things out. He was proud of his beautiful boat.

"Here's your cabin, and there's the head – you know, the bathroom. The rule is everyone takes a shower before hitting the sack. I like to keep my boat clean. Just don't waste water – you get wet, soap up, rinse and get out. Then there's Brigitte's cabin. Got all that?"

Harmony nodded but didn't reply. Florent swept his eyes over her stained dress, her sandy, salty skin and scraped hands,

120

then handed her a towel. It smelled wonderful, like lavender. The rules on a boat imposed extreme order and cleanliness, and he sighed to think of the bottles still rolling around overhead, and the dregs of beer spilled over the bridge. Brigitte would get her ears boxed tomorrow.

"Excuse me, but would you have some pajamas or nightgown I could borrow?"

Florent disappeared for a few minutes, then came back grinning. He handed her a T-shirt with a big red heart on it, which couldn't look more juvenile, as well as a toiletries kit, the kind hotels offer. His eyes full of wonder, he took out a miniscule tube of toothpaste, mini toothbrush, and a soap the size of a cherry. Then, from a plastic bag, he pulled some jeans shorts with frazzled edges and a pair of pistachio green thong undies of questionable taste.

"Here are some clothes a client left behind. The underwear isn't brand new, sorry, but I washed it with bleach. I usually throw out stuff people leave, but I didn't this time, I don't know why. Maybe the green color – I like that. The toiletries are new, a gift from Air France."

He smiled, sure he would earn a smile, but Harmony was too sick at heart. She could only manage to thank him with a thumbs-up.

A few minutes later, she was sitting like a Buddha in the shower, tepid water flowing over her. Hypnotized by the waterfall, she meditated, until some loud knocking at the door put an end to her tranquility. An angry voice, distorted by the rustling of the water, reached her.

"Come on, you're not in a hotel. Water is precious on a boat!"

Jolted back into harsh reality, she instantly turned off the faucet and started crying. Tears of relief, tears that freed her from all the intense stress of the last hours.

*Max, where are you? What did I do to deserve this? I never should have gone to buy that dress and leave you alone.*

She got out of the shower and stood naked in front of the sink. The round mirror resembled the boat's porthole, but she couldn't see herself through all the steam. She dried off with the sweet-smelling towel then wrapped it around her body, its perfume making her recall how Max wanted to show her the lavender fields of Provence one day.

In her private cabin was a high, wide bunk framed in wood, solidly fixed to the bulkhead. Cubbies occupied the space above the bunk, where she found only pillows and bedding, nothing heavy that could fall and injure someone if the boat rolled or pitched drastically. Florent had thought of everything. She was surprised at the how cool the cabin was, as she'd been afraid she wouldn't be able to sleep without A/C. With her sunburn, she was thankful it wasn't hot.

She pulled on the kitschy t-shirt, stretched out on the bunk, and pulled the blanket up to her neck. She had to rest, so she turned off her phone and began repeating her mantra: clear your mind, stop thinking, let the fatigue fill you.

She fell asleep, and fell into a weird dream.

She was paddling in the ocean. The turquoise water was delicious, and she felt wonderful, swimming next to Max, diving down to discover angelfish, surgeon fish, starfish. But suddenly, he let go of her hand and started sinking into deep water. A few seconds later he came up, panicking, twisting and turning in superhuman efforts to stay afloat. She drifted, petrified, watching the scene like a spectator in a cinema, powerless to change a storyline written in advance. She screamed, "I love you, never anyone but you!" and while still in the dream, in complete contrast with what she was going through, she started to smile and even to rejoice. Why rejoice like that?

At the same instant, screaming erupted, real screams that pulled her out of her nightmare. A couple was about to climax, and their moans and cries grew indecently loud, then stopped. A few seconds later, she heard some whispering, but that was all. Almost total silence, aside from the rhythmic slapping of waves on the hull. Exhausted, she fell back to sleep, only to enter a new dream.

Max and her brother were sitting with her in an open rollercoaster car, about to start a ride. Her brother sat in between them, and they both held one of his hands. They were laughing, having fun, happy. The train departed with a frightening lurch directly into its top speed, and continued at that crazy rate. The teddy bear her brother had tucked firmly between his knees was ejected and crashed into the ground. Then she saw herself leaning over to look at the bloody teddy bear, and when she straightened up, she found herself face to face with Jonathan Clark, who was staring at her with sad, sad eyes.

# Chapter Nineteen

"Live for what tomorrow offers, not for what yesterday took away." Anonymous

January 1997. Jonathan Clark's chauffeur Emilio parked in front of the Lycée Français. Emilio, who was born in El Salvador, was a discreet, polite, ever-punctual young man whose boss insisted he drop off little Harmony Flynt at least a half-hour before classes started. Clark wanted her change of schools to be an easy one. Meeting her new classmates and especially, immersion in a foreign language was, for him, stressful enough. He hadn't forced her to choose this high school, although his deceased daughter Kimberly had attended it. Harmony liked the idea from the start. She looked forward to the challenge of becoming bilingual, as it would keep her mind busy and prevent her from brooding on the tragedy she had lived through a few weeks earlier. So was about to turn a new page in her life.

"Here we are, Miss," Emilio said, pulling up to the school. "I hope it all goes for the best today – I'm sure it will."

He turned around and gave her a big smile of encouragement. He had two girls of his own, one of whom was her age.

"Thanks, Emilio. See you this evening."

She would have liked to hug someone, and get a kiss on the cheek like her mother always used to do. Instead, she politely said goodbye as she got out, trembling slightly. The freezing mist didn't help matters. And yet she had awaited this day so impatiently during those long days in the hospital and the weeks confined to the Clark's home to get physical therapy and talk regularly with a psychologist. Talks where Harmony had been annoyed by the doctor's insistence; she just wanted to go back to real life, including school. But now that the moment had arrived, she had to force herself not to jump back in the car, return to the Clark's bourgeois home, and shut herself up in her room.

She'd felt comfortable in her old school, even if she had only a few friends. It was her milieu, her familiar social environment of working-class families with modest incomes. They watched the same TV shows, had the same interests and spent their free time in the same way: playing basketball or skateboarding.

This high school was another world entirely, a higher social class with different codes and activities. Horseback riding, classical music, ballet. She would have to relearn everything. Plus, if all went well, she would enter the dormitory. Jonathan Clark was a charitable man, but his wife Katreen wanted to set limits to their generosity, notably emotional limits. Harmony was not to "replace" their deceased child. She would soon move into the dorms, and go home only during school holidays and long weekends.

After high school, they would pay for college and help her find an apartment, so she could become completely independent. All this was Katreen's plan. The epitome of the bourgeoise wife, Katreen had never worked outside the home, as Jonathan owned numerous car dealerships spread around Chicago. She had no interest in his business concerns, preferring to nurture her interests, watch her weight and do charity work. The death of their daughter was an atrocious heartbreak for them, but Harmony was not to become a substitute for Kimberly. Plus, their girl had been full of life, with a bright, cheerful personality, and Katreen had not picked up that kind of positive vibe from Harmony, with her eternal hang-dog look. Of course she understood that what Harmony had gone through was hard to bear for a child of twelve, and that's why she insisted on psychological care after the terrible accident. Mr. Sherman, the therapist who had advised them, also recommended the greatest prudence concerning this preadolescent, considering her to be "in denial and defending herself by plunging into an imaginary world that went beyond the norm."

Harmony forced herself to open the school gate, where a young monitor pleasantly greeted her in French. His face was pale and he shivered with cold under his long waterproof coat, hood raised, but his tone put her at ease and bolstered her courage. She headed to a courtyard as big as a tennis court, to be alone while she observed everything around her. The three- and four-story buildings were of gray stone, built in the seventies, rectangular and functional. Altogether it lacked color, and the bare-branched trees added to its mournful appearance, she thought it looked like a real French high school.

She dug through her backpack and fished out the cell phone the Clarks had given her, the first phone she'd ever had, and called Shirley Connors. She'd been trying to reach her since the night before. But once again, she only got voice mail. Shirley's family must already be on the road to work and school. Harmony thought of calling her mother, but there was no use in that, and she couldn't really talk to her anyway. How long would she stay in that condition? The doctors and the psychiatrist might repeat all they want about how she had to be brave because her mother would never be quite the same person she used to be, but she didn't want to believe them, those liars, those pessimists. Everything would soon be the way it was before, and she prayed that her mom would emerge from her awful silence. And her brother, too.

The central courtyard gradually filled up with laughter and shouts. Harmony saw faces turn toward her, curious to know who this timid new student was. The girls seemed prettier and more elegant than the girls in her old school, maybe more arrogant as well. Her stomach hurt. She looked for the bathrooms, but didn't dare to ask anyone, not knowing what language to use. Finally, she recognized the little signs showing a girl and a boy at the end of an interminable hallway. Some older girls were doing their hair in there, and some were putting on eyeliner, regardless of their mothers' prohibitions. After classes, they would come back and wash it all off, to look like obedient little girls again.

Harmony went straight to the last stall and shut herself in, sat on the toilet and opened one of her backpacks. She'd brought two; one had her school supplies, the other was for her gym clothes, even though she knew there was no PE on Mondays. She took out her worn teddy bear. The fur on its face was nearly worn away. It was her brother's. She hugged it tightly against her heart. Her life had turned upside-down, with doctors, a psychologist, a new home at the Clark's, people she'd never seen before the accident, and this new school.

For the moment, Harmony was simply trying to survive.

The bell rang to signal the start of class. She took a deep breath and let it out slowly, then left the bathroom to search for her class, amid the throng of noisy, happy kids. She was about to enter seventh grade in the Lycée Français. Mr. Clark would pay all the expenses, because his daughter was the cause of all this turmoil in Harmony's life.

# Chapter Twenty

"Short absence quickens love; long absence kills it."Honoré Mirabeau

What time was it? Daytime, certainly, but at this tropical latitude in December, the sun rose around six-thirty. It was hard to tell, especially after a night of bad dreams interrupted by the noise of lovemaking. It must have been the other tourist, Brigitte, with some companion she hadn't seen when she came aboard.

Her stomach growled, and she realized how hungry she was. She rolled off the bunk, with a wry smile at the t-shirt Florent had given her. The huge heart on it was even more ridiculous in full daylight. But she had no choice than to keep it on; she couldn't wear her elegant gown or put on yesterday's outfit, stained from the black rocks and excessive perspiration. She resigned herself to wearing the green thong undies, bleached, yes, but used by a perfect stranger. She struggled to squeeze into the jeans shorts and pull up a zipper corroded by sea salt.

She'd felt like a vagabond the previous night, and now she felt like a pre-teen. Clothes like that looked vulgar on a woman her age in her opinion. How was it all going to end? She searched through her canvas bag, whose dancing dolphins and embroidered sun no longer amused her. There was less than a hundred dollars left in the threadbare coin purse, so she would have to withdraw some money from the first cash machine she came across.

Up in the cockpit, she smelled an agreeable odor of coffee – such a reassuring, everyday kind of smell that she could hardly believe the preceding day and night were real. For a few seconds, she imagined Max waiting for her, one hand around his coffee cup, the other holding *Le Canard Enchainé*, the

French newspaper he managed to procure every week. But no, the table was empty of his presence.

"Finally, Madame Flynt arrives! A few minutes more and I was going to call the doctor."

"Why? Is it so bad to get a little sleep, Monsieur Van-something?"

"Van Steerteghem, but call me Florent. It's sounds friendlier, and I hate hearing my family name mispronounced. And no, it's not against the rules to sleep in, but it's getting on to one o'clock!"

"No! Why didn't you wake me up?"

"As it happens, you told me last night not to wake you up. So, coffee or tea?"

"Black coffee, no sugar. It's incredible – I didn't expect to sleep so late. I need to get back to Gustavia right away. Could you take me, please?"

"Sure, no problem. But we have time. You know the next ferry isn't due to leave until five-forty-five?"

Did she know! Those figures obsessed her. Yesterday at that time, they should have been arm-in-arm on the ferry to Oyster Pond, ready to land, to dress up and have fun and make love all night. A dream vacation…

But why had the gendarmes not contacted her? Her telephone – as always, she had shut it down before going to sleep, without thinking. She never thought she would collapse like that and sleep all morning. They must have been trying to reach her for hours. She kicked herself for being so stupid as to turn off her phone. Under these circumstances, she should be reachable at all times.

She went back to her cabin, where the phone was lying on the deck. She could have stepped on it and broken it. She turned it on. The battery was almost dead, and she didn't have the charger, having left it at the hotel because they were only going on a day trip. Her heart started pounding when she saw there were some messages. She had to listen to them before the battery died.

"Hello, Madame Flynt. This is Yves Duchâteau, from the gendarmerie. This is my third message. We started searching again at dawn, with a helicopter, and made a ground search too, but haven't found a trace of your husband yet. Call me as soon as possible, or find me at the fort. I hope you're comfortable at Florent Van Steerteghem's."

She went back up to the bridge, dejected, and wondering how they knew where she was. In the meanwhile, Brigitte had come up and seated herself at the breakfast table. Unlike Harmony, she looked refreshed and happy. Her yellow pareo barely hid her breasts, which were too round and perkily high to be natural. She was sipping fresh orange juice with her botoxed lips, leaving lipstick marks on the glass. The night before, Harmony had estimated her age at forty, but she upped it to fifty now that she saw her in sunlight.

"Hello, mate," Brigitte said. "Sleep well?"

"Yes and no. I slept too long, but badly."

"And people usually sleep so well on Florent's boat, even if it did toss a bit last night," she said with a chuckle, remembering her nocturnal adventures. "This is the third year straight I've stayed on his sailboat, the first time right after his parents bought--- or rather, helped him buy it. And you, Harmony – is this your first time in St. Barts?"

"Yes, the first time."

"You'll be back. Everyone adores St. Barts. But you seem bothered by something. It's no big deal to miss the ferry, and get to spend a night on this paradise of an island! You can take the next one. Are you alone?"

"No..."

"Oh!"

"And you?" Harmony quickly added, so the other woman wouldn't have time to ask for more details.

"Alone with myself. Otherwise it wouldn't be a vacation, you see."

She started giggling in a way that made Harmony uncomfortable. Who had shared this woman's bunk last night, not Florent surely? She was at least twenty years older than him.

He emerged from the galley at that instant, a little unsteady, as his tray had almost tipped over. But he managed to set it down with a sigh of relief. Steaming coffee, hot croissants, grilled toast and jams. A copy of the *Kama Sutra* next to Brigitte's plate. She glared at their host, who ignored her or pretended to.

At that, Harmony concluded they had slept together that night. Hadn't Brigitte admitted she was vacationing alone on purpose? And there wasn't anyone else aboard the catamaran. What kind of place was this? At "only" two hundred bucks a night, there must be something fishy about it. She spread a thick layer of local maracuja jam on her toast, hastily ate it and drank some coffee. Hungry but without appetite, she ate some croissants, hoping they would make her feel better. She always reserved the best for last. Max had quickly detected her little glutton's mania, and had fun pretending to grab the treat from under her nose and laugh while she tried to get it back. A game that had started when they met in Miami. She remembered his irregular hours as a chef, and how he had put aside the hours between seven and nine in the morning to spend with her, magic moments when the joy of seeing him made her forget waking up so early. She wouldn't get to see him again until after his late shift ended around eleven at night.

She thought he would forget her once her vacation was over, but right after returning to her lonely house in Milwaukee, he surprised her by calling several times a day. They spent hours on the phone, until the middle of the night sometimes, talking about how much they missed each other, how painful their separation was. He sent hundreds of text messages, to which she immediately responded. Her daily life brightened up.

He came to visit a few months later, and after that, everything happened quickly. His job resignation, their intimate marriage in Las Vegas, life as a couple in Milwaukee.

Harmony bit into another croissant, but it was tasteless. She nibbled it slowly to gain time and not have to join the conversation. Brigitte talked enough for all three, and had launched into a thorough review of all of St. Barts beaches. As she started in on her analysis of Saint-Jean Bay, where you could admire the planes landing and taking off, Harmony suddenly leaped up. A helicopter was flying by, just overhead. Craning her neck, she spied it turning south. Shivers ran down her spine. She grabbed yet another croissant as a diversion.

"Florent, did you notice that helicopter?" Brigitte said. "Probably from a yacht. I saw one yesterday on the bridge of a boat with a black hull and black masts. It looked like a bad guy's boat from a Bond film. The wealthy sure enjoy their caprices!"

"I know that yacht. But this helicopter was from the gendarmerie."

"Why, what happened?"

"They're searching for a drowned guy, a tourist who disappeared yesterday."

Harmony felt the blood leave her face, but she wasn't about to confide in Brigitte or this Florent, who slept with his clients. She could only trust this kind of secret to Shirley. It would have been such a comfort to unburden her heart, but she couldn't call her. Shirley was pregnant, and she didn't want to saddle her with this kind of drama, especially since her due date was so close. No, she had to hold it all in until Max was found.

She finished her breakfast in silence, anxious to get back to the gendarmerie. She felt devoid of energy, and wished the coffee was stronger. The sea was calmer but still heaved a little. She was surprised to realize the rolling motion no longer bothered her, though. Maybe the gravity of the situation allowed her to forget or ignore her aches and pains, like her still swollen ankle.

After thanking Florent for the meal, she went back to the shower cubicle. She wondered if the luxury yachts anchored at Gustavia had bath tubs. She loved taking long, hot, relaxing baths. But she settled for a quick shower, then got busy washing out the many stains on her white dress. With its thin fabric, it would quickly dry. After rinsing it, she wrung it out as best she could and hung it to dry on the trampoline between the twin hulls. She wasn't going back to Gustavia and the gendarmerie in that loopy t-shirt with the big red heart.

It was now two o'clock, exactly eighteen hours after she'd reported Max's disappearance at the gendarmerie. The longest stretch of time they had ever spent apart since their wedding day.

# Chapter Twenty-One

"Events are like trapezes: there is one coincidence and one alone allowing passage from one event to the next."

René-Salvator Catta, *Le grand tournant (The Turning Point)*

An hour and a half later, Harmony was hanging on to the gunnel of the rubber dinghy, uncomfortable in her damp dress. Brigitte had insisted on joining them. The following day, she would fly back to Belgium, so she wanted to live her last day "to the full," as she put it. As she said this, she grabbed Florent's chin, as if he were a doll she could turn this way or that. Florent grinned, showing his perfect teeth. Harmony had to admit he was a handsome man, and he could pour on the charm when he wanted. In a fit of jealousy, Tempest pushed Brigitte's hand away with her paw, making her lurch and almost fall in the water.

Florent wouldn't have minded, and was glad he had brought his dog. Brigitte was getting far too familiar with him, and a dip would have calmed her enthusiasm. Tempest would have been the first to jump in after her; Newfoundland dogs were called the "St. Bernard of the Sea" for that very instinct. It was one of the qualities that had convinced him to adopt her when she was a puppy. He would have made thought twice if he'd know how big she would grow.

He purposely turned his attention from Brigitte to Harmony.

"Are you going to sleep on the boat again tonight? I prefer knowing ahead of time if possible."

"Sorry, I don't know yet."

She would have liked to add that she hoped never to set foot on his boat again, or hear them wrestling in the sheets, but it all depended on how the investigation turned out. She might have no other choice than to hang out with them a bit longer.

Reaching the beach, Florent tied the dinghy to a wall serving as a breakwater. Brigitte's hilarity was attracting notice. Any pretext served for her to burst out laughing, and this time, it was Tempest licking her face. "What a fool!" was all Harmony could think about her behavior.

The Chevy wagon looked a different animal in the glaring light of day. A real antiquity. The body, especially the undercarriage, was so rusty it was crumbling away, and the once-plush upholstery was ravaged from mud and claw marks. Florent obviously devoted more attention to his boat than to his car.

Tempest jumped in the back, Brigitte slid into the middle of the front banquette seat, her flaccid thigh pressed against Florent, and Harmony sat on the right, wondering if last night was their first time together. Or was that included in the weekly rate for single female clients, given Florent's seductive demeanor? Harmony forced her thoughts elsewhere, but their physical presence was too overtly sensual to be ignored.

"Brigitte, where shall I drop you off?"

"In Lorient, *mon petit chéri*."

"And where do I pick you up?"

"At La Pointe. I'll hitch a ride there, and wait for you in front of the Barnes bookstore in less than an hour."

"And you, Harmony?"

"At the fort please."

"Perfect, I can pick you both up in the same area."

Harmony noticed that Florent used the French polite form "vous" with her, but the intimate form "tu" with Brigitte. Another subtlety of the French social code she had perfected with Max's help. She'd attended the Lycée in Chicago for many years, but nothing worked so well as daily practice with a French person.

Florent took off like a rocket, back in reckless driving mode. These narrow winding roads scared Harmony; they felt dangerous even in the daytime, especially the tight scrapes with each oncoming car, when Florent would swing the car back onto his side of the road. He stopped at the Minimart in Lorient, one of the few supermarkets on the island. Brigitte clambered over Harmony to get out, instead of waiting for her to move, not without tittering, and once on the sidewalk, she looked at Florent with a beastly look followed by a wink. He shook his head back and forth, with a smile of disgust.

"What a nut, that Brigitte!" he said.

Harmony closed her eyes, thinking the situation grotesque. Brigitte now looked even older and Florent even younger. In Milwaukee, she often had a hard time judging the age of a Black person, whose skin resisted the marks of time, but she would bet Brigitte was at least fifteen years older than Florent.

As they took off, she couldn't help sighing with disdain.

"Is something wrong, Harmony?"

"I don't know what you're talking about."

"When someone says that, you know very well what they're talking about. Otherwise, you would have simply said no."

"You must know a lot then."

"I can read humans like a book."

"Oh, really."

"Let's take you for example. A tourist on vacation does not 'forget' to board the last ferry. You don't risk being left without a roof when night falls, particularly on an island with such exorbitant prices. It doesn't hold together, not for you, a woman who must usually be highly organized, thinking ahead all the time. Plus, you're married, seeing as how you're wearing a wedding ring."

"Think whatever you want, if it amuses you."

"Why didn't you tell me right away you're the wife of the man lost at sea?"

"How did you learn that?"

"News spreads here faster than fire, especially a search for a drowned person, plus I heard it on the radio this morning. They deployed helicopters to search the more dangerous trails, too."

"Would telling you have changed anything?"

"It's strange, that's all," he said. "Most people would have been a wreck, and looking for support."

"Of course I'm miserable, and I'm dying from worry, but not to the point of confiding in the first comers," she said. Then, unable to hold back, she spit out, "Especially not to that Brigitte!"

"What has she done, my Brigitte? She's a fun girl, full of energy."

Florent stepped on the accelerator; content to have gotten a rise from this woman with the impassive face.

He climbed the steep road leading to the fort in first gear, happy he had recently checked the brakes. He parked on the left with his side of the car brushing the bushes. He cracked the windows a bit for Tempest, then scooted across the seat and climbed out the passenger door after Harmony. Parking was an art in itself on St. Barts.

Harmony didn't lose any time, immediately hurrying over to the speakerphone A muffled voice responded, and she identified herself. The gate opened, and they took the graveled path up to the building. Her third trip here in twenty-four hours. The place had been sinister enough the previous evening, but she'd attributed that to the darkness and her anguish at not finding Max. But even now, the old fort had the look of a high-security prison with its massive, coal-black rocks and heavy bars protecting the windows. Only the coconut palms and the panorama of Gustavia's bay cheered up the place.

She went into the lobby, where she found Gendarme Jourdan looking even chubbier than she remembered. His doll-like face revealed a budding double chin. He instantly came forward, but awkwardly, an attitude that fit badly with her image of authoritative men in this kind of job.

"Hi, Florent. So you finally got here, Madame Flynt. That is, uh, hello. Did you receive my colleague's messages?"

"Yes, that's why I'm here. But even without his phone call, I would have come. Where are you at with the search?"

"The ocean search led to nothing, absolutely nothing. Your husband remains missing. I'm sorry, but in drowning cases, that sometimes happens."

"Right, now you're going to tell me his body will wash up somewhere, eventually. We've wasted enough time. Something's happened to him, and it's not drowning. We have to search for him on the island, or somewhere else."

"I'm not heading the investigation. We're waiting for the Commandant's orders."

"What a waste of time! It's the first twenty-four hours that count in a missing persons case."

"That's for the disappearance of a minor. This is a missing adult, and if he has neither drowned nor fallen ill, then maybe…"

"Maybe what?"

"Perhaps we must consider the possibility he simply wanted to disappear," Jourdan said, dropping his voice. "And if that's the case, we can do nothing. Adults have the right to vanish."

"What in the world are you saying? You're insane!"

"I can tell you nothing more than that. The Commandant's coming to explain things to you."

Jourdan's telephone vibrated, which wasn't normal. He must have pushed the wrong button and put it into silent mode. He hoped he hadn't missed any calls, especially from his wife. He withdrew to have more privacy and put some distance between himself and Harmony Flynt. He hoped she wouldn't get more upset with him than she already was. What could he do if her man had left her on purpose? These women never wanted to admit their husbands could pack up and leave like that, alone or with another woman. Some men didn't like being married, but they didn't like being single either. He knew, for he himself thought that petite brunette who wandered the beaches selling bikinis was truly too cute for words. He would love to pack up and leave his wife. She might be an excellent housekeeper, but they hardly ever made love anymore. Any excuse served: the kids, their homework, the ironing, her period, a migraine, a meal to fix...

Pack up and leave. That was it: open a suitcase, throw in the essentials and go, to start again somewhere else, a place that would be better. Every now and then, he thought about disappearing. But not alone. Once again, he fantasized about the little bikini-seller who liked to flash her white teeth at him and show off her firm buns. Any man could throw it all away for that kind of dream, but of course, he could not explain it to Madame Flynt as brutally as that.

It was Madame Aubin on the line, another regular caller, to report that the man house-sitting for the Wallaces had brought in several people. What an old dragon that lady was, constantly ratting on her neighbors. He went to Duchâteau's office to report the news. He hadn't yet come to that kind of duty. But they had to be polite with the locals, the "Babarts," or "Barthians," or rather "Saint-Barth," the name they called themselves.

Thierry Roland finally showed up, looking tired but wearing an impeccably ironed uniform, all insignia shining, and his commander's expression on his face. As Harmony tried to speak, he came forward and greeted her, then turned to Florent.

"So, Sherlock, what are you on now? An unfaithful wife, or a cheating husband?"

"Nothing at all."

"You wouldn't tell me if you were!"

"You know it!"

"You rent cabins on your boat, now, eh? Thanks for lodging Madame Flynt, by the way. We were worried; she didn't want to accept our help to find a roof."

He looked at Harmony with a discontented air.

"I know," Florent said. "I saw one of your guys following her. He could do better at it – I immediately noticed him hanging around the Sunset hotel."

140

"Nothing escapes you. I merely wanted to make sure she found something for the night. Seems your floating bed-and-breakfast is working. The taxman may need to do an inspection."

"Is that a threat or a joke?"

"You choose!"

Harmony listened to them without interrupting. Their attitude left her perplexed. Two roosters fighting? Humor in the second degree? And was Florent really a private investigator? But she was impatient, and wondered when the commander was going to have the decency to occupy himself with her.

Seeming to read her thoughts, Roland leaned toward her, his knuckles on a desk.

"Madame, we have found no trace of your husband, unfortunately, and your beach basket has disappeared. The servers at the restaurant didn't find it. As theft isn't likely, we've turned to other hypotheses. We advise you to register a complaint in the logbook in the interest of the families involved. That will permit us to carry out our administrative checks. As soon as we have news, we will contact you. Will you be staying in St. Barts or going back to St. Martin?"

Harmony paused a few seconds before answering. She had to figure out what he was saying. Had she heard correctly? Was he talking only of bureaucratic affairs?

"But what are you going to do about finding my husband, concretely? You need to search the island, organize a hunt, send out missing-person notices."

"My men carried out a sufficient number of searches and the helicopter flew over all dangerous spots. It's a small territory – trust me, we would have already found him. Don't worry, we've done everything we could do."

"Everything? Right! That means you file some paperwork and that's the end of it?"

"I just explained we've working on other hypotheses."

"Yes, like the one where Max disappeared on purpose."

"Madame, no one has reported anything disturbing or suspicious. No assaults, no fights, no traces of blood. I'm very sorry, but yes, it is possible your husband left you. That could be why no one has found the basket. Either because he left with it or got rid it. Have you at least called your hotel? He may have made a stop there. Come back as often as you wish, but at this time, I can add nothing more to help you!"

Harmony was floored. What more could she do all by herself? A wall of obstinacy hemmed her in. She'd seen this before in special news reports that reconstructed criminal investigations. Someone disappears, and instead of taking it seriously, the police wait for more unsettling elements to surface. And she couldn't always understand the attitudes of victims' families. Some were extremely active, distributing flyers and putting up posters, while others seemed paralyzed, without reacting at all. She guessed she was in the second category. This unbelievable situation had left her bewildered, especially since she wasn't home and didn't know a single person here.

She couldn't leave the island. She had to wait, but she didn't have the courage to go look for a hotel room. This so-called private eye's boat wasn't a great solution, but it was the best she could come up with. They were about to leave when Duchâteau came up.

"Madame, pardon me, but would you have a recent photo of your husband?"

"I don't have any photos of him."

"How's that? No selfies, no Instagram photos or anything?" he asked, incredulous.

"I don't have one photo of him, I assure you. He hated being photographed – call it the caprice of an artist, since he started writing his novel. The only photo of him is on his ID, which he has in his wallet."

Commander Roland shrugged in disdain. Artists and writers! That whole world annoyed him, those nuts who could never be realistic or reply clearly to questions. They were unreliable, and made you suspect them just by their preposterous attitudes.

"Artist or not, we need you to bring us a photo of him as soon as you can. At least we'll be able to check with the Dutch ferry company. The crew may have seen him embark. Dig through your emails, or somewhere. Contact his friends and family – they must have some photos of him!"

"He has no family. His parents died when he was a boy, and he has no siblings."

"What bad luck! But I want you to do whatever you can, nonetheless. Find me a recent photo."

The commander watched them walk off. Fortunately, this was a case of a missing adult, so he had no obligation to launch a formal investigation. Nothing pointed to the disappearance being criminal in nature, aside from the convictions of an American woman about whom they knew nothing and who didn't even have of photo of her beloved husband, a fact tending to prove their marriage was not all roses and sunshine. He saw no use in alarming the residents and tourists on the island. Especially the wealthy, even though they tended to travel with bodyguards. It wouldn't do to have them imagine one could disappear that way in St. Barts.

Plus, the husband was French; the case would seem insignificant, as a middle-class Frenchman who disappears wouldn't disturb the rich residents as much. He was an orphan, too, an important factor in mental illness in adults. Yves had spoken to him about that kind of pseudo-disappearance. Men and women searching for their identity who suddenly take off. Really, there was no reason to be alarmed; this could only be the banal story of a couple breaking up, and hadn't this woman professed to being "worried to death" and yet turned off her phone for hours? She'd only arrived for news of him late in the afternoon. That didn't sit well, and all the better…

But why did Yves have to interfere, asking for photos? If she did end up bringing some in, then what? Put up posters all over St. Barts? The island had to retain its reputation as super clean and super safe. He also hoped Florent Van Steerteghem wouldn't get entangled in this. Now that he had some wealthy clients, he took himself so seriously, and he was capable of going overboard with zeal. The commander had to admit it: he was jealous of Florent's bachelor life and his job without a hierarchy, without having to answer to anyone, and he had it from a private source that Florent was raking in the bucks with his private investigations. But then he remembered his retirement account awaiting him, a carrot leading him by the nose and preventing him from changing his life. Security over liberty.

Before entering his office, he surprised Jourdan devouring another takeout cheeseburger. Mayonnaise dribbled from the corner of his mouth.

Roland immediately decided to address the problem. He had to keep his men physically fit, at least minimally. He would organize a joint operation with the marine brigade, a staged exercise of a cocaine delivery and confiscation between the islands. His team got bored fast here, and he did too. He suddenly felt homesick for Lille. His wife's depression must be infecting him, or was it the horrible night and lack of sleep? His wife claimed that the sight of everlastingly turquoise water crazed her. He'd never heard that before – only the reverse, that gray caused depression. Even Jacques Brel sang about how "a sky so gray a boat hung itself."

But his transfer here hadn't been by chance. He had too often criticized the disastrous state of the equipment at his former station, and that hadn't pleased the hierarchy or the local politicians. They'd sent him here as a punishment, to serve his sentence in the sunshine.

Back in his office, Yves Duchâteau took a seat behind his massive teak desk, a unique piece dating from the colonial era, a nice change from the soulless gray metal desks he'd always worked at. He considered Harmony's behavior strange, too. He was ready to help her, but he could tell she hadn't told him

144

everything. Las Vegas weddings, as everybody knew, ended in divorce, and then, not one photo of her husband? How was that possible? But on reflection, he admitted his wife Nadia didn't carry a photo of him in her wallet. Only a picture of their daughter. A child's photo quickly replaces that of the husband.

Something else had been bothering him since hearing the details of this disappearance: the missing man's name. Max Rousseau. But "Max" didn't fit. He'd talked on the phone several times with a friend of his deceased brother, Olivier Rousseau, who had also figured in his brother's blighted visit to the Caribbean. Was that last name purely coincidental? He had to find out more about this enigmatic Harmony Flynt.

# Chapter Twenty-Two

"Time passes and waits for no one. All the cords and cables of the world could not hold it back. It has no port of call, time; it's but a gust of wind that passes by and does not return."Mohammed Moulessehoul, aka Yasmina Khadra, *Cousine K (2003)*

Florent was ecstatic. Commander Roland often chafed him, so he'd enjoyed the chance to poke back at a representative of the law. The officer didn't like private investigators or what they did, even though Florent didn't interfere with their police work. The inquiries he dealt with were not in the same category. The gendarmes were there to make people respect the laws, give tickets, respond to complaints, but he was more involved with people's private, sometimes intimate concerns. There was not necessarily any law-breaking, or "guilty parties" involved. Often, someone wanted to know something, at any price, or someone wished to make sure nothing had been disclosed or become a subject of gossip, or wanted to make some indiscretion or other quietly disappear. His clients were usually wealthy St. Barts residents or jetsetters. Florent didn't ask them too many questions. They paid him well, so he no longer depended on his parents, who had helped him get started on this new life. But the umbilical cord was cut at last.

His last case, an original for Florent, had been to recover a compromising video of an actor very much in vogue, a man the ladies fell for in droves. His looks had helped him snag publicity spots that paid him royally. These brands stressed his virility to the point that if a video showing their milk cow wrapped in the arms of another man, he would have been put out to pasture.

Florent's partner "Fat Boy" was a computer wizard, and together, they had managed to get the video back and stop it from going public. His nickname wasn't exactly politically correct, but that didn't matter in the Antilles, where names like that were common. His mother was also Congolese, from Kinshasha, and whatever a person had a complex about, became their nickname. Ugly, Stutterer, Fatso…

Tomorrow, Florent was going to pay Fat Boy for his computer prowess – three thousand dollars cash. In the old days, private detectives worked with hired muscle, guys who inspired fear and if necessary, used their guns, but nowadays, computer geeks were most sought-after. And Florent had found the best of them. Fat Boy was from St. Martin, where from boyhood, he'd spent all his time at the computer. His neurons functioned with HTML, URLs, metadata – everything Florent detested. He preferred handling concrete things, like the sails of his boat. He had to face it though – in this world, he couldn't do without digital technology. And Fat Boy could worm his way into any computer, any social network, a talent much more effective than a Beretta nowadays.

Florent had been cogitating so long that Harmony began to fidget, so she asked him, point-blank, "You've been hiding things from me, too – like the fact you're a private investigator. "

"So it seems."

"What do you think of my husband's disappearance?"

"Absolutely nothing. It's not my problem."

"How can you answer me like that? You sure don't have any tact."

"Why should I be tactful to someone who wouldn't confide in me, even though I took her in as a guest? But if you insist, I think you better not expect any miracles. They don't like to stir up trouble here, and they'll merely pretend to do a few verifications, and then let time take care of it."

"What do you mean?"

"If he didn't drown, they'll say he left, maybe under the pretext you had a massive fight."

"Massive?"

"A fight to the death, if you want. And after this fight, he took off somewhere to calm down. Two possibilities follow. First scenario is that in his rage he walked too far along a trail, and either fell ill, hurt himself, or had a bad fall. But that seems improbable, as they would've already found him. So, scenario two – he cleared out by some other means, by plane maybe. If I were you, I'd check at the airport, or as Commander Roland suggested, ask around at the docks whether any boats left for Philipsburg in Sint-Maarten."

"I swear we had no argument. We love each other. We've never even raised our voices to each other."

"That's hard to believe! And if it were true, I'd tell you it's abnormal. A relationship isn't some long tranquil river of love. All couples quarrel from time to time, then patch things up. But an argument can be a make or break moment, too."

"I don't see that," Harmony said.

"If you knew how common it is! Sometimes, people have no warning, but get dumped all of a sudden. They can't wrap their heads around it. They didn't see it coming, thinking everything was going along fine, and meanwhile their partner had long been ruminating about running away."

"You have a rather negative view of relationships."

"My view is realistic, and it's the most prevalent, as I know personally. I see it all the time in my line of work. The boredom of ho-hum daily life causes a kind of gangrene in couple."

He suddenly turned and searched her face.

"Why didn't you check to see if he had gone back to your hotel to get his stuff?"

"Why would I do that? I'll repeat it again – it's impossible my husband left the island without me. He disappeared from here, St. Barts. We never had any massive fight like you say. Why won't anyone believe me?"

She shouted this last question, and it was only with an effort that she stopped herself from crying. She had to be a block of marble, like Katreen Clark had so well taught her.

They would find Max and break this evil spell. To cry meant to mourn, to attract despair, the evil eye.

*Max had disappeared, but he would come back. Max had disappeared, but he would come back. Max had disappeared, but he would come back.*

She repeated it three times, because that was what she always did for her brother. Another one of her tics. But one day, after repeating it three times, he had come back. He disappeared again later on, but that was because she no longer needed him.

Max had made her understand that.

Florent's conscience pricked him. He'd wanted to test her to see how much this crisis really affected her, but maybe he'd been too direct. Was she feeling anguish, sadness, relief or indifference? These emotions were important, as they said much about a missing person's loved ones. Sometimes they adopted paradoxical attitudes, which the police usually misinterpreted. She did seem believable when she insisted their marriage was a happy one, but he'd also thought that about his former relationship.

His ex, Lise Clijsters, had also pretended sincerity: "I can never live without you" and "I will never love anyone else." He had gone on, floating in complete happiness, but it was all a lie and a dream. In the end she decided she could easily live without him and love someone else.

He believed Harmony was truly grieving and sad, but something was amiss. His instinct told him she was somewhere else.

They approached Barnes & Nobles, where he spied Brigitte's seductive figure, recognizable a mile away. She had caught a ride there from Lorient the instant she stuck her thumb out. Even at fifty-something, she could still pull off an outfit like that: micro-mini-shorts and matching tank top, of a fabric so thin it showed every curve of her firm body. Florent drove past, pretending not to notice her, but put on the brakes a few seconds later when he saw her in the rearview mirror waving at him desperately.

He hesitated. Should he pick up his sports journal, then go back? He finally decided to pull over and wait for Brigitte to catch up. He preferred newspapers over surfing the net; the smell of the paper reminded him of his childhood, when his father, an extremely solemn man, would sit in his hunter-green chair leafing through the medical journals. He couldn't complain about those years growing up in their fine house on Avenue de Tervueren in Brussels, in the cozy atmosphere of Europe's capital, rocked by the mellow ding-ding-ding of the trams.

Both his parents were doctors, able to give him the means to succeed, and he had done brilliantly in his law studies. And when he became passionate about sailing, they had done all they could to encourage him, including weekend lessons at the Knokke-le-Zoute sailing club. When the ocean was too rough, he made do with sand yachts at low tide on the gigantic beach. Later on, when he worked in a Flemish law firm, his colleagues scoffed at his enthusiasm for the sea, which didn't fit their clichéd ideas, until he ended up slamming the door on them all and sailing off to Martinique with Lise.

He chased that name from his mind, but the word "bitch" replaced it. For so long, he had cried and yearned for her to come back, but now all he felt was hatred, and if he ever saw her, he would spit every possible insult into her face. Proof he wasn't quite over her, but he hoped that one day soon he would reach the stage of indifference. The stage of healing.

After their explosive separation, he'd moved to St. Barts, alone. Three years already! He occasionally thought about lifting the anchor and sailing back to Europe, but when you've tasted liberty, it's hard to stick your wrists back into the handcuffs of a job he'd have to perform day in and day out, held to account, forced to beg his superiors for vacation dates. To look at his watch, not daring to leave five minutes before his hours were up.

Brigitte climbed in the Chevy, sulking. She was no longer Brigitte the "fool" who laughed for no reason but Brigitte the "pouter." She pushed Harmony to the middle seat. Florent thus had for company a woman who was pining and a woman who was peeved. The kind of passenger he detested. The boat would fill with bad vibes, and in such an enclosed space, quickly become suffocating. He still had to figure out dinner for that evening. The ladies obviously hadn't thought of anything and he wasn't about to make an extra trip to shore to go shopping. He headed toward Chez Mayas, a restaurant where you could buy takeaway food. A giant poster displayed tantalizing photos of paella with seafood and chicken. That should do the trick. He asked the two women what they preferred, but they barely reacted, one sighing "chicken," the other "seafood."

Florent walked into the restaurant, pensive. Why hadn't Harmony contacted her family and friends? Shouldn't she be hanging on the phone trying to move heaven and earth? Instead, she passively waited for the results of the official searches. This was one of the paradoxical reactions people in her situation sometimes exhibited.

A missing husband – that was enough to make a person go crazy. But who was she? Only time would bring him the answer.

And what about his own case – when would he raise anchor and flee somewhere else? He too was starting to turn in circles. It was about time someone hired him for a new investigation.

# Chapter Twenty-Three

"The more original a discovery, the more obvious it seems afterwards." Arthur Koestler

"Okay, fellas, no more need for a leg up – I think I got it."

Theo, only ten years old, talked like his father. That impressed his buddies Mael and Julien even more than his height and size. For several months, the three of them had been treasure-hunting in the richer neighborhoods, which to them meant digging through the big trash containers close to luxury villas. They'd learned that rich people threw out just about anything. The other day, it was a Nintendo Switch that worked perfectly. This dig was a little different. Mael, a master at trailing people, had gotten a lead, and their homework done, they had hurried over to here to get started.

Theo loved bossing over his little group. His mother was the school principal and his father a local politician, so he'd learned a thing or two about it. After hauling up the treasure, he announced their find in a loud voice: two towels, one purple and one navy-blue, and a brand-new mask and tuba rolled up in each; two pairs of black fins. This gear alone would have made their day, as they loved swimming and watching the fish at Colombier beach, but there was even more loot. They nearly had to pinch themselves to believe their luck. An iPhone 6! The equivalent of a gold ingot in that digital era. Their biggest take of all time. The other day, Mael had stopped in front of a boutique selling phones, and had seen that very one on sale for more than six hundred euros. A real catch, like when he went fishing for dorado with his dad.

The purple towel was spotted with suspicious stains. Julien stuffed it back into the trashcan with a scowl of disgust. The son of an esthetician and a nurse, he'd been raised to fear germs and love beauty. His clothes were always impeccably clean and fashionable, even to go play with his friends. His hair was always shampooed and his perfectly even bangs frequently trimmed, his nails were never black, and before eating, he washed his hands without even been told to. The whole game of taking stuff out of the trash was already against his nature, so he was not about to keep a dirty towel.

Aside from that one towel, they kept the rest. Julien thought for a moment. He considered himself the cleverest of the trio because his father was a "microbe specialist," so he pried out the telephone's SIM card. As he was about to throw it as far as possible, spinning around like an Olympic disc thrower for the fun of it, he had a change of heart. He'd seen in a movie it wasn't that easy. They weren't far from his house, and the police could trace you via the SIM card, and he wasn't so sure what to do now. He didn't share his doubts with the others, but he decided to dispose of it more efficiently.

They chose Mael for the task. Mael, the most athletic of them, usually wore soccer clothes and the latest model Nikes. He chose OM, the "Olympique de Marseilles" team, for his favorite French team, and Brazil's national team for upper-league games. He knew St. Barts and its beaches like the back of his hand, plus he ran everywhere. That's why his calves were so wiry.

Mael took the SIM card and his mission orders. He would go to Pointe Milou by his cousin's house, where there was a great, tall cliff. His mother had forbidden him to go near it, but that was back when she still worried about him and his doings. That was before he turned nine. Since then, she let him wander around by himself or with his little band, and she was left in peace to watch her soap operas, especially when his dad was out fishing, and she didn't have to put up with all those soccer games on TV.

During those two years of total freedom, Mael had learned a lot by delving into the best trashcans on the island. He had a certain flair for it; he could smell treasure a mile away, which is why he had followed Antoine Brin, who was carrying a beach basket that day. He seemed too excited. Had he stolen it?

Everyone knew Antoine lived in a strange world, and had since childhood. He hardly ever spoke, and when he did, it was always about the same things. You had to be very careful not to vex him – he would start screaming or even smashing his head against a wall. People had learned to accept his temperament and not contradict him, especially during the main tourist season, as it made the island look bad. Antoine wasn't mean, just different. Woven baskets were his latest obsession, and he collected them.

Earlier that day, seeing Antoine pass his house, chuckling to himself, Mael shadowed him, and saw him dump the contents of the basket into this trashcan and then leave, even happier, to bring his swag back to his room.

Mael had insisted they go dig through the container right away, as the trashmen would go by the next day, and it would've been bye-bye to the iPhone 6 and the snorkeling gear. All they had to do now was throw the SIM card into the waves crashing into the bottom of the cliff at Pointe Milou. The cops could always go find it there if they wanted to.

His friends shouldn't worry – they hadn't stolen anything. Mael's dad had explained that "anything thrown in the trash is free for the taking."

But still, Mael was a bit uneasy. He wondered where Antoine had found the basket, and hoped some tourists had left it behind, and not any St. Barts residents. Mael was convinced the towel was stained with blood, as it looked like the rags he and his dad wrapped around the fish they were lucky enough to catch sometimes. He thought he'd better not tell the others, though, as they might panic and go tell everything to their parents.

It wasn't that big a deal with Theo's parents, because they never asked questions. They never had time – they worked like crazy. His mom always looked sick, with gray circles under her eyes and a face the color of aspirin, as if she still lived in Normandy. But Julien's parents were jerks, and that would be

155

more of a problem. Like all self-respecting jerks, they always asked troublesome questions.

It would be so dumb to have to give up their treasure.

# Chapter Twenty-Four

"One downpour does not guarantee the harvest." Creole proverb

Brigitte and Harmony waited in the car, shoulder to shoulder, neither of them feeling like talking to the other. Florent seemed to be taking forever to get the paella. Brigitte ended up getting out and calling someone, then she paced up and down the sidewalk with her phone bonded to her ear.

Harmony noticed a blue bench not far away, half-hidden by a poinciana tree. It looked inviting. The Chevy was like an oven, even with the windows down, so the tree and the bench was just like an oasis in the midst of the vast parking lot, with its asphalt and concrete. She unglued her back from the seat, got out, and headed straight to the shady spot, where she sat down on the bench, taking care to choose a place where Florent could see her when he came out.

The sun was starting to go down, and some clouds, still far off, looked menacing. The dark gray clouds, the orangey sun and the azure sky formed a glorious combination of colors. It was out of place in the circumstances, but she couldn't resist pulling out her phone and taking some shots of it in the hopes of capturing its beauty. In the shade of the poinciana, and with the light trades blowing, the air felt balmy, nothing like the hellish temperature inside the car. Harmony imagined the suffering of babies left in the backs of cars in summertime, found dead when their parents came out, like she'd heard about. How was it possible to forget your child? What kind of bizarre life must those parents lead to be capable of an atrocity like that? To park, get out, leave your child in its car seat and not think of it again until it was too late. And yet you never heard of kids forgotten in cars during the winter. Was it because the outcome was not fatal and so it didn't interest the press? Or were people more stressed in the summer? No, in general, it was the opposite. So could it be, in some cases, a camouflaged infanticide? A father or mother at the end of their wits, who knowingly leave their offspring to die of heat or thirst. But what investigator would dare to think that, except one with a twisted mind? And yet, the police were supposed to get into the skin of their criminal suspects, to think and act like them in order to unmask them. She shivered. What a horrid job. She much preferred crunching numbers. And this Florent – how had he ended up a private detective in St. Barts? Why did a young man like him live year-round on his sailboat far from his family, without any roots?

Lost in her thoughts, she didn't see him approach and sit next to her. A blond boy around six or seven, a bit skinny. He wore a white tank top and navy-blue shorts, and he was staring at her with sparkling blue eyes. Harmony tottered, her eyes wide.

"Hi Harmony!"

"Ben! What are you doing here?"

"I'm on vacation, like you."

"It's been so long!"

"That's normal. You never invite me anymore."

"You know life isn't always easy. Adults are often very busy."

She was lying, but what else could she say to keep from hurting his feelings?

"I'm so happy to see you, Ben. You haven't changed a bit."

"You have! You look like a real woman since you got married. By the way, why didn't you invite me to the wedding?"

"We wanted to celebrate it alone, darling. We didn't invite anyone."

"That's strange. You always wanted to have a fairy tale wedding, with lots of people and a band."

"True, but our childhood wishes don't always come true."

Her eyes filled with tears. The boy took Harmony's hand, a comforting gesture that she needed right then. She wanted to envelop him in her arms, but held back, because that might make it start all over again. A few seconds later, he pulled his hand away and ran off.

Her name being called louder and louder made her start. Turning around, she saw Florent with his arms loaded with the bags of food, raging for someone to come help him. Brigitte was only a few steps from him, but she was sealed off from the world as she talked belligerently on her phone. Harmony jumped up and ran toward him.

"I'm sorry, I didn't hear you!"

"I could tell. Are you deaf or what? Who were you talking to?"

"Nobody."

"Harmony, I saw you from the side, leaning down with your lips moving. You were talking to somebody hidden by the tree trunk."

"That was just a little boy on vacation I was chatting with."

"Well, hop in. As a punishment, you'll carry these boiling hot paellas on your lap," he said with a sadistic gleam in his eye.

Brigitte finally climbed into the Chevy, looking furious, even more a contrast from the relaxed, carefree woman of a few hours ago.

Night fell as if someone up above had flicked a switch, and along with the darkness came a tropical downpour and strong gusts of wind. Harmony didn't expect such a change in the weather; it had been so calm on her bench. She shivered with cold. A sweater would be nice. She really needed to go back to Oyster Pond and get her suitcase and clothes.

Florent switched the window wipers to their highest speed, but that wasn't enough, and driving became dangerous. The few vehicles they encountered were visible only as flickering headlights. Her face white, Brigitte dug her long, red-polished nails into Harmony's thigh. At last, they reached Corossol, where Florent parked the car in a safe position like his mother had taught him, the front facing the road to take off quicker in case of emergency. She'd had that drilled into her during her missions with Doctors Without Borders. But the rain was now cascading down, making it impossible to take the dinghy. They would have to wait. This was typical December weather: capricious, with blue skies suddenly turning to black. They could see the catamaran rolling and pitching far worse than before.

At least Brigitte could relax now and unhook her nails from her neighbor's flesh. Harmony hadn't cried out from the pain because she didn't want to upset the paella dishes, and she hadn't taken her eyes off the road, as if that would help Florent see, so she was relieved when they parked. But nails like those should be outlawed!

Right then a man sidled past the car and went into the neighborhood market across from where they had parked. With his raincoat hood up, he looked like a lost ghost, but Harmony had glimpsed his face, and thought she recognized the Antillean deckhand from the ferry. She needed to know. Avenging herself for Brigitte's nails, she set the still-hot paella on her thighs and stepped on her toes as she scrambled out, without a word of explanation. As she slammed the door, she caught Brigitte's explosion of "Goddammit!" An eye for an eye, a tooth for a tooth.

The heavy, tepid shower instantly drenched her. Her white dress became transparent and her hair started streaming as if dozens of buckets of water were being thrown over her. But she ran into the market, which was crammed with merchandise, so yachties and nearby residents could buy whatever they needed, fresh or canned food, cleaning supplies, odds and ends of all kinds, including a huge selection of umbrellas near the cash register.

Sure enough, it was the young Antillean, taking some dollars from his pocket for a Présidente beer and Palms cigarettes. The unkempt cashier seemed never to have known a moment of stress. He had a trick of tossing his blond dreadlocks out of his face every few seconds, and when he spoke, there were so many words in patois that Harmony understood nothing.

She hesitated to step off the welcome mat because of the water streaming down her body, but finally lost patience.

"Excuse me, guys!"

The two men looked her way, astonishment and then amusement in their eyes at the vision of her wet dress and what the rain had immodestly revealed.

"Just you, actually," she said, pointing to the young man in the raincoat. "Can I talk to you a minute?"

"Yes, what is it?"

"My name is Harmony Flynt. Yesterday morning, I took the nine-fifteen ferry from Oyster Pond. I was with my husband. Do you remember me?"

"Of course, your dress was flying up. I would've liked to see more, but you held it down too well. No big deal. It's see-through today, and that's just as nice."

Harmony blushed, not knowing how to respond. Right then, Florent barged in, helping her overcome her paralysis.

"What's up with you, to bolt like that without saying anything?"

"This guy served juice to Max on the ferry and kept passing by us. I wanted to ask him if he had seen Max since then, and why he was looking at me so strangely on the ferry."

Florent turned to the Antillean, saying, "So, Brandon, did you see her husband again?"

"No, I never saw her 'Max.' I only remember her."

"My husband disappeared yesterday – you've probably heard about it. The gendarmes are searching for him. We were supposed to go back on the five-forty-five boat, but he didn't show up. I'm positive something's happened to him here. Are you sure you didn't see him again?"

"No, I don't remember your sugar bear, sorry. There are so many passengers. We do plenty round-trips a day. Some faces

161

stay with me, others don't. And women more than men, especially if they're sexy."

She fumed. Men always had the same refrain on their lips. Giving up the bit of hope his appearance had inspired her with, she dropped her useless questions.

"Come on," Florent said, grabbing her arm and pushing her out of the store. "The rain stopped, but it might start again. It's now or never if we want to get out to the boat."

Brandon Lake peered through the window to make sure they were leaving. It had been a chore to seem natural while answering that woman's questions. He lived a serene life between the two islands; he liked his job and the tourists tipped generously. This missing person business smelled like trouble to his sensitive nose, and he wanted no part of it. The gendarmes would just have to do their job. That's what they were paid for.

He took out his phone, scrolled down the list of recent calls and chose that of Tania, his girlfriend, who had insisted he pick up cigarettes for her. He sent her a text message, "I didn't forget your stupid smokes," with a smiley face sticking out its tongue. He sure wished she would quit, but telling her about this disappearance wouldn't help her stop. He hadn't yet told her about yesterday's crossing. He'd only pretended to focus on the pretty blond, whose name he'd just learned was Harmony Flynt. It was her husband who interested him. Every time he went by them, Brandon observed him from the corner of his eye. He reminded him of someone; at least their faces looked alike. The haircut made him hesitate – it was unreal how much it could metamorphize a person. But his eyes were the same, a blue so innocent he could trick God into opening the gates to Heaven without even having to confess.

He had to tell Tania tonight though. She would have to keep quiet, just as they had done all these years. If anyone asked her questions, she had to say, "I don't know. I just don't know." A Black, even in the Antilles, and an illegal immigrant

162

from the Philippines with false papers would be perfect scapegoats. He couldn't afford to get mixed up in that murder case, even if it was practically a cold case, and it was even more important he to avoid getting involved in this new disappearance.

Brandon hated this December weather, constantly changing from gray to blue and blue to gray. And when he lifted his eyes from the phone screen to look one last time at the sea, his eyes met those of Florent, staring at him through the window. Brandon did all he could not to act bothered, and gave him a naïve smile. But when he stepped away from the window, he banged into the counter. All the post cards fluttered down to a floor wet and dirty from shoppers' feet. He really did detest this weather and these tropical downpours, which brought nothing but evil.

# Chapter Twenty-Five

"Drunkenness is nothing but voluntary madness." Seneca, *"Moral Letters to Lucilius," 63 AD to 65 AD*

After scrambling aboard the catamaran and sitting for a while with the others, Harmony felt she could do with some time alone. She went down the companionway to her cabin. Strangely, the boat's roll no longer bothered her; it was more like being rocked in a cradle. Just what she needed, along with the safe, enclosed space of her cabin. And some dry clothes. She peeled off the damp dress, put on the silly t-shirt and shorts, then lay on her bunk, thinking.

All those years before meeting Max, she had lived alone. Not even a pet cat or dog, just some fish. Mostly platys and swordtails that swam round and round in the aquarium she'd decorated with a few stones and purple plastic seaweed. She could only watch them, not pet them, but they did help calm her. Her psychiatrist had recommended the aquarium as a therapeutic tool to help her get over the trauma of her fiancé's brutal death. He was right. She never admitted to him that she didn't care Steven had died. What she needed to overcome was the humiliation of his betrayal. How long had Meg and Steven been sleeping together? How long had he been soiling her body by juggling his sex life between two women? The aquarium idea was such a cliché, but sometimes old remedies prove to be perfectly efficient.

She was hungry, reminding her the only meal she'd had in the last twenty-fours was the late breakfast Florent had prepared. He was turning out to be an ideal host, she had to admit. Neither Brigitte nor she had given a second of thought to shopping for dinner. The image of seafood paella was tantalizing. She hadn't eaten paella since her vacation in Miami.

Miami… Max.

Las Vegas…Whirlwind romance and wedding.

Milwaukee... Their simple life, no one but the two of them.

*What is happening, Max?*

Skipping to another subject, she started thinking about Brigitte, who seemed a different person now her giddy mood had abandoned her. Sullen but more stable, more serious, more of the woman she must be in her official life as a respected executive at Longchamps, the luxury leather goods company. Brigitte had divulged this and more about her life to Harmony up on deck after they got back, as she was opening a fresh bottle of rosé. She had divorced her boring, homebody husband three years before, and blamed him for ruining so many years of her youth. He had dumped her for a "fresher" woman, and the ironic part of it was that he left on the day of their twentieth anniversary, which coincided with their son's sixteenth birthday.

She found these coincidental dates in families such a mystery. A child born on a symbolic day, the day a relative died, or a marriage was celebrated, even though there were three hundred and sixty-four other days that birth or death or marriage could have taken place. Her accountant's bent corrected herself: every four years, there were three hundred sixty-five other days. But no, human beings persisted in doing everything on the same key dates. That included Harmony and her brother, who were born years apart but on the same day: the twenty-third of August. Was that why they'd been such close friends?

She ought to go up and find Brigitte, the woman of free morals who bedded down with a man the age of her son. The Frenchwoman was single, so why should Harmony snidely accuse her of doing wrong? The effect of her upbringing, she supposed. But then she wondered why she even questioned her attitude toward behavior like that, and realized these islands and their singular tropical atmosphere must have something to do with it. Norms and codes of social behavior lose their importance, as if the sun burned them up or the buckets of rain

166

washed away all sin. In Milwaukee, she wouldn't have been so quick to find excuses for Brigitte.

Now the gendarmes' "leads" started trotting through her head. Florent had calmly reminded her of them earlier as he set the table: a breaking point, a dispute, a fit of anger that could have provoked Max's departure. The hypothesis he'd run away from her.

No one wanted to consider a kidnapping. Yet it could be that. Why would he leave the island when their relationship functioned so well? Functioned...the word was poorly chosen, as it supported their "runaway husband" theory. A functional couple, a bored husband who found the chance to turn his back on everything during a fabulous trip-for-two to the Caribbean.

Their theories made no sense, though. Max loved her. He couldn't possibly have faked his feelings. Why would he do that? Florent had explained, in his detached tone, that you don't realize it until it's too late and the spouse has already abandoned you, that mentally they left you months or even years ago. The physical disappearance was but the final step, the one way to cut ties with a life they no longer wanted. He also said that some men couldn't come right out and look in their wife's eyes and announce they wanted to break up – their love may be dead, but they don't have the courage to say it out loud. Instead, they disappear.

Florent had stopped setting the melamine dishes on the table, and stared into space, articulating each word: "The worst, and I believe it's rare, is when they do still love their spouse, but for some reason they don't know, they have to flee as if their life depended on it."

He spoke as if he were telling his own story.

The episode of the strange phone call a few months earlier popped into her head. Sonia! She would always remember that name. Was there someone else in his heart – someone he couldn't forget?

She remembered attending the fiftieth wedding anniversary of her friend Shirley's grandparents, and in a solemn speech, her grandpa had proclaimed that even after fifty years of life together, the person sleeping next to him every night was a perfect stranger. A stranger with her secrets, things left unsaid that she would never reveal, that she would bring to the tomb or perhaps confide to him in her last words, a confession made so that her soul would rest in peace. Some of the guests laughed heartily, others meditated on his words.

In hindsight, the memory of that speech made her blood run cold. Did Max have someone else in his life, this Sonia perhaps?

But at this stage, she could only imagine one theory: a kidnapping. Max didn't roll in riches, but they were on an island filled with rich people, and he had the look of a wealthy man. Plus, he wore a fake Rolex he'd picked up on the black market. She thought about that regrettably famous gang from Paris, the "Barbarians." Max had been obsessed by that affair, and had spoken to her about it many times. One of the accomplices, a beautiful girl, had seduced the victim to draw him into a trap. The "Barbarians" had picked him because he was Jewish, meaning he had to be rich, a prejudice that would have heavy consequences. He was not rich at all, and the abduction spiraled down into a tragedy. He was tortured to death. A subject worthy of a thrilling crime novel, the kind of book Max dreamed of writing one day.

Had Max been kidnapped like the "Barbarian's" victim, for the same reasons and prejudices? He had to be rich because he looked rich and he was on the island of the richest of the rich. Maybe a ransom note would arrive soon. That's what she hoped, because even if the gendarmes got to work searching St. Barts from top to bottom, they weren't going to find him under some trees, having succumbed to some attack of illness. If any surveillance cameras were installed around the island, they should be busy searching the video records for clues. In short, they should get investigating as if they meant business, as if it this *could* be an abduction. Was he being held prisoner somewhere?

Florent hadn't brushed off this hypothesis, but simply shrugged as if to say, "Why not?" before sliding the paella into the oven to reheat it while they drank their *aperitifs*.

Max, the love of her life, for whom she'd waited so long. *Max, don't abandon me, please. Wherever you are, stay strong. You and I will be united once again.*

She had to dry her tears, keep hope alive, and imagine the best of outcomes, to draw it to herself. She had to face this trial, just like she'd faced others in her life. That terrible car accident, when she was twelve; Steven and Megan's betrayal when she was twenty-two.

She had turned thirty-two this year. Was she cursed to go through an upheaval every ten years? Impossible. Pure coincidence. Meeting Ben on that bench under the poinciana tress added to her stress. She had to hide that from Florent as best she could. It was lucky the tree had hidden part of the bench, otherwise what would he think of her?

A bell started clanging – dinner must be ready. When she went back up to the cockpit, she could hear dogs barking in Corossol. Maybe Brandon Lake lived in one of the gingerbread-trimmed *cazes* there. She could swear he was lying when he said he didn't remember Max. She didn't trust him. From the minute she laid eyes on him, she'd gotten a bad vibe. And why had Florent so abruptly swerved around to stare at him through the store window? People on this island sure acted weird.

Her mental wanderings ended there, for Brigitte had regained her liveliness in front of a cool glass of rosé.

"We were getting impatient, Harmony! We're getting drunk without you – at least I am. Florent's a lightweight – he hardly drinks at all. Help yourself! As much paella and wine as you want tonight."

They ate with good appetites. Brigitte's glass was never empty, and she patted Florent on the back regularly. He was now her bosom-buddy. On reaching the dregs of the third bottle, she started to ramble.

"I'm a ol' wreck, a tramp, nobody wants me more'n a week, 'n Cédric Deruenne's a bastard."

Feeling awkward, Harmony tried to console her and prove her wrong with what few arguments she had at hand, pointing out the positive side of her career, her life as a mother, full of sacrifices for her son. An exemplary life, even though she hardly knew anything about it. But she knew moms liked to hear that kind of thing.

She'd also been drunk the night she met Max, but she hadn't shared anything compromising, or so he said. He also assured her he'd seen her to her room as a gentleman should, and nothing else. She had not had another drop of alcohol during the rest of her vacation in Miami. The very first encounter puts its stamp on the life of a couple, otherwise why would people constantly ask couples, "How did you meet?"

They had met when she was drunk and depressed, but he brought her back to life in the following days. Touching bottom meant you could only go up. But if she had started to ramble that way in her state of inebriety, could she have talked about Steven Reardon? Max always insisted that she hadn't, and she believed him. He would never have married her if he knew.

Without transition, Brigitte started talking gibberish. The only thing they could make out was a general insult to males: "They're all bastards!" She ended up with her cheek flat on the table, eyes closed. Florent threw his head back and guffawed. Harmony liked his deep, warm laugh.

He shook Brigitte by the shoulder. No reaction. He got up, slid her onto his back and brought her to her cabin, where he chucked her onto the bunk like a sack of potatoes. They went back on deck, where he supplied her with more background on Brigitte.

"Her French lover, one Cédric Deruenne, skipped out on their date tonight, so she won't get to see him again before her departure. He claims to have urgent business to take care of. I wonder what that could be! That slacker takes advantage of people left and right. He's house-sitting a mansion right now –

all he has to do is water the plants, check the water in the pool, and get the mail while the Wallaces, the Scottish owners, are away for a few weeks. There's nothing to stop him from coming out to see her one last time. In my opinion, he's already latched onto some other woman."

"So that wasn't you…"

"No, that wasn't me making her moan loud enough to wake the dead. Oh, no!"

"I thought…"

"You thought that since I'm black, I'm randy, I'll jump on anything that moves, it's in my genes."

"Not at all! I never thought that. When I got up, there were only the two of you here."

"So you decided it had to be me. You'd make a terrible cop. Don't ever trust appearances. You need material proof, direct witnesses. Did you see her on me or me on her? Did she tell you it was me?"

He was evidently enjoying playing the interrogator.

"But the facts are the facts," Harmony argued. "No one else was aboard."

"Cédric was in her cabin. He was resting when you came aboard in the middle of the night. Brigitte had come up into the cockpit for a beer, more than one in fact. Then they went at it again. He got up around eight and left in his kayak. The sea was rough, and he flipped it a few times."

"Wouldn't his clothes get all wet?"

"He was wearing swim trunks and his stuff was in a waterproof bag, like that one," he said, pointing at a sack in a corner. "I recommend it – very practical. Anyway, my advice as a detective is to not trust appearances."

"I'll remember that. Florent, I have a proposition to make. I'd like to hire you to help me find my husband."

"The fee is out of your range. My clients are extremely wealthy, and I won't lower my rates for you. It could get around. The rich will think I'm destitute – meaning my business is going badly, meaning I'm no good as a detective. The old vicious circle."

"I have some savings. I'll spend everything I have, if only I can find Max as soon as possible."

"You've got five thousand euros?"

"Twenty-five hundred to start and twenty-five more if you manage to uncover a real lead."

"And you're a negotiator, too!"

"An accountant, that's all. Inflow, outflow, profit."

"Alright, but you have to engrave this on your memory – in France alone, fifty thousand adults are reported missing every year. Ninety-five percent of them are found, but five percent remain missing. I'll do my job to my utmost, but whatever the result, I want my money. You can sign a contract right now so it's all up front, and you'll see there's even a confidentiality clause. And you'll have to wire me the money as soon as possible."

He went over to a drawer by the stove, and after digging a while, came back with some papers.

"Here's a blank contract that I'll fill out, then you can sign it. And here's my bank info. Good accounts make good friends, as they say. But keep this in mind – I can't guarantee I'll find your husband."

"I heard your statistics," Harmony said. "Mathematically speaking, I have much more chance of finding him than not."

She signed the contract without even reading it, then went back to her cabin, where she sat on the bunk feeling profoundly disappointed. Florent's reaction had offended her. She would have preferred seeing him as more of a "heroic knight." A bit like Max. Instead, he had immediately launched into the business of money, contracts, outcomes.

He was just a private eye, end of story. She shouldn't have expected more. The dinner between pseudo-friends, the wine and laughter – what a load of rubbish!

Feeling a blue funk coming, she decided she better try to sleep. She should have followed Brigitte's recipe: chug wine until drunk, then fall in a heap.

# Chapter Twenty-Six

"Insomnia is a bad counsellor; especially how it exaggerates images. It easily transforms worry into fright, and fright into terror." *Yves Theriault*

It was her second night aboard Florent's boat, a full night this time. But it wouldn't be a full night of sleep, because she could only toss and turn. She regretted having rushed to hire Florent. She decided to count imaginary sheep leaping over imaginary fences, which had worked when she was a kid, although her mother's hugs were more efficient. But she'd gotten those only when her mother was under the influence of alcohol, when she no longer saw her children as burdens, as mouths she had to feed every day. Once the alcoholic effluvium evaporated, she became inaccessible, immersed in the daily grind.

To please her, Harmony had tried to be the perfect daughter. Forever the brightest in her class, always obedient, watching over her little brother like a second mom. Her teachers vaunted her extreme maturity, how fast she was growing up, and often pointed it out to the other students. One time a classmate had drawled, "Yes but 'more haste, less speed,' as my dad says," getting a hilarious reaction from all the class.

Harmony sometimes wished her mother would get drunk more often, to get more affection from her. Most Saturday nights, she did get drunk. Like that evening they'd left in the car after dinner, at which her mother drank more than a little wine. She wanted to treat them to a movie, and they had happily watched a film, taking turns grabbing handfuls of popcorn from a huge bag. But after they left the theater, Jonathan Clark's daughter had crossed their path, and their lives had fallen apart.

She decided to call Rosanna the following day. Even if they couldn't hold much of a conversation, she was still her mother. Of course she wouldn't mention Max's disappearance. She mustn't worry her. Harmony visited her every weekend, and Max usually accompanied her, using the time to write or walk around the institution's park-like grounds.

Midnight, and Harmony had counted up to three thousand sheep, so she went up deck as quietly as she could, then crept to the bow. She hung onto the lifelines, appreciating even more at night the benefit of that cable making the tour of the boat. On the trampoline, she discovered Florent rolled up in a blanket on a mattress. The Newfoundland slept at his feet, a biological hot water bottle.

Seeing her, Florent instantly ended a vehement telephone conversation.

"Sorry, I hope you didn't hang up because of me."

"No, I was done."

"What language was that?"

"Lingala."

"The same as the name of your boat. Is Lingala spoken all over Africa?"

"Mainly in the two Congos, but because it's unusually sing-song, it's known throughout Central Africa and even farther."

"So how did you end up here?"

"My mom left the DRC in the eighties, when it was still called Zaire, and went to Belgium to study medicine. Then she met my dad, who was also studying medicine, and I was born eight years later. He's Flemish – that's where I get my unpronounceable name."

"Have you been to your mother's country?"

"Several times, to visit our family there."

"That doesn't tell me how you landed in St. Barts. It's odd, and living on a boat is unusual, too."

"I've always been attracted to sailing, and the Caribbean, and warm waters. And here, nobody asks me where I'm from. I could be a local, born on the islander. It's so nice to feel anonymous and not have to justify my origins. Even my last name is inconspicuous, because of the former Dutch colonies around here."

176

"I can understand. I have to reprimand my husband sometimes for saying such and such a person isn't Breton or Corsican or whatever, because their name or physique isn't typical of the region. That's typically European. In America, you're simply American."

"You're simplifying matters. Americans also categorize people by community, like 'Blacks,' or 'Latinos' or 'WASPs.' Anyway, excuse me for changing the subject, but why is it you don't call your family, or friends?"

"I have very few friends. The one person I can talk to is pregnant, and I don't want to make her go into premature labor."

"And your family?"

"My father left us, and we haven't been in contact for a long time. And my mother isn't in her right mind – she's seriously handicapped. I'll call her tomorrow, but just to see how she's doing."

"I'm sorry. Sounds like your life hasn't been easy."

"My husband pampers me, and I don't need anyone else."

"That's not healthy – a symbiotic relationship eventually drives people batty, plus it often hides something."

"It's not hiding anything!"

"Oh yes, it is. Usually, one person is extremely possessive, and keeps the other in a protective but perverse bubble of love. You no longer dare to do anything, and you get cut off from your family and best friends. Unconsciously, a form of terror reigns. You can't get out of the relationship once the gears are in motion."

"Now you're a psychiatrist, huh? There's nothing like that between us. I didn't have many friends before meeting him, and he's never prevented me from seeing anyone. What do you know about love, seeing as how you live all alone on your *Bisó na bisó*, aka *Between Us*? You should have called it *Between Me and Myself*."

Enraged, she marched off, ignoring the lifelines and almost tumbling down several times. That guy had almost won her over. Explaining the difficulty of his life as a mestizo had drawn her pity, but then he'd had to trot out his pet theories about relationships. Plus, his parents were doctors. Papa and Mama had opened their purses so he could realize his dream and go live on a boat, leaving everything behind. No risks – he could always fall back on their money. And his job? Private eye for the super-rich. He was no philanthropist.

The only positive side to all this was that he had tired her out. Yawning, she stretched out on her stomach and counted hardly a dozen sheep before falling asleep.

# Chapter Twenty-Seven

"Everyone should keep a journal. Starting with bandits and criminals. That would simplify police investigations." Philippe Bouvard

Hot rays of sunshine struck the porthole of Harmony's cabin and brightened her peaceful face. No nightmares had perturbed her sleep. She'd better not dawdle anymore, as they had to take the ferry to St. Martin at ten that morning. The sailboat would have taken too long.

About a half hour earlier, Florent had jolted her out of deep sleep by setting a radio in front of her door, blasting the new Kungs song. Then a series of home-spun ads, Radio St. Barts-style, featuring desperate requests for rentals or roommates. Rents were exorbitant on this island; sharing a house had become the only way to avoid handing over your entire salary to a landlord.

All three of them were taking the ferry. Brigitte was flying back to Monaco out of Juliana Airport, and Florent was going to launch his investigation at the Flynt's starting point: their landing at Sint-Maarten. He planned to retrace every step of their voyage. Harmony couldn't see the use of it, as nothing particular had happened, but she didn't want to contradict him. Considering the price she'd agreed to pay him, she figured he knew what he was doing. She still wondered at her blind confidence in signing his contract, which wasn't like her at all.

She put on some clothes Brigitte had spontaneously loaned her, like an old friend. Beige cotton shorts and a pale pink linen shirt. She would return them through the mail as soon as she could, even though Brigitte had insisted she could keep them as long as she wanted. But Harmony detested procrastination. If you have to do something, get to it right away.

Her ankle had returned to its normal size, so she didn't bother wrapping it with the compression bandage. She left the cabin and encountered Tempest, who lay in front of the companionway. She caressed its long fur, smiling at the gallant dog, harmless despite its imposing physique, then climbed over and went up to the deck.

Black coffee and toast awaited her next to a jar of fresh mango jam. Florent hadn't had time to bake croissants; he was busy writing on an electronic notepad, but looked up when she sat at the table.

"Good! You're up a lot earlier than yesterday."

"Hard to sleep with that music, thank you very much. And I was able to sleep soundly after our conversation last night."

"I hope you're not mad about it, or things aren't going to go too smoothly between us. I'm not used to mincing words. That goes both ways though – when you don't agree, just shout it out. It's better than keeping it to yourself."

Brigitte displayed all the symptoms of a bad hangover. She was silent, she winced at noises and her movements were gingerly. Instead of eating, she swallowed a giant spoonful of antacid and a couple of aspirin with a cup of sugary tea. She kept her opaque sunglasses on to counteract the glaring sunshine. Harmony pitied her being in that state right before a transatlantic flight.

Harmony was taking her first sip of coffee when she noticed a boat heading straight toward them at high speed. It was the gendarmerie's launch, which slowed and held steady at the port stern.

"Hello on board, can you hear me?" shouted Yves Duchâteau. "I have news for Madame Flynt-Rousseau. Is she there?"

"I'm here," she said, getting to her feet.

She made her way to the stern to talk to him.

"I have some good and bad news," Duchâteau said. "We think we found the contents of the beach basket you spoke of. These towels and snorkeling gear, and especially the iPhone 6 – are they yours?"

He waved triumphantly at the pile of gear in the bottom of his boat. Harmony took a step down the aluminum swim ladder and looked closely at the objects, even squinting to make sure, even though she had recognized them instantly.

"Yes, those are our belongings. Where did you find them?"

"Three kids fished it out of a trashcan. One of their mothers was smart enough to ask her son where he got the iPhone, and she called us."

"But where's the basket?"

"The boys don't have it. They claim to have followed a teenager, Antoine Brin, who dumped its contents into the trash. But it's difficult to question him, as he's autistic. You can't push him too hard. For the moment, he doesn't respond, and he goes into a fit if you try to get to the basket, which is in his room. His mother asked us to be patient, and she'll persuade him to talk."

Florent had come up behind Harmony to listen, and he asked, "What's the bad news, then?"

"They threw the SIM card into the ocean from the top of the cliff at Pointe Milou. We can't get information from the phone company anyway unless we open a missing-person criminal investigation."

"And you're still reluctant to do that?" Harmony exclaimed.

"The commander doesn't want to rush into things. Monsieur Rousseau is an adult, and he has the right to disappear without us running after him."

"But what more do you need? His dead body?"

"What makes you think he's dead?" Duchâteau said, alarmed.

"A kidnapping that goes wrong – has that never happened?"

"Listen, it's only a question of a few days. I'm sure to find new clues that will clear this all up. Will you be remaining on Saint-Barthélemy, Madame Flynt?"

"I'm returning to St. Martin today, and we'll be back here tonight. Right, Florent?"

"That's right, Inch 'Allah."

The "Inch-Allah" made Yves smile. He was familiar with Florent's tendency to provocation. In this era of Islamophobia, Florent never hesitated to invoke God in Arabic, especially with representatives of the French Republic's authority, like him. Yves liked rebellious characters, going against the flow. His wife Nadia had Tunisian ancestors, and she felt the accusatory looks thrown at her every time there was a terrorist attack on the news, and she had to bear in silence the shocking comments on social media sites, especially when they came from her Facebook "friends." She felt more at ease in the Caribbean, blending in with the mass of women naturally tan, or bronzed by the sun.

"Florent, if you hear anything new, will you call me?"

"Why would I have news?"

"Because Madame is looking at you as if you've become the master of her destiny. She hired you, no?"

Florent said nothing and Harmony didn't deny it, so Duchâteau concluded his guess was correct.

"Have you found a photo of your husband?" he asked Harmony.

"That's what I'm going to look for. Maybe there's one in his luggage."

"As soon as you have one, send me a copy to this email," he said, handing her his card, and staring at her with eyes both serious and searching.

She stammered, "Yes, yes, of course."

The gendarme and his colleague from the Marine Brigade took off. Harmony felt anxiety filling her heart, her chest, her head. Their beach gear had turned up – finally, a lead! But no one could reassure her about what had happened to her husband. Duchâteau had spoken to her in a different tone – was he coming around to her hypothesis, or still stuck on the idea of a voluntary disappearance? She latched onto the statistics Florent had given her: ninety-five percent of all missing persons are found…

Florent cleared the table and gave water to the dog. He had analyzed his new client's reactions. A gleam of hope had surged up for a few seconds only to make way to an anguish he knew well. That's why he didn't tell her about the dark spots on one of the towels, which he'd identified right away. He also thought about the scrapes on Harmony's palms. She had mentioned hurting herself, "probably" while climbing onto some rocks during the Shell Beach search.

Thirty-six hours had passed since she had last seen her husband. The enigma of Max Rousseau was starting to jiggle the pieces of an imaginary chessboard, and Florent was leaning more to the possibility of a kidnapping. But in any investigation, as plausible as a scenario seemed, you always had to go back to the essential question: who would profit from the crime? If there had even been a crime. For, as of now, there was no cadaver.

# Chapter Twenty-Eight

"People are always on the cusp of revealing something, but in the end, they don't want to let it out, they put on airs. And sometimes they can't hold on; it sweats its way out. You have to seize the occasion, gather up the scraps, and reconstitute it."
Chloé Schmitt, *Les Affreux (The Frightful Ones)*


Wednesday, December 7, 2016. By the time they dropped Brigitte off at Princess Juliana Airport, she looked her radiant self again, relieved that her medications had erased all trace of her hangover and that her trip was about over.

The road from the airport to the resort was the same Harmony and Max had taken on their arrival. Harmony couldn't recall anything out of the ordinary about that whole morning... After landing, they went through customs, and the officer on duty, a corpulent, aloof woman, stamped their passports after a mere glance at their landing cards, duly filled out in capital letters, indicating where they would be staying and the motif of their trip. Harmony had drawn a cocktail and beach chair in the space, which earned them a half-smile from the customs officer. They went to the one baggage area next, and by chance, theirs were the first suitcases disgorged onto the ramp. A spanking-new matched set bought especially for the occasion, purple and pink stripes for Harmony, blue and white for Max. Since they had been the last to check in for their flight in New York, Max had laughed and proclaimed, "and the Last shall be First." Before continuing into the main hall, they put away their heavy coats, Harmony's beige fake fur carefully folded; Max's gray trench stuffed into a ball. She told Max he'd better hang it up as soon as they got to the hotel so it wouldn't get too wrinkled. She hated wrinkled clothes, and it was such an elegant trench coat. When the automatic doors opened, they saw all those people, the same as in every airport, peering at, around and over the heads of the new arrivals, searching for a familiar face. A parent or a child, a spouse or lover, perhaps a mistress. The giant, brightly lit hall was comfortably air-conditioned, but when they went outside, the heat blasted down on them. The blue sky and the glaring sun made them squint and fumble among their bags to find their sunglasses. They climbed into a Mercedes taxi, white like almost all the cars on the road. A sense of well-being enveloped them as they sat close together in the back of the car, holding hands. Their vacation had just begun, the sky was magnificent, and tropical air rushed in through the open windows.

Harmony remembered that detail, and told Florent she had asked the old Antillean driver to turn off the A/C so she "could feel the tropical breeze and breathe in the warm air." He had rolled his eyes but smiled, saying he liked seeing happy people, especially a couple in love, like them.

Forty minutes later, they had climbed out of the Mercedes in front of the hotel, right where she now found herself in Florent's company. The resort seemed less enjoyable than when she'd arrived with Max, but Harmony knew it was because she was so heavy-hearted. Why do we miss others so much more when they've been wrested from you?

Florent realized this was the first time he'd set foot in the Oyster Bay beach resort. He'd seen it many times when he took the ferry from Captain Oliver's Marina or when he anchored his boat near it. The resort was a landmark that all boats had to go past after leaving the dock, and on return trips, the sight of it meant they'd reached their destination. Built in the seventies during the demographic and economic boom on the island, it sported an audacious color: pistachio green. They'd probably tried to match the turquoise water it looked out on. At the left end of the hotel complex was a dome with stained glass windows that attracted all eyes, and Florent had always wondered what was in there.

He wasted no time to find out. He headed to the security office, and Harmony hurried after him. The security guard, one Anthony Gumbs, was lunching there on ribs and rice, a typical

St. Martin meal. Luck was with them, as Gumbs was a person Fat Boy had mentioned. His partner knew Gumbs from elementary school, and in Florent's book, "a friend of a friend is a friend." He called Fat Boy on the spot so he could talk to Gumbs, and after this, the guard dropped the administrative formalities and attitude, and let them watch the security footage from the day the couple arrived. The video was too gray and blurry to make out much, and when Harmony pointed out her husband, he looked like a ghost as he crossed the lobby and headed to the elevators. He'd already put on his straw hat, so his face was partially hidden. Harmony had entered the hotel before him to check in while he paid the taxi driver, and he'd had to search for his wallet. By the time he came in, Harmony had already gotten their room keycard. She had been caught on film via a different camera, with a better image. It showed her smiling happily, her face that pale color of people newly arrived from the wintry north. Checking in had taken less than three minutes, as there was no one in line, and the desk clerk was a highly efficient Dutch woman.

All Florent could glean from the security footage was that Max Rousseau was a man of average height with wide shoulders, so he thanked Mr. Gumbs and slipped a bill into his hand as they left.

Next, they spent some time talking to the front desk clerks. A young intern took a long while checking the computer and finally confirmed that their credit card hadn't been used since eight in the morning on the day they went to St. Barts.

They also learned that Max had not come back, and no messages had been received.

"I already knew all that," Harmony said wearily. "It couldn't have been otherwise."

All that remained was to check their room. As they were about to enter the elevator, Florent heard a hissing whistle, Fat Boy's signal, which he hated. He turned around, irritated. He'd asked him so many times to not whistle like that, but the more it annoyed Florent, the more malicious pleasure it gave Fat Boy.

Looking at him with a frown, Florent was struck by how thin his partner was – his new diet was really working. Bizarrely, Florent missed the old "Fat Boy." With fifty pounds melted away, he no longer seemed the happy-go-lucky islander he knew. He'd have to rethink that nickname.

"Hey man," Fat Boy called out. "Got the envelope for me?"

"So that's why you came," Florent said as he handed him his pay. "It's all there, thirty one-hundred-dollar bills, but count it anyway. And let me introduce Madame Harmony Flynt-Rousseau, our new client."

"*Enchanté*, Madame. Wow, you score jobs fast, Florent."

Fat Boy spoke English and French fluently, but as if he'd picked them up on the streets of New York or Paris rather than in the classroom. Yet he'd lived in the Caribbean all his life, and even his Information Sciences degree was from a school in Martinique. A true local boy, he would never set foot in Europe unless it was under general anesthesia.

Once they were all in the elevator, Florent addressed Harmony. "Could you give us your email address and cell phone number? Oh, and we're going to stay on St. Martin tonight, then go back tomorrow. I have some things to take care of here. I'll let you know about our program later. First, let's visit your room."

They got out on the third floor. Harmony's legs started quavering, and she stumbled a few times. Florent watched her closely. This reconstitution of the couple's first day of vacation hadn't brought him much in the way of material elements, but that hadn't been his main goal. He wanted to shake her up, get her to reveal her secret, for like the majority of people, she had one. She had revealed nothing, not a hint of it, but he had a feeling it was a serious one.

Florent hated it when a client didn't tell him everything. He wasn't a cop, so what was she afraid of?

# Chapter Twenty-Nine

"Nothing seems more like a lie than the truth." Harry Bernard, *Dolorès*

Chicago, November 18, 2006. The residents of Chicago's Pilsen neighborhood were having a tranquil day, and it was now Sunday dinner time: those hours between noon and four o'clock when people raised in the old style felt the obligation to sit quietly around the table. People who had never benefited from that type of education chose what seemed most natural, and they lounged in front of their televisions after or even during the meal.

Phil Peterson and his wife chose the second approach. Their two kids were seated on his ample lap, trying to keep pieces of hamburger meat or onion rings from falling on the carpet. Their mother handed out containers of barbeque sauce, worrying there was not enough.

They munched away at their fast food while watching the Chicago Bulls play basketball against the Indiana Pacers. Phil would have liked to bring his boys to watch their favorites in person, but that was wishful thinking. Their rental contract was about to expire, and the house was up for sale. If they didn't buy it, they had to move, and they had neither the money nor the credit to get a loan. It was too bad. Phil loved living in Pilsen on the Lower West Side, where his Czech ancestors had settled. He felt at home here, even if the Mexicans, who were now the majority, marked it with their more conspicuous imprint. The children liked their schools, and took off in the mornings cheerfully, plus, his wife worked at the National Museum of Mexican Art just a few steps away. Only Phil had to make a long commute, out to Northwestern Memorial Hospital.

The house was blessed with a narrow but long back garden where the kids could play. They were in their teens, so that was far less often now. Still, having a yard was important. They had a few chickens, and fresh eggs, giving the place the feel of the countryside. In the summer, barbecuing was sacred to them. Phil grilled the meat, bought cheap straight from the slaughterhouses Chicago was famous for. His wife Sarah brought out the deck chairs with the yellow striped cushions to create the illusion of being on vacation, even if they stayed home for it. Phil had never liked apartments. They would be deprived of their barbecues. Sarah had already started looking for another house, afraid of finding herself and her family without a roof, but so far, she'd found only duplexes and triplexes, all of them atrocious. Cages where they would feel more cooped up than their beloved hens.

That Sunday, the Bulls were vanquished, only by a fraction, but vanquished, nevertheless. That only reinforced his depression of the last few days. Phil zapped channels until midnight before deciding to head upstairs, where Sarah was already sleeping. For some reason he never figured out, he looked out the front window. The little accountant Harmony Flynt wasn't yet in bed. Her window was still lit up, and he saw her graceful figure moving behind the curtains. He had always admired the care she took in decorating the windows at Christmas time, with snowmen, polar bears, shooting stars, Rudolph and his reindeer pulling Santa's sleigh.

He got up in the middle of the night to get up and use the bathroom. He'd drank quite a few cans of beer that evening. His wife didn't stir when he tiptoed out. He respected her sleep, especially when Monday morning was at hand. As he was about to slide back between the covers, he heard steps outside. It was amazing how well you could hear at night, and he now clearly heard the tapping of high heels on the sidewalk. He approached his window and discreetly pulled back the curtain to peer out. It was Harmony, opening the door to her Ford Ka. She often parked in front of their house. They didn't have a car and since they'd always found Harmony friendly, they reserved their spot for her, even putting a chair there so no one would steal it. Tonight, she was dressed for a party, braving the freezing cold weather in a thin black dress barely longer than her red coat, which didn't look very warm. She had wound a thick scarf around her neck and put on gloves, gray or black. It was hard to tell at night, despite the street lighting.

She raised her head before getting into her car, and their eyes met. They both waved. Phil felt a little embarrassed, as it was late, and he hoped she didn't think he'd been spying on her. He thought he'd explain this to her as soon as he could; it was only the noise of her high heels that had made him look out on the street.

A few hours later, his wife and the kids left at seventy-thirty as usual. As he kissed them goodbye on the front step, he noticed that the Ford Ka wasn't there, and figured that Harmony had slept at her fiancé's house. Youth was made for love and amusement, he thought, and recalled they'd been invited to the marriage in May.

At eight-twenty, he saw her pull in and park, rather haphazardly, in front of their house, then take off again just minutes later. She must be late for work, he thought. Phil was an ambulance driver, and didn't start until the second shift that day. He liked the afternoon shift, as it gave him a little time to himself, and he could hang out at home watching a film or two. His wife didn't care for erotic films, inhibited as she was by her education, so he took advantage of these solitary hours to watch them. But that morning, he didn't even do that. The fear of having to move, of having to break with all his little habits had completely stifled his libido.

After that slightly strange night, he got the feeling Harmony was trying to avoid him. As a result, he never had the chance to explain why he'd been watching her from his window.

A few days later, an elegantly dressed man in his sixties had knocked at his door. Phil almost didn't answer, thinking it must a Mormon proselytizer, but the man's gray flannel slacks and long beige coat spoke of wealth, and his confident voice, that of a rich man, commanded respect, so he let him in.

Jonathan Clark had something important to ask him concerning his neighbor. On the street, Emilio Garcia stood by the black limo waiting for his boss.

Six months later, the home that Phil Peterson didn't want to leave became his. All he'd had to do was tell a certain life insurance agent that Harmony Flynt had been home all that night. After all, he had seen her in her room in the middle of the night, and she had left as usual for work in the morning. Aside from a few little details, it was all true.

A half-truth isn't the same thing as a lie....

# Chapter Thirty

"Losing acquaints you with the void." Gilbert Dupuis, *La Marcheuse (The Walker)*

Harmony closed the heavy security door behind Florent, holding it so it wouldn't slam. Most hotels used them now, but it intensified her sense of isolation in a hotel room already so anonymous. And the double bed looked too vast, especially since she would have to sleep in it without Max at her side. She missed her little bunk on Florent's boat.

The suite was just as they had left it two days earlier. His clothes still hung in the closet, and she grabbed an armful and took a deep breath. They smelled like Max. The odor of Chanel's "Allure" cologne wafted up. Max loved to splash it on, to the point it seemed he wanted to erase his own odor. She didn't know his true smell, as there was always a hint of "Allure" mixed in. Secretly, she thought it a bit girlish for such a virile man, but excused it because "he was French."

The king-sized bed had been remade, the pillows carefully tucked under the thin yellow comforter. The bathroom had been cleaned, rid of their hair, smears of toothpaste, their fingerprints on the mirror. She had scrawled "I love you" across the whole thing after taking her last shower. Max had added, "I love you 2." All wiped clean, of course. The used towels had been replaced by pristine white ones. The room cleaner must have been surprised at having nothing more to do since then.

Their suitcases and hand luggage hadn't been moved from their precise arrangement next to the closet, where Harmony saw that all of Max's clothes were still there, neatly arranged on the various shelves: shorts, t-shirts, underwear, bathing suits. His trench coat hung there, ready to face winter back in Milwaukee, and his Italian dress shirt seemed ready and waiting for the famous casino soirée that might never happen. When someone died or disappeared, their belongings existed still, at the ready, unaware a drama had occurred. At worst, they would undergo a change of ownership.

Without asking for her permission, Florent opened the hand luggage, then Max's suitcase. He found nothing out of the ordinary, and no photos. As he leafed through the brown notebook Max used for his writing, Harmony told him about how Max always used Clairefontaine notebooks, a French brand that reminded him of his childhood. Expatriates often hold dear the products of their former homes; they help them keep in touch with their roots.

Max wrote his ideas on these pages, the kind that surge up out of nowhere and that could be useful to his book. This one didn't hold many words yet, being brand new, but there were four huge capital letters written across the width of the flyleaf: M.I.T.T. Harmony wondered what that meant.

On the first page was written: "Injustice, Birth, Rebirth. Why do some of us succeed and others do not? Must a man be born under a lucky star? And for that, does he simply have to change his skies and find the one star that will bring him luck? Under a star of Western Africa?"

On the second page he'd written: "Can love be sincere if it's built on secrets? Will you be the one who throws the first stone, you who also hide a terrible secret? But I love you anyway."

Harmony felt a quiver run through her body on reading these words. Was she becoming paranoid? She could have sworn they were addressed to her, but that was impossible. He knew nothing; he couldn't know – she had never shared her secret.

On page three: "Where do you want to live the last days of your life? Appearances are often mistaken, Princess. Sometimes you have to imagine the other person in an exact opposite situation. Will you remember this?"

When Florent read this aloud, she was vaguely reminded of something, but it wasn't until after he and Fat Boy left after a half-hour of fruitless searching that it popped into her mind.

Shell Beach! Before going shopping for her dress, Max had insisted she memorize those phrases. Was it a coincidence to find them set down on paper almost word for word? And should she tell Florent about it?

She did nothing of the kind. She could swear these notes were addressed to her personally. Couples had a secret language, like twins, that only they could understand. Should she try to discover the message hidden behind them?

She decided she needed to rest instead; she was exhausted and didn't have the energy to figure out their meaning right at the moment. But before resting, she needed to eat lunch. Not wanting to go down and mix with the happy vacationers or listen to lively island music, she leafed through the flyers on the nightstand, most of them for restaurants offering takeaway, and chose pizza.

An hour later, she opened the door to the delivery boy. She got through half the pizza, covered in anchovies and herbs, but gave up when she realized tears were running down her cheeks. She stuck the rest of it in the minifridge, where she discovered several tiny bottles of Saint-James rum. In lieu of sleeping pills, she drank them all, upending each little bottle one by one.

Before lying down, she decided to open her suitcase. She wanted something she'd hidden under a beach towel – her brother's teddy bear. A sight that always moved her. It traveled with her most of the time, even if she never let anyone see it. Today was different. Max wasn't there. When the cat's away, the mice will play...

She set it next to her pillow and contemplated its fixed expression, the half-smile and benevolent gaze that seemed to say, "Sweet dreams."

She remembered the time Max had grabbed it from her, screaming, and hurled it out their bedroom window. And then took her by the shoulders and ordered her to stop all that. She had cried, her head on his chest, and he'd consoled her, saying the teddy bear was part of the past, that they were both going to start a new life.

That was at the beginning of their marriage. She had obeyed him, and put the bear away with the rest of her brother's stuff. Everything was to be out of sight; everything was to gradually fade from her memory. But today, the stuffed bear gave her a feeling of well-being and calmed her down, like in the old days. Max would surely understand there were times a person is forced to disobey. She ended up sleeping the afternoon away.

When she awoke, it was dark outside. She felt disoriented and completely empty. Like this hotel room, without his presence. Max had not reappeared. Hearing her phone beep, she dragged herself to the nightstand to reach it.

An email had arrived from an unknown sender, and the subject heading gave her a jolt: "Concerning your husband."

# Chapter Thirty-One

"In searching for Heather, he was faithfully reproducing her movements – and quite possibly her mistakes as well. In following the same clues as her, he might well be heading for the same destination."Robert Goddard, Into the Blue


December 7 – 2 P.M. After his boat trip to see Florent and Harmony, Yves Duchâteau had decided to do some checking around before returning to the gendarmerie. He hadn't wanted to involve Commander Roland, who was convinced Max Rousseau had disappeared for some reason that concerned only himself. If he'd fallen ill, they would already have found him, especially since the helicopter had scoured the island the day before. Finding his belongings in a trashcan was all the more proof to him that the man wanted to break with his past. If he'd been the victim of criminals, they would have taken his iPhone.

But Yves wanted to cover all the bases, discreetly of course, and Roland wouldn't be happy to see him investigating as if this was an abduction. Yves wanted to interrogate the principal witness, as was only proper. His instinct as a cop told him so. It would soon be forty-eight hours since Rousseau had disappeared. Madame Flynt had taken the morning ferry to Oyster Pond, and he hoped she would send him a photo of Max soon. As a precaution, he had verified there was no police record. As soon as he got the chance, he would check at the French embassy. Maybe they could snag a photo or more details about him.

He found his witness sitting on a little red chair in the shade of a lemon tree. The fence separating the garden from the road was only about knee-height, so there was no privacy. Passersby looked into the garden, and people in the garden looked at the passersby, but it was probably the way they wanted it. Owners established their territory, but could see what was going on in their street. You had to entertain yourself as best you could in St. Barts.

"Hello, Antoine. *Kommank t é?* Good?"

The teenager understood patois, but he didn't answer or even look at Yves. The question had no interest for him – no one cared if he was doing good or not. Other details attracted his attention, however. He scrutinized the gendarme's pockets. The edges were worn, and a few threads hung down, and to Antoine, that meant the gendarme often put his hands in his pockets. Did he put things in there? Like a keyring or a handkerchief or snacks?

Next, he detailed the gendarme's nose, which he considered too long, like a lot of *métros*, or people from France, and it wasn't in good shape: the tip was red and the nostrils irritated from excessive blowing. In fact, Yves had been quite cold the previous night, for the first time since his transfer to the tropical island.

Antoine left the face and went back to his visitor's pockets, imagining them as little baskets glued to people's thighs. Not as prized as the big beautiful woven baskets he collected, though. What did this man want? Antoine was no idiot, and wouldn't let himself be duped. Like the others, the gendarme would be sneaky and try to get into his room and touch his belongings. Then what? Would he try to steal them?

Noticing the boy's gaze, Yves looked down at his pocket. He could tell Antoine was on the defensive. He needed to get into the boy's head, put himself at his level, tame him and get him to disclose where he had found the basket with the American and her missing husband's personal effects.

"So my pockets intrigue you. I know, they're very deep, but even so, sometimes there's not enough room. When I want to carry something really big, like my fins, it's impossible. I can't put them in there, you know! But maybe I should try."

Yves forced himself to laugh, then surprised himself at laughing naturally. Antoine stared at him even more keenly, at his lips and teeth, one of which grew lopsidedly and pushed

198

against another. The way lips moved revealed a lot, and Mr. Duchâteau had ended up laughing "for real." Antoine could discern between fake and true emotions. All of a sudden, he laughed at the image of the gendarme trying to stuff fins into his pockets.

"Are you thirsty, Antoine?"

"A little."

"I have a few cans of Oasis soda if you want one."

"Is it the purple one?

"I've got orange and purple. You're in luck."

Moving slowly to preserve the fragile link he'd just forged, Duchâteau walked over to his police car and opened the trunk, where he'd stowed a cooler. He came back with two cans of Oasis. Antoine's mother had told him it was the boy's favorite drink, especially "the purple one." He'd taken care to put them in a basket shaped like a hen, canary yellow with red handles. A unique piece that his mother-in-law had given to his daughter for Easter. He thought it a horror.

Antoine lit up as Yves handed him the can and proudly showed off his "hen basket."

"Do you like it?"

"Yes, it's so, so beautiful."

"Well, let's make a deal. I'll give you this one, and you give me one of yours in exchange, like the one you found the day before yesterday. You dumped what was inside into a trashcan. You know the one I'm talking about?"

Antoine scratched his head, reflecting. He liked the one he'd gotten in front of the Wallaces' house. A car had stopped, the kind he hated because it had dark windows you couldn't see through. The people got out like they were in a hurry and afraid to miss the start of a soccer match. People were so weird sometimes. He knew one of them, Cédric, who had gotten very mad because he couldn't get the remote work to make the electric gate go up, and he'd rushed through the little gate instead. A man and a pretty lady with short legs, a "munchkin," his mom would say, had followed him through the gate, and in their rush, they'd forgotten the basket next to the car.

In two seconds, Antoine had grabbed it and was running off. He didn't care what was inside – he just wanted the basket – so when he saw a trashcan, he turned it upside down and shook it. He knew Mael had followed him; Mael was always hanging around and he was a fast runner, but Antoine didn't care about that either.

He gazed hungrily at the giant fake hen. It was magnificent, so original, and he finally decided the one from the Wallaces didn't even come close to it. He agreed to the exchange and went up to his room. A few seconds later, he came back as proud as a peacock with the Flynt-Rousseau basket. Yves thanked him, took a step out of the garden, then turned around.

"Say, Antoine, could you show me where you found it?"


The Wallace villa was built on a rocky hillside in Colombier. You could see it from the coast, its tennis courts, pool and three modules with red roofs shaped like pointed hats, a typical St. Barts luxury villa. He suddenly remembered Madame Aubin's call to the gendarmerie reporting an usual "coming and going" there. Her home looked out over it, so she had a view of the entrance.

Antoine had not wanted to explain the circumstance in which he'd found the basket, saying only, "on the ground in front of the Wallace's gate." The boy didn't want to be accused of theft, and risk losing his new hen basket, so when the gendarme rang the bell, he took the opportunity to run off.

No response.

Yves rang a second time more insistently, and scowled into the video camera above the intercom. He was about to leave when the door next to the gate opened. Cédric Deruenne seemed to have dressed hastily, t-shirt backwards with the label showing.

"Hello! How can I help you?"

200

"Sorry to bother you. Yves Duchâteau, from the gendarmerie."

He held out the basket. "We found this in front of your place. Does it belong to you?"

"No, straw baskets aren't my style – they're for old folks. What made you think it's ours? Or rather, theirs, as I'm not the owner. I just watch this place."

"A kid found it and emptied the contents into a trashcan, and some other kids dug them out. There was an iPhone, some towels and snorkeling gear."

"The rascals!"

"Exactly. But these things belong to a man who's disappeared, and his wife claims he's disappeared in suspicious circumstances."

Cédric showed his astonishment, then quickly added, "A disappearance in St. Barts? That'll get some tongues wagging."

"Exactly. Are you alone in the villa?"

Cédric smiled roguishly before responding in a low voice, "Not really. I wasn't about to stay here all by myself. I'm with a girlfriend and two other guys. One of them sleeps all the time, and the other likes to go pick up girls, day or night."

He winked, as if the gendarme were a staunch supporter of seducers. He reminded him of someone. His face was familiar, but that could be his imagination tricking him, or they had crossed paths on the streets in Gustavia.

Yves knew Cédric by sight and by reputation, like all the people who lived year-round on the island. He wasn't a bad fellow, just lazy and a bit of a moocher, with no real qualifications. He seemed to get by as a borderline gigolo, considering the average age of the women he was seen with. Yves couldn't see any obvious link between him and Max Rousseau, so for now he contented himself with knowing the basket had been found in this immediate area, but not why. He said his goodbyes and left.

Cédric calmly shut the gate and picked up a few giant latanier palm leaves marring the pristine gravel path. He had to keep the place looking neat so the neighbors wouldn't discern anything out of the ordinary.

What talent he had shown in lying in such a natural way! He'd fooled the lieutenant with ease. That damn basket, though – it had caused them nothing but trouble; and now it had led a gendarme to the villa. Filthy kids! But he would have done the same at their age, especially for a new iPhone.

It was Fernando's fault for not coming to open the gate, lounging on the deck with his headphones on instead of keeping an ear out for the buzzer. They'd all had to get out of the car and walk through the side gate, forgetting they'd left the basket on the curb.

What a jerk! Sonia shouldn't have let him in on it. But it would all be over soon. Ah, Sonia. She had gotten under his skin and into his heart, too. No other woman managed to please him like she did, not even Brigitte with all her energy. And Brigitte was twenty years older than him, so what future could he imagine with her? It had been a real hassle to get rid of her. After that last night on Florent's catamaran, he had spent a long time explaining to her he couldn't see her before she left. What a scene she'd made on the phone the day before. Luckily, he hadn't given her the Wallace's address.

It had been hard enough cajoling Sonia, who couldn't understand why he didn't spend her first night there with her. He'd made up a story about a damaged boat and a big black dog to take care of. It wasn't very clear, but Sonia had let it drop, being tired from her trip and the race against time since the second she'd landed.

He heard the gendarme's car start up and pull away, which relieved him. Doubtless Sonia was paddling into waters too deep for her own good. What had she gotten them into? But she'd looked at him with her black doe's eyes and promised him they would be together for a good while this time. He and Sonia, a real couple? He liked the idea, and this was perhaps the first time he'd ever pictured himself with a ring on his finger and a few kids of his own.

He couldn't thank his lucky stars enough for having won that school lottery in Gustavia – the trip to Miami that had brought him such happiness, for it was there he fell in love with Sonia, the instant he met her. She worked at the hotel reception desk and had spent every night of his vacation with him.

After his departure, he'd tried to remain in contact, but she answered only a few of his messages. And then she had called him a few months ago, expressing her regrets and asking him if she could come to St. Barts to see him. Since then, he thought only of her, although he'd had to console himself in the arms of other women until her arrival. There were so many temptations here that a single man couldn't resist.

So without an ounce of tact, he'd sent Brigitte packing. It wasn't his style to run after two women at the same time. And with Sonia, he ran a marathon – just the kind of woman he liked.

She was in the bedroom with the other guy, putting together that video of theirs. She'd better get it sent before that cop came back to sniff around again.

The fuzz always had a sixth sense when it came to smelling anything fishy.

# Chapter Thirty-Two

"True love is pure, sincere, fair-minded, serious."
Henri-Frédéric Amiel, *Journal intime (Amiel's Journal)*

"You see, Max?" Sonia said, tapping him on the cheek. "It's not that hard to talk in front of the camera. You did it like a big boy, and you look so sweet when you put on your scared face."

Max had been cloistered in the bedroom at the end of the hall for the last forty-eight hours. Sonia planned to keep him there until those pathetic sea and helicopter searches were over. She had gone to the bar L'oubli on Rue de France to listen to the local gossip. The gendarmerie seemed to have lost interest, and were no longer moving heaven and earth to find their man, obviously convinced he'd disappeared of his own volition. This had reassured her.

Max didn't have much to complain about. He had the biggest room, an ocean view, and Sonia had even had couscous delivered. She now had to send the video to his "naïve" spouse, as she categorized Harmony. It would all be over in a few days. She would have her money and a new life would open to her. And to think that coward Max had dared to hide himself from her for almost two years! Having a good time in Milwaukee while she slaved away at her exhausting hotel job, wheedling clients who were more and more demanding. You had to keep them happy and smile all the while, and then there was her boss, controlling everything with an iron fist, making all the decisions, fixing her hours, even her vacations. She felt like a prisoner at her job. But without other qualifications, she couldn't hope for much else, and she hadn't found a man rich enough to set her up in style.

If she wanted to buy an apartment, she had to borrow money and pay it off every month. For how long – fifteen, twenty years? Stressed all the time, terrified of losing her job and not being able to pay the mortgage. But with the sum she was going to extract from Harmony Flynt, she could pay cash for a little nest on Collins Avenue, overlooking Miami Beach.

She pulled out the USB drive from the Wallace's computer, so she could send it from a safer location, one that couldn't be traced to this address. She'd learned how to create a floating IP address, and planned to make use of one from a cybercafé on Rue de La Liberté in St. Martin.

"Is it really necessary to lock me in?" Max said. "What are you afraid of, with two bodyguards, and then where would I go anyway?"

"It's more sensible to avoid temptation. You have to keep out of sight, and the less contact you have with the outside world, the better. Do you really think she'll pay for you?"

"Of course! She's attached to me."

"How touching. You seem pretty sure of yourself. I hope she comes through; if not, we go to Plan B, and that will be worse for her. You remember?"

"Of course – you're constantly reminding me. But she'll pay. She loves me, not like you."

"Good, we'll soon be all set."

She lowered the electric shutter outside the French doors, leaving a crack for some light to filter through, then took the remote control and left the room, double locking it behind her. Maybe it was a bit much, as it wouldn't serve his purposes to leave, but she didn't want him consorting with the other two men. She had lost confidence in him, and had never trusted Cédric or Fernando. The less they knew, the easier they were to handle. It reassured her to know he was locked up, because she knew what Max was capable of. His past actions made her tremble. Why did he scare her all of a sudden? She had borne with him all these years without ever feeling fear.

She went out on the terrace to avoid thinking about him. Fernando wasn't back from his walk, or she would have seen him lounging on a deck chair sipping a cold beer or a rum Ti-punch. At least he knew how to enjoy his pseudo vacation.

Thinking he had the right idea, she threw off her transparent green wrap and dove into the pool. The other sucker was probably snoring in his room. She had to put up with him a few more nights and then good riddance. Cédric had supplied them with a superb hideaway, though, and for that she had to keep him happy. When he made love to her, she gave herself to him one hundred percent. The act had to be perfect. And by dint of simulating pleasure, she ended up really feeling it. Cédric was addicted to her; too bad he had no future. He scraped by, skipping from job to job, and that wasn't good enough for her. She would never set up a home with him.

Why did she use men this way? In the beginning, she genuinely thought she loved them, at least a little. She had loved Max for a few years. But he'd never had any real ambition. Not only had he contented himself with a job as cook in a Miami hotel, but he was also a coward, running away to get married in secret, living off his wife and worst of all, lying to her. It was pitiful. He should be wary of naïve women, because they can transform into vipers once they understand what's really going on...

In all her relations with men, Sonia looked for benefit to herself, but maybe that would change once she got all that money in her pocket.

She would finally love a man sincerely, without ulterior motives, and she wouldn't even have to tell him. It would be obvious in her eyes and in her every gesture.

# Chapter Thirty-Three

"Spying among friends is never acceptable."Angela Merkel

Carolina Monteira stopped dancing. He wasn't looking at her anymore. His eyes were closed, his face wreathed in sweet beatitude. She wasn't surprised, as this special client never demanded more. She just had to be sexy and bewitch him with her slow, sinuous dancing.

Like her eyes and her hair, her underclothing was black: lacy bra, string bikini, thigh-high stockings. Black high heels with red soles gave her a passionate, spicy air. She had put on his favorite playlist, old RnB hits from the nineties. She loved that style of music too, and perhaps that was why she was more attached to this man than she should be.

He always relieved himself without touching her. Afterwards, he asked her to lie down next to him. He kissed her forehead, hugged her and fell asleep, satisfied, for an hour or two. She'd seen him cry, in the very beginning, when he confided in her as a friend, telling about his first love. A girl named Lise, who had promised him they would spend their lives together. With her – and for her – he had crossed the Atlantic. Lise, who flew away, her arms flung around the neck of an airplane pilot. Florent had become reserved, hard, after that, his heart closed off. He had become a man, or so he thought.

Florent kept his eyes closed, without moving, peacefully breathing but not sleeping. She lay down next to him, feeling like she was the one who wanted to cry. Carolina wanted him to love her. The dreaded phantasm of women who sell their charms for a living.

"Hey, you handsome boy, when are you going to take me out to a nice restaurant?" she said with a sigh, caressing his chiseled torso.

"Never, Carolina. That's not part of our deal. We don't mix things up, as I already explained. It's simply on principle, nothing against you. You're a great girl."

"You don't want to be seen with a stripteaser, huh?"

Florent didn't want to hurt her feeling by stating that she was in fact a prostitute. He stroked her silky coal-black hair and opened his eyes, only to be shocked by her angry glare.

"Shhh, Carolina. I need to rest a little. I didn't come to have a scene with you."

"I know, just to jerk off. Don't forget to pay my pimp Bernard the three hundred dollars!"

She got up, vexed, and imagined driving a knife into his icy heart. That soothed her and released some of her rage. She wriggled into her tight black dress, so short, low-necked and immodest it did away with any and all mystery. When she opened the door, dancehall music filtered into the room. She didn't look back – he wasn't going to see her cry! She went into the pole-dance room, hesitating whether to dance or go sit at the bar, then decided to dance, where men couldn't piss her off as much.

Florent closed his eyes again. With regret, he decided he would not come back again. Too bad, as he preferred La Casa Rosa, the "adult entertainment" club on the Dutch side, for its laxity and its Latino and mestizo girls. He avoided Russians and Blondes, as they looked too much like his ex.

Visiting Carolina had seemed the best solution, as she would have no grand illusions of being a couple. All he had to do was take his pleasure, relax, and then pay her boss. And Carolina Monteiro was such a sassy, curvaceous brunette. She could really swing. His ex, Lise Clijsters, was a gray-eyed blonde with tiny breasts and a flat butt, a terrible dancer, completely disjointed, and yet he'd been madly in love with her. Until she dealt him her knockout blow.

Carolina was his antidote, one of his little habits when he came up to St. Martin. But he'd begun to detect certain signs that smacked of real affection: she would pull the sheets up to his shoulders when he fell asleep, and adjust the thermostat so he wouldn't be too hot or too cold. Yes, she was getting attached to him, and that was a deal breaker.

He ended up falling asleep, but not long enough to dream. His cell phone vibrated and awoke him. Fat Boy's profile photo still displayed his triple chin.

"Dude, what's so important you have to wake me up in the middle of the night?"

"First of all, it's only ten o'clock, man. And yes, it's urgent."

"You already got into her emails?"

"What do you think? I got started as soon as we split up. Although I don't get why we're spying on her when she's our own client."

"I know, but she's not telling me everything. Something's off, and I don't want to be mixed up in anything suspicious. Plus, she reminds of someone who took me for a ride once, and you know I like being in the driver's seat…"

"Nice play on words. Anyway, her password is ridiculous, so it was easy. Harmony0821. First name, month and day of birth."

"And?"

"Our girl receives very few personal emails. Plenty of professional contacts, and they're listed by category, so that makes it easy. And there's a 'love' category with messages from someone called Steven Reardon, all from a few years ago. No uncertainty about their relationship – they were supposed to get married. Then, which seems bizarre, after exchanging several emails a day between 2003 and 2006, it stops entirely. The last one was from November 18, 2006. From that time on, under the category 'friends,' she gets a ton of messages from people with their 'sincerest condolences.'"

"What, the guy died?"

"You catch on quick."

"So, she has a fiancé who dies just before their marriage, and now a husband who disappears. Did you try searching for the keywords I gave you?"

"Of course. Under 'insurance,' I found emails from Jonathan and Katreen Clark. Those are her guardians, who've taken care of her since she was twelve. There's an interesting message where Mr. Clark advises her to keep the life insurance money, even if she considers it blood money."

"I guess it must be tough to spend money you've gotten from your fiancé's death. We should find out exactly how he died. And what's so urgent? You could have told me all this tomorrow morning."

"There are more recent emails having to do with 'insurance,' but I didn't have time to read them. I've been trying to reach you for over an hour, and your client has too. You told me you'd come by my place at nine. I assume you're with Carolina?"

"You assume correctly. She just left."

"Ooohh, I see."

"You don't see anything. Just continue."

"Better talk to me nicer than that – don't forget I've been babysitting your dog all this time. Man, can she eat! Weren't you supposed to put her on a diet?"

"Come on, say what you have to say. I'm all ears."

"Harmony is freaking out. She says she received a ransom demand for her husband."

Florent took a minute before reacting. "So that's it. He's been kidnapped."

"They want two hundred fifty thousand dollars."

"Oh, lord!"

He didn't know why, but the vision of Brandon Lake behind the mini-mart window flashed into his mind. He felt sure Brandon knew something about it, and when he surprised him, he pretended to be Mr. Jovial. There was something shady about the guy. Why had he pestered Harmony on the boat, and then pretended not to remember her husband?

"Do you know Brandon Lake?" he asked Fat Boy.

"Yeah, why?"

"Can you check him out?"

"What's gotten into you? You want to spy on everybody."

"I just want you to check his background. Especially where he's lived as an adult, and if he's ever been to the United States. And where he sleeps in St. Barts, and if his place is suitable for holding someone hostage. I'll meet you at Mrs. Flynt's hotel in fifteen minutes."

He hung up and took a quick shower, meditating the while as to how he could get out of La Casa Rosa without meeting Carolina Monteiro murderous gaze.

# Chapter Thirty-Four

"The clutter of an attic sometimes resembles that of one's memory." Claudie Gallay, *Les Déferlantes (The Breakers)*

December 8. This was the first time Florent had ever embarked on such a last-minute trip, especially for such a long distance. He'd snagged the last seat in business class at six-thirty that morning and taken off at one o'clock that afternoon from Sint-Maarten. After a stop in Atlanta, then another in Chicago, he was now in the air again, waiting for the Boeing to land in Milwaukee, a city he knew nothing about. Twenty hours so far – long enough to fly round-trip to Paris. And after landing, he would have to take a taxi to the Flynt-Rousseau home. Luckily, it was close to General Mitchell Airport, about five miles south of the city. Of course, it wasn't the miles that counted, but how long the drive took, with traffic and all the rest.

He thought about the previous evening again. After the call from Fat Boy, he had left Casa Rosa with a bitter taste in his mouth, thinking of Carolina. Any other normally constituted man would have screwed her by now. Was he afraid of getting too attached if he went that far sexually?

A half-hour later, Harmony let him and Fat Boy into her suite. On entering, Florent was more than ever convinced that places take on the mood of their occupants. The room was imbued with the sadness of a wake before a funeral. Harmony sat cross-legged on the middle of the bed while showing them the ransom demand – a video sent to her phone. Florent had never seen her so pale. At that instant, her close resemblance to Lise shocked him, especially the ivory satin nightshirt and the mussed hair. She was the very image of his ex, and that upset him so much that if Fat Boy hadn't been there, he would have told her to find some other detective, politely of course, then given back the money she'd already transferred to his account.

But he held back. He needed a continuous supply of money to make it in St. Barts, and others relied on him, like Fat Boy – or rather, Josuah, his real name, seeing as how "Fat Boy" no longer applied. And he wanted to prove to his parents he could succeed without their money, an adventurous but independent adult, which his mother sometimes doubted. The other night, she had gotten angry about that very subject. She wanted to send him some money, but he'd refused, and she didn't like that. She still needed to feel that her only child needed her.

In the video, Max Rousseau was visibly tense and spoke in a serious tone. According to his wife, he was wearing the same white linen shirt he'd worn at St. Barts, and looked as he had the last time she saw him, except for the dark circles under his eyes. In the background, they could see a smooth taupe wall and part of a painting of a sunrise. Fat Boy had tried to determine where the email came from, but the kidnappers had used a floating IP address. So they were pros or trained amateurs. And after downloading the video, Harmony had deleted the email with the attachment, blindly obeying their orders.

Florent had tried to get her to alert the gendarmerie, but Harmony surprised them by categorically refusing. She would do exactly what they required: stash two hundred fifty thousand dollars in an ordinary cardboard box among some clothes, then send it via DHL to their service point in St. Martin.

It would soon come to an end. Harmony had always wanted to get rid of that money anyway. Even though Florent and Fat Boy knew the story from reading her emails, she described the terrible car accident that had carried off her fiancé five months before their marriage, and how the life insurance settlement had ended up in her account. She and Steven had signed the policy because they planned to buy a duplex. Had they attracted the evil eye? That's what Fat Boy thought. He remembered how his friend Jimmy had signed a funeral insurance policy and a few months later, had buried his father, dead from rapid-onset cancer.

Florent noticed that while telling her story, Harmony didn't look them in the eye. This little detail upset him, as it reminded him of the day his ex – that lying bitch – swore there was nothing between her and that seducer of a pilot. She had avoided his glance while denying his accusations. Was Harmony lying too, and if so, why?

The insurance money was sitting in her home in a safe behind a painting. The worst possible hiding place, he had exclaimed, making her jump. Why hide it at home instead of in the bank? he'd demanded, and she said her guardian Jonathan Clark had recommended it, saying it was important to keep a large sum of ready cash hidden somewhere, that you could draw from without filling out forms or having to waiting for your bank to open. Florent remembered thinking that only peasants or mafia types acted like that, and since Clark lived in Chicago, he opted for the mafia.

Harmony had followed Clark's advice and hidden that huge sum of cash, like a bandit hides his dirty money, and then she concluded her story by saying it was a relief to be able to make use of it. In a few hours, Max would be free, and they would take up their peaceful life again, just how it was before. The death of her first love would save her second love. She had looked into the distance as she said that, fixing on some ghost of the past.

The two men had shared a look: Fat Boy's wide eyes expressed wonder, Florent's frown expressed puzzlement. Her fragility perturbed him, and he set aside all her unfortunate similarities with his ex, who had a character of steel.

Against all expectations, Florent had agreed to go get the ransom money himself, as Harmony simply lacked the strength. He wanted to satisfy his curiosity about this woman, and take advantage of the chance to escape the closeness of his boat and these tiny islands. Fat Boy was taking care of his dog, to whom he was quite attached, despite all his grumbling about the enormity of the task.

The plane was already starting to descend. Less than a hundred miles separated Chicago and Milwaukee after all. The flight attendant went up and down the aisles checking that everyone wore their seatbelts, even though everyone knew that in case of a crash, they would all die. Florent tightened his hold on the elbow rests. He much preferred sailing to flying.

Once outside the airport, the cold gripped him. He fastened the black down jacket Fat Boy's brother Josué Hamlet had loaned him. Josué often traveled to Europe. The Hamlet family liked Biblical names, like many Caribs who shared this trait with Africans.

Over two years had passed since he'd confronted freezing temperatures, which acted like a whip to his neurons. They seemed to work sluggishly in the tropics. He worried he didn't have enough warm clothes, having brought only one carryon bag with t-shirts, underwear and a couple of sweaters for the three days he intended to stay.

He dove into the first available taxi and barely fifteen minutes later, reached Max and Harmony's home in the heart of a quiet, clean residential district. According to the inscription on the façade, the house dated from 1928, which gave it a certain cachet. A tiny garden separated it from the icy sidewalk. What a difference from the Caribbean!

He found the house neat and spotless, but lacking in human warmth. The furniture was too new, too modern. An impression due to the owners' absence, he decided. He headed to the alarm before it went off. He had only three minutes to type in the code, 0821, Harmony's birthday once again. He then made a tour of the ground floor, his carryon slung over his shoulder as if he were about to take off, although he would be sleeping there at least two nights.

A kitchen with a stylish central island opened to a huge living room, where a plush gray sofa in the shape of an "L" faced the usual flat-screen television enthroned on a white stand. Florent eyed the sofa as the ideal place to take a siesta, and soon – he was exhausted.

The small room to the left of the entrance was evidently Max's office. A solid plank of wood on trestles served as a work desk, and it held a laptop and a Clairefontaine notebook, its pages filled. A multitude of post cards were tacked to the wall above it, like in a company's break room. He read several. Most had been sent by colleagues at his old job, vacationing in California, the Bahamas, Mexico, Hawaii, the usual destinations for Americans.

Some papers lay on the floor, creating a little disorder that contrasted with the immaculate house. He picked up and read one of the hand-written notes. It was a scene describing some students sharing a meal on a boat, probably part of the book Max was writing. He opened the computer and turned it on, and found it had no password. The background showed a black sand beach and someone's bare feet.

Several Word document shortcuts showed up on the screen, one of which was named M.I.T.T., the same initials in the notebook Max had packed in his suitcase. Florent wondered what it meant. Something to do with the famous university? He clicked on it and looked it over. It was the manuscript of a novel. The first chapter was about some young students preparing for a trip after graduating from the Paris Institute of Political Studies, an elite university commonly known as "Sciences Po." The second chapter described their arrival in Indonesia. Florent copied the document to a USB key, then closed it, seeing nothing of immediate interest and figuring his emails and internet history would be more informative. Too bad Fat Boy wasn't there, but one last-minute plane ticket had cost their client enough.

He went back to the foyer, up the wrought iron spiral staircase, and into the guest room, where he would sleep the next few nights. The painting that hid the safe in there was a reproduction of Gaugin's *Piti Teina*. Two Polynesian girls, the elder sister looking up dreamily, with a protective arm wrapped around her younger sister's back. Its vivid colors made him think of the celebrated works of the painter from St. Martin, Sir Roland Richardson. He dropped his bag on the massive bed, which looked like a family hand-me-down, seeing how unfashionable it was compared to the furniture downstairs. The only other furniture was a clothes rail with some empty hangers, and a worn-out leather ottoman. It looked like the room didn't often receive guests.

He got busy with his main errand, unhooking the Gauguin reproduction carefully, even if it had no real value, then opening the safe. Packs of one-hundred-dollar bills filled it. What stupidity to keep all that here! But then, the couple didn't entertain much and there was no inquisitive cleaning lady. Max took care of everything, like a good house spouse. The only people in on the secret were the Clarks, and according to Harmony, they were not the kind of people who would reveal information like that. But her never having shared it with Max was pretty brazen, eroding the image of their symbiotic relationship. She had at least one secret.

Now he needed a cardboard box and some clothes. Harmony had told him he could find both in the attic. Following her directions, he went out to the garden behind the house, located a lightweight retractable ladder, brought it in and set it up in the hallway under the attic trapdoor. Once he'd managed to open the ladder and get through the trapdoor, he discovered there was enough headroom to stand up straight, at least in the middle. Empty boxes were stacked up on the left, exactly as she'd explained, as well as several huge plastic bags full of clothes, mostly summer dresses that she planned to donate some day. Today, though, they would serve to camouflage the wads of money. He grabbed one of the bags and a cardboard box, and was starting to back out toward the trapdoor when he noticed something strange – the length of the attic was shorter than that of the house.

The right wall was bare brick, which looked new, while the other three were painted drywall. A dresser against the brick wall contained board games like Scrabble, Monopoly, Clue. The same games he'd grown up with, as in many families, only these were in English. On the ground, he saw tracks in the dust made from moving the dresser. His intuition told him to try it himself, and there it was: an opening in the wall right behind it, as wide as a door but only about a yard high. Obviously, the dresser was there to hide it. Any room with such restricted access was intriguing to Florent, so he got down on his knees and crawled through. He couldn't find a light switch, so he activated his telephone's flashlight.

It was a child's room, a little boy's room to be exact. A bed shaped like a sportscar, red and blue, shelves around the walls holding lots of Lego constructions, and oddly, a sandbox filled with tiny paper umbrellas, the kind that decorate ice-cream desserts.

The room was spotless, a sort of well-maintained sanctuary. Meaning someone visited it frequently. Tacked to the wall above a little desk of yellow wood was a photo of a blond, blue-eyed boy about seven, his smiling face cheek-to-cheek with that of a girl, a bit older and more serious. He immediately identified her, as she still had the same aspect. He sighed, moved to the core.

A few words were written on it in red marker, in a round hand, "To Ben, my lost brother. I will always love you. You will always be with me."

# Chapter Thirty-Five

"You have to be a bit of a mythomaniac, even very much a mythomaniac. The problem with mythomania is that at times you lose contact with reality [...]. It's a notion that's difficult to explain [...]. You also have to embellish, you also have to cheat, you also have to lie to tell the truth."

Robert Lepage, *Episode 6, Contact, l'encyclopédie de la creation, Canadian television series hosted by* Stéphan Bureau

Florent compared the clinic's address to the magnetic card he'd found on the Flynt's refrigerator door. On the back was written, "Visit Mom every Saturday!!!"

It was correct, so he waved to the taxi driver to let him know he could leave. So this neuropsychiatric institute was where Rosanna Flynt lived. Like many establishments of this kind, it was located on the outskirts of the city. Was it so the residents could find more repose or so they would be farther away, less visible to normal people? It was definitely restful, being in the middle of a magnificent, wooded park. Swans floated across a pond, and along its banks, a peacock paraded in complete freedom. The place was quiet, peaceful, and the personnel Florent encountered were young and cheerful.

He'd contacted the head nurse the night before. Nurse Jenkins recommended he visit at four o'clock, as there were no meals, treatments or leisure activities then. It would be calm, plus it was a Saturday, so a lot of patients would be away, spending the weekend with their families, not to return until late Sunday afternoon. But Rosanna Flynt mostly remained there. Her case was too challenging for Harmony to lodge her every weekend, but she tried to bring her home for a day once a month or on a holiday.

Florent had fallen asleep on the sofa. Completely befuddled when he awoke, he wondered where he was, with whom, what day it was, but after two expressos, his spatial-temporal bearings adjusted. He then tackled the most urgent task: packing the ransom money into the box. Harmony had sent him countless messages, wanting to make sure he was doing everything necessary to deliver it. He took a taxi to the DHL office to make things easier, and feeling reluctant to wander a strange city carrying two hundred fifty thousand in cash in a box. Now that he'd sent it off, he felt greatly relieved. There'd been one problematic moment, when he had to list the value of its contents. He'd roughly calculated the worth of the summer dresses and "two books" he'd added to the list to justify the box's weight, then entered the sum of five hundred dollars.

In forty-eight hours, the box would be waiting for pickup at the DHL office in St. Martin. Florent would be back by then to go with Harmony to collect the box and discreetly complete the transaction. Should he alert the gendarmerie, even though his client refused? Max's kidnappers must be hiding in St. Martin or on one of the nearby islands to be able to collect the ransom money. They could nab them.

An attendant showed him the way to Rosanna's studio. It was extremely bright, as the curtains were wide open, and the south-facing windows showed nothing but wintry blue sky. Rosanna sat in an electric wheelchair, looking out. A news station blared its predictions for worsening weather and heavy snows. The attendant was obviously embarrassed by the volume, by how it showed he wasn't doing his job of looking after a resident, and after looking all around for the remote control, he grabbed it out of Rosanna's hands and lowered the sound. She looked at him, annoyed, then dove back into the news stream.

"Mrs. Flynt, you have a visitor."

"Is that you, Harmony?"

"Sorry, no, I'm…"

"Ben?"

The attendant broke in, "Of course not, Rosanna. You know that's impossible. It's a friend of your daughters, Florent Van Stetregum...?"

He looked at Florent, an appeal in his eye.

"Florent Van Steerteghem," he said, slightly irritated about his name being mangled once again, then approached the woman in the wheelchair so she could better see his face, discovering in turn a thin woman with the same blue-gray eyes as her daughter.

"So I can leave you two for now?" asked the attendant.

"Yes, thanks," Florent replied.

Mrs. Flynt scrutinized the newcomer. Aside from her daughter and Jonathan Clark, she never had visitors. After the accident, her colleagues from the fast-food restaurant had come in one long solemn procession, then their visits became fewer and finally stopped. Twenty years had elapsed since then.

"Excuse me for bothering you, Mrs. Flynt. I'm passing through the area. Your daughter Harmony suggested I stop by to say hello for her. She's on vacation in St. Barts, where I live."

He felt guilty for lying to this handicapped woman. Harmony had not asked him to make this visit, but he had to continue his search for the truth. Too much mystery, too many secrets, and as a result, lies hovered around her daughter. To relieve his guilt, he held out a bag of chocolate-covered almonds.

"Chocolate! Thank you, really too nice of you, sir. And did you also see Ben?"

"No, unfortunately."

"Too bad. He's an adorable boy."

"I'm sure he is, especially if he resembles his sister."

She smiled. She liked it when people flattered her children. They were her sole treasures. Harmony had succeeded in life, but more than that, she was a wonderful person. Rosanna was a little sad that Ben no longer visited his sister, because Harmony couldn't bring her any more news of him. That's why she constantly watched the news channels – sometimes, she would chance to see him in the breaking news.

Before leaving the institution, Florent talked to the head nurse, a severe middle-aged woman, tall and heavy in the waist. Nurse Jenkins was bursting with energy that animated her big brown eyes, which always looked astonished. She'd been furious with Harmony for a long time, even though she felt this was highly unethical – a medical professional must listen, and not judge others, even if they could not pardon them.

When Florent wanted to know more, she had been reticent at first. Patient confidentiality was sacred. But he had gently insisted, lying about working with the French gendarmerie in investigating the disappearance of Harmony's husband, and hinting they imagined some kind of maddening situation within the couple or their families that had proved too hard for him to deal with.

She ended up telling him all about the family drama. Florent had noticed this more than once; people who are reluctant to speak become especially talkative once they get started. He just had to prime them.

On November 30, 1996, the little Flynt tribe had decided to go to the movies. Rosanna, Harmony and Benjamin had been delighted with the latest Disney film *The Hunchback of Notre Dame*. The trip home would take no more than a half-hour. If they had only left a few seconds earlier or later, the tragedy would never have occurred. While they were watching the movie, the weather had abruptly deteriorated, and on a straight stretch of road, a car had skidded right into their path. Its driver, Kimberly Clark, was only nineteen, and she'd had a drink, several actually, in a bar with some friends. On leaving the bar, she had admitted to one of these friends, Betty, that she was tired and had had too much to drink. Betty had told her to wait a while, but Kimberly, impatient to go home, had just shrugged. Rosanna had not been able to avoid the collision. Everything had seemed to slide away, and she lost control of the steering wheel.

When she woke up from her coma several weeks later, the doctors doubted she would ever again sit up or speak or even communicate with her eyes. But by some miracle, she had sat up, after many long months of therapy in a private clinic in Chicago. She couldn't walk without assistance, though, and she suffered from severe cognitive problems. Her reasoning was off. When Harmony could finally talk to her, Rosanna had believed everything she said: that Ben was still alive, and lived with Harmony, who helped him with his homework and made sure he brushed his teeth, some of which would soon be picked up by the tooth fairy. And that she read him stories every night so he could sleep.

Since she was twelve, Harmony had lived with an imaginary friend, no other than her brother, who had died next to her, whose blood had splashed her clothes. Harmony felt guilty because she had served an extra glass of wine to her mother, and wondered if that had altered her mother's reflexes at the instant the accident happened. Blood tests proved the contrary, but her guilt could not be assuaged, not for all the scientific data in the world.

Luckily, Nurse Jenkins told him with a sigh, since her marriage, all that pretense had come to an end. Max Rousseau had been resolute, and convinced his wife to stop living in that painful mythomania. But for Rosanna, it was too late. Her damaged brain could not admit that Ben was dead, especially after so many years of believing the lies.

Florent had thanked Jenkins for the information, but as he left, he had the feeling she regretted having said so much. He didn't care – he had learned enough to help him proceed.

Harmony had reconstituted her brother's bedroom in a secret part of the attic. Did her husband know of its existence? And the day he'd bought the paella, she had said she was talking to a little boy on a bench. Had she relapsed? What else was she hiding from him?

He hailed a passing taxi, eager to get back. He wanted to contact EasyJet and buy a return ticket. At that instant, Fat Boy called him. It must be urgent, as he knew his partner hated spending his money in roaming charges.

"What is it, Josuah?"

"Hold on to your hat. Harmony and Max also signed up for a life-insurance policy after their marriage."

"You found that in her emails?"

"Yeah, man. I made a copy of the contract from the attachment. There's one interesting clause – she'll receive the benefits even in case of a disappearance, on condition that its duration is over six months."

# Chapter Thirty-Six

"Reason commands us far more imperiously than a master; for in disobeying the one we are unfortunate, and in disobeying the other we are fools."

Blaise Pascal, *Pascal's Thoughts*

Monday, December 12, 2016 – 3 P.M. The sky was clear, the sun had returned in all its vigor. But it hadn't been a bright idea to take the shared taxi bus. The spacious Hyundai van easily held ten or so customers, but Harmony felt suffocated between two corpulent Haitian women. Crossing Orleans, one of the island's most thriving neighborhood, was laborious, with so many stops, people bumping into each other, and double-parked cars preventing traffic from flowing. Wanting to avoid attention, she had overdone it by choosing shared transport. A blond woman among the black and mestizo population attracted attention. The trip seemed interminable, but finally she recognized the spot where she had to get out. She paid the two euros and made her way out, slowed by her fellow passenger's nonchalance.

The hotel receptionist had drawn a detailed map so she wouldn't go astray. At the roundabout, she took the third road on the left, then followed a road past a small commercial zone. She noticed a woman in fuchsia running clothes on a ladder, putting up a poster for a fitness club. She took Zumba classes in Milwaukee, the last one only a few days before leaving, but that time seemed to belong to some imaginary past. Max had waited for her in the cafeteria. He liked bringing her there so she could do the exercise she liked without the stress of city driving.

Coming to a second intersection, she turned right then immediately to the left to enter the Hope Estate commercial zone, a fairly recent development where dozens of buildings had sprung up, like mushrooms on a misty autumn day. Another vast development was nearing completion, a mall of some kind.

The air was charged with dust, most likely from the quarry on a nearby hillside, scarred and disfigured from mining.

She was glad she'd dressed in jeans and a dark polo. She was more comfortable like this, and she walked fast, her ankle held stable by her tennis shoe, with only an occasional ache to remind her of the terrible events that had taken place so recently.

Her heart started to race when she reached the DHL office. She glanced around to make sure no one was following her. Florent wasn't with her because the weather had gotten so bad up in the Northeast that his flight had been cancelled. He was stuck at the airport in Chicago, waiting for more favorable conditions. But she was glad he wasn't there. She didn't want to take any risks, and she had sensed how reluctant he was to act without notifying the gendarmes. It was better to make the exchange by herself. She would give them the money and Max would come back. It would all be over.

She had emailed the mysterious kidnappers with the date and time she would go to the Hope Estate office to pick up the package. They had responded with one word, "OK."

She pushed the door, but it wouldn't budge. She hadn't seen the sign saying you had to ring to enter. The employee behind the counter stared at her a second before opening, then welcomed her with a chirrupy voice completely at odds with the nervous tension shaking her. Enchanted at doing business with an American woman, he launched into a story of his happy voyage to San Francisco. He was curious about Milwaukee and asked her questions as to whether it was a city worth a visit, so she mentioned a city landmark, the Art Museum's "Burke Brise Soleil," a retractable sunshade that looked like wings, and the Basilica of St. Josaphat in Lincoln Village, created by Polish immigrants. That was about it for ideas, so she said Chicago was close to Milwaukee, and had many sites worth visiting.

Detecting a slight irritation in her voice, the clerk asked if he could help her with something. After showing him her passport and signing a receipt, he put the precious box in her hands.

Out on the sidewalk, she hesitated, not sure what to do, since the kidnappers hadn't given any other directions. She wandered about the area trying to figure it out. Was it safe to take public transport with that amount of money on her, even if it was in a banal cardboard box? Who would want to steal that?

Finally, she decided to head to the roundabout and wait where she'd gotten off the taxi bus earlier. She could always get into another and go back to the hotel. Concentrating on that, she didn't hear someone walking up behind her.

"Don't turn around, Harmony! Put the box on the ground and keep walking as if nothing was wrong."

"And my husband? Where's Max?"

"Don't get all excited! If it's all there, you'll soon see your sweetheart. And don't contact the cops, whatever you do, get it? Go back to Milwaukee on the date you'd planned, and he'll find you there."

She set the box down and stumbled on, feeling drops of sweat running down her back and face. She didn't at all like the mocking note in that voice, even if it was a woman's, a priori less dangerous than a man, and after a few seconds, she disobeyed the order and turned around, but the woman had disappeared. She caught a glimpse of a white Golf whose back door had just slammed shut. It took off fast.

Her clothes suddenly felt too tight and close to her skin, and even the air felt dustier, too thick to breathe. The roundabout seemed miles away and the sun too close to earth. She remembered Max's illness after they visited the Gustavia museum, and she felt she was in the same state. But she had to be strong, and push this dizziness away before it became an uncontrollable whirlwind. She absolutely had to get back to her hotel.

When would they free her husband? Why didn't they do it immediately?

She regretted not having awaited Florent's return.

# Chapter Thirty-Seven

"If I had to choose between a woman or a final cigarette, I would choose the cigarette – it's easier to throw away!" *Serge Gainsbourg*

"Still no news, Harmony?"

"No, Florent, none. I've sent emails to the address those guys used, but no answer. What really worries me is that my last email came back with an 'address not found' error."

"Why do you always say 'the guys' when it was a woman who picked up the money?"

"A reflex, I guess. I can't believe one woman, or even several, could do a thing like that."

"That's a bit sexist, but maybe you're right. The hardest thing to imagine was your husband being forced to follow someone in the heart of St. Barts. And then, he had to be locked up somewhere without awakening the least suspicion. There are plenty of day-trippers, but the island is so closed off to the outside world that everyone ends up knowing everything. At times, other people know more about the way you spend your day than you do."

"Maybe they brought him somewhere else, like St. Martin. Don't you think so?"

"You have an answer to everything. But you shouldn't have handed over that money all by yourself. That was stupid!"

Florent wanted to add that she'd done it deliberately, but he held back.

"I feel guilty for being out on this sailing trip with you," Harmony said. "I should have stayed at the hotel. I can't get any news out here or check my emails."

"Don't feel guilty. In two days, you fly back to Milwaukee. It's now or never, and I wanted to give you this little gift. I know your heart isn't in it, but you'll see – you'll feel more relaxed, and that often helps clear the mind."

Harmony didn't argue. After she had handed over the ransom money, she had returned to her hotel in the shared taxi, which was not so crowded then. In her room, she had taken off all those oppressive clothes and lain down naked on the bed, the air conditioning on full blast. Her faintness had dissipated, but then the frustrating, anguishing wait had begun. The woman had ordered her to go back to Milwaukee "as planned." She had wavered about calling the gendarmerie, but feared the kidnappers would hurt Max if they learned of it. And how had they learned she had that much money in the first place?

She had hoped for a new video with news about Max, and kept fantasizing about seeing him burst into the room. But nothing happened. No phone calls, no one knocking at the door. She had sent messages demanding proof that he was alive, and that night she'd awoken abruptly several times to check her phone. Nothing.

Once that long night was over, she went into a compulsive phase where she sent a storm of emails without a break. Still no answer. After one last try, she received the message, "The email account that you tried to reach does not exist."

Only then had she notified Florent, full of remorse. His flight had still not left for St. Martin. After a long silence on the line, he had hung up on her, and she hadn't dared to try him again.

Josuah Hamlet, aka Fat Boy, had paid her a visit with Tempest, and asked her all kinds of disconcerting questions, one of them being, "Are you absolutely certain you don't know Brandon Lake, the ferry deckhand?"

He had repeated it, asking her to concentrate on remembering. Why was he so insistent? It was the first time she'd ever been to the Caribbean. Josuah explained that Brandon had lived in the British Virgin Islands when a young Frenchman had disappeared from there. He was trying to find a link to Max's kidnapping, but Harmony saw no relationship. Lots of people disappear all around the world, so it must be a coincidence, nothing more.

Josuah had stayed with her a while, determined they should dine together. He brought her to a creperie in the little town of Oyster Pond, so she could get away from the hotel a bit. Tempest had stayed in her room with the TV on. Josuah claimed that distracted her, and when they got back, the dog was reluctant to leave her cozy spot on the bed, as if she had settled in for the night. Harmony wouldn't have minded – it would be less lonely.

Florent seemed different on his return from Milwaukee. In just a few days, his skin had lightened, but apart from the physical change, his bizarre behavior troubled her. He had landed Wednesday, the previous night, and gone straight to her hotel. As soon as she opened the door to her room, he had shocked her by shouting and calling her reckless for rushing into the ransom exchange without him. Then he'd abruptly calmed down, like a tropical downpour that unleashes buckets of water for a few minutes then veers back to clear skies.

His proposing this sailing adventure made him seem even more erratic. She had accepted though. She was desperate to fill the hours until her flight home, and being shut up in her hotel room was making her despondent.

Florent had picked her up that morning at Captain Oliver marina. As she watched *Bísó na bísó* maneuver through the deadly reefs into the port, she admired its lines and great size, especially when it moored next to a little motor boat. Tempest ran toward her, expecting pats and play time. Harmony had fended off as her drooling mug as best she could, generating loud laughter from other boaters strolling on the dock.

They had been sailing for six hours. Florent concentrated on steering, and rarely spoke or left his post. The wind had come up, and as far as they could see, the water was flecked with foam, the troughs between waves getting deeper, and the sailing trickier. They had just passed Dog Island, an uninhabited bird sanctuary.

Harmony took several pictures to divert herself, but she felt disconnected. An experience like this should have been a highlight of her vacation with Max. She tried to console herself by thinking that only a few more days of waiting separated them. They would both be home soon.

Florent left the helm on autopilot and went to the bow, and a few seconds later, called out to her.

"Harmony, could I take our picture with the ocean in the background? It's an old tradition – I like to keep a souvenir of my clients. And if you don't mind, I'll post it on my business Facebook page. You know, a little publicity."

Amused by his offer, she wrapped a flowery pareo over her bikini and started making her way to the bow from the deckhouse, where she had taken shelter from the spray flying over the trampoline. She looked around for Tempest, but remembered he'd gone down the companionway, most likely to snooze in his master's berth. She was about to go down and roust him out, as she wanted the dog in the photo. But Florent called her again, saying he had to get back to steering. He stood near the port bow, gripping a lifeline with one hand and his telephone with the other. She clambered to the bow and joined him.

Harmony felt like a regular vacationer for a brief instant, as they tilted their heads close together and smiled while he took several shots. She wanted to look at the selfies, but she never got the chance.

She suddenly felt herself lifted up and propelled into the air, then she fell backwards over the lifeline. Stunned, she fixed her gaze on Florent, whose eyes were fixed on hers. It was like one of those stupid games kids play, to scare each other by teetering on the edge of a pool and trying to push each other in. She couldn't understand why, though, and she had no time to react.

She hit the surface of the water, sank in and started dog-paddling toward the boat, struggling to keep her head above the choppy water.

# Chapter Thirty-Eight

"Why would you use poison if you can kill with honey?"
Bosnian proverb

"Are you busy?"

"Yes, Jérôme. Why, what is it?"

Yves Duchâteau had given up on requiring others to knock before entering his office, but it still startled him every time Jérôme Jourdan shoved his door open and rushed in.

"Will you come with me? Bernard and Eric are busy. The fire department called us to report a death in a rich guy's mansion. A woman had an allergic reaction to some seafood and died, even though they did all they could to save her."

"And why should we go? According to your report, it isn't a violent death."

"No, but there's a problem identifying her. There are two guys there, one of them a Colombian. He's the one who called and gave her name as Gloria Sanchez."

"Just because someone is Colombian doesn't mean they're suspicious."

"Except when the other guy says that's not the woman's name, and wouldn't stop screaming, and calling the woman by a different name."

"So they won't give up the woman's true identity?"

"Right."

"Let's go, then."

He didn't much mind taking a break, as he was frustrated. He wanted to send an email to the Montpellier mayor's office to verify his missing brother's birth certificate with the civil service department, and that of the friend who had accompanied him to the Caribbean, and since it was eleven at night in France, he wouldn't be able to get the documents anyway. Too bad – he'd do it another time. He hadn't even had time to work on the Max Rousseau case this last week. The commander had ordered him to prepare the mock training exercise, including the procuring of a cargo of cocaine at sea. Roland hadn't left him alone for a second, making sure he was getting everything prepared.

The days had flown by, and it was already the middle of December. He was annoyed, and impatient to find the answer to this case, and discover any possible link to his brother. He was convinced they were related, and he wanted to know the whole truth now – was François dead or alive? And what were Florent and Harmony Flynt up to? The missing man's wife said she didn't want to file an official complaint, and she had acted bizarre that last week, as if she'd accepted Roland's theory that her husband wanted his freedom. But Yves wasn't fooled – she was hiding something. Then Florent had suddenly left on a trip. He was back now, but wasn't answering his phone.

Yves checked his gun, then made a quick call to his wife to let her know he would be late for dinner. She liked him to warn her. In Paris, that had been nearly impossible, with his heavy workload and the risky interventions he was constantly making. Here, things were cushy. Nadia would give dinner to their daughter, then wait for him; she loved spending "alone time" with him on the terrace. The view over Chevreau and Frégate islets was superb. She never tired of it.

He followed Jourdan, who seemed unusually motivated for the end of a workday, alert, cheerful even. It must have been Claudia's visit a little while ago. Claudia was a street vendor, who once again had reported losing her identity card. She'd probably let it fall out of her bags of merchandise on the beach at Saint-Jean bay. Someone would eventually turn it in or advertise it on Radio St. Barts – they were good at relaying information like that. And for once, Jérôme had rushed to take charge of the case. The way he gazed at Claudia left no doubt. It upset him to catch his colleague lusting after another woman, especially since he was friendly with Jérôme's wife Christine. It's true she was a bit acrimonious, but she'd immediately taken a liking to Nadia, and they were constant companions, always up on all the doings of the island and supermarket specials. That was important, as on St. Barts, you had to strictly adhere to the household budget in order to make ends meet.

Ten minutes later, they pulled up in front of the Wallace villa. Normally, this road in this neighborhood was so calm. Nothing ever happened, aside from an occasional iguana getting squashed by a passing car. But since Max Rousseau's disappearance, things seemed to be converging around the villa: Antoine Brin found the woven basket there, a neighbor reported "commotion" there, and a woman died from an allergic reaction there. A woman with aliases...

The fire department had sent an entire team, quickly joined by the emergency room doctor, Ghassan Nasser, who had only been able to confirm the death. The body, covered by a gray sheet, was strapped onto a stretcher, and they were all waiting for the hearse to arrive – contrary to TV dramas, it's not the ambulance that transports the corpse.

Cédric Deruenne was caressing the inert body where the shoulder bone jutted out, tears streaming down his face. Several feet behind him, a good-looking Latino man was observing the scene with an incredulous air. Yves guessed this must be the Colombian, but he hesitated before going over to question him. This kind of dramatic situation required considerable discretion, and he always felt terribly awkward about starting in with his practical, concrete questions. They made him seem so heartless. But the sooner he got to it, the sooner it would be over with. He took a deep breath and launched in, choosing to approach the Colombian first, as Cédric seemed much more affected by the young woman's death.

"Hello, sir. Sorry for troubling you, but did you know the victim?"

*"No entiendo."*

Yves continued in rudimentary Spanish, the remnants of high school classes. All the man had to do was confirm the woman's identity and it would be over.

*"La signora, como se llama?"*

The Columbian paused for too long a time. Cédric stopped crying for an instant and the two men stared each other down. The Columbian finally lowered his eyes.

"*Esta 'Sonia Marques,'*" he said, holding out a passport.

Yves was about to continue when Jourdan decided to enter the conversation. Whenever that seductive Claudia got under his skin, he was filled with unusual energy, and as he spoke to the Colombian, he mimed his words with movements of his eyes and hands. Yves had to look away to repress a smile.

"But why did you tell the firefighters her name was Gloria Sanchez?"

Fernando Sanchez responded in a loud voice, broken English and Spanish, "*Muchos emociones*, the lady is get all balloon, *estaba panico. Gloria, es el nombre de mi hermana.*"

"If I've understood, you panicked and gave the name of your sister to the firefighters. Is that it?"

He nodded.

Jourdan turned to Cédric. "And you, sir, do you confirm that this is truly Sonia Marques?"

"Of course it's her, so stop hassling me about it," Cédric shouted. "You're driving me crazy!"

The two gendarmes didn't react to his anger. At least it proved his sorrow wasn't fake. Out of questions, Jourdan looked at Duchâteau, who in turn looked at the stretcher. He was in doubt, trying to convince himself this was merely another coincidence, but no, that name, that passport photo – it was impossible. He walked up to the stretcher and lifted the sheet from the face.

It was her. Yves had met her only once, in Tortola, when she gave him François' personal effects. Her face was swollen twice its normal size, but there was no mistaking it. It was Sophia, his brother's girlfriend at the time he'd gone missing. Her death here in the Caribbean, a few years later, couldn't be a coincidence. And then, that name: Rousseau! It had already startled him when he'd heard it at the gendarmerie the first time. But there were a lot of people named Rousseau, so he hadn't given it as much attention as he should have. Plus the first name was different. His brother had left France with his friend Olivier Rousseau. Yves had never met Olivier. His brother had only recently re-entered his life, and e hadn't had time to get to know his circle of friends. He had spoken to Olivier by phone before flying to Tortola. He had lamented leaving François alone in that bar, and felt guilty as hell about it, but all the same, he couldn't hang around the islands to meet Yves because he'd found a job as cook in the U.S. He had left his email address, and they had corresponded from time to time, but their correspondence had grown rare and then stopped altogether. The last he'd heard, Olivier was in Thailand. Yves wasn't yet a gendarme at that time, but now he had resources – he would locate Olivier, at any cost. He needed to contact Florent Van Steerteghem, too. He might have something new.

He called Commander Roland, who nearly choked when he insisted on having an autopsy performed for a suspicious death. Yves said nothing about his missing brother or his link to Sonia Marques. He needed to figure it out before they did. If he could only close this chapter of his life – whether it had a good ending or a bad.

What if Sonia had been poisoned? If the autopsy confirmed it, he would arrest Cédric and the Colombian. But he had to be patient, and not cause any trouble without solid proof. Not in St. Barts. Especially since they knew absolutely nothing about this Fernando Sanchez or his social standing.

He went over to the group standing around Sonia Marques.

"The body will be transferred to the hospital, as we're going to perform an autopsy," he said, before turning to Cédric and Fernando. "In the meantime, I recommend you two don't leave the island. You have to be available in case we want more information."

Fernando stammered that he had to leave in four days, and didn't see any necessity for an autopsy, as everyone knew she was allergic. He pointed out that they weren't the only ones present in the villa. Sonia had invited a friend over for a few days. A quiet man who had stayed in his room almost all the time, and whom she called "Stéphane."

Yves immediately sensed the Colombian had already had dealings with the police, with his smooth attempt to mislead them with a supposed roommate who was no longer there. But then, Cédric had also mentioned another guy, "who slept all the time," when he had come by to ask about the basket Antoine found. Another thing to check on.

But his priority was on getting the autopsy done as fast as possible, to rule out any poisoning, and then to find the connection between this affair and that of his brother.

For the first time in nearly seven years, he had a solid lead.

# Chapter Thirty-Nine

"You have to lie if admitting the truth results only in unhappiness."
Michel Leiris, *Fibrilles (Fibrils)*

"Florent!" Harmony shouted as she flailed in the water alongside the hull, which was rapidly sliding past her. "Are you insane? Come back! What are you doing? If this is a game, it's not funny!"

Harmony shouted louder, but to no avail. He was deaf to her cries, and merely watched her drop into the boat's wake as he nonchalantly walked back to the stern. Then he disappeared. She tried to stay calm, but the waves frightened her. She had competed in swimming when she was a teen, but being an excellent swimmer in a pool didn't guarantee the same ability in the ocean, especially when it was rough. She took a deep breath in between each wave, preparing for the next crest.

The sailboat was getting farther away. What was he doing? If this was a baptism at sea, it had lasted long enough. She absolutely must not panic, and she forced herself to keep breathing like she'd learned in yoga: swell out the stomach as you breath in, suck it in as you breathe out. Stay Zen. There had to be some explanation. It was all a stupid game Florent liked to play – what else could it be? It was a dangerous game, though, and as the boat got smaller and smaller, it was hard to play it down.

Suddenly, she saw Florent back on deck, a bullhorn in his hands.

"Harmony, you've been lying to us from the start. I'm going to come back close enough to talk with you, but this time, you'd better tell me everything. Otherwise, I swear I'll leave you here. Without fins or a lifejacket, I wouldn't bet on you surviving very long. The sea is going to get rougher and you'll get tired out, and even if there aren't many dangerous sharks out here, there are false orcas who won't like your being in their hunting grounds. You get it?"

Florent dropped the sails and motored the catamaran around until the stern was near her, close enough to talk without running her down. She searched for the rope ladder, but it was no longer in place.

"You can look for it, but it's up on deck, and I guarantee there's no other way up, especially with these waves. You must have heard stories of ghost ships floating around with no one aboard, because they all jumped off for a dip, and forgot to put the ladder down."

"Have you gone mad? What do you want with me? I'm going to drown here."

"Not right away you won't. I saw your swimming medals on the mantel in your living room. Bravo! By the way, I learned a lot about you in Milwaukee."

"What did you learn? I didn't pay you to investigate me! You were just supposed to send the money."

"Overzealous, I guess. Wanting to play at being a real cop. I discovered a boy's room hidden in your attic, and I visited your mother in her institution. You lived a lie, pretending your brother wasn't dead."

"How dare you go through my home?" Harmony said, between gasps. "What is all that to you anyway?"

"I needed to know if you were out of your mind, and what you were capable of doing."

She was starting to tire out, but launched into a loud reply. "My brother – that's as far as it ever went. I was twelve when we got into the accident, when Kimberly Clark crashed into us."

She stopped to gasp some air into her lungs before continuing.

"She lost control of her car because of the weather. My brother died instantly, and my mom almost died. You saw her – she's only the shadow of what she was. Jonathan and Katreen Clark, the girl's parents, took care of me after that."

She choked on some water, coughed for a while, and took a deep breath.

"I wasn't brave enough to tell my mother the truth, so I told her what she wanted to hear. Ben became my imaginary friend, but when I met Max, I had to end all that, so I moved his room up there."

She was hardly able to see through the foam now, or keep her head above it. She screamed her next words hysterically: "Let me come aboard – I'm cold and I don't want to drown! I want to see Max again. I didn't go through all that just to die out here!"

Florent stared at her, wanting to believe her words. She was only half-crazy, then, like most people. He didn't feel she was capable of organizing her husband's abduction just to collect from the insurance company, and she had never touched the money in her house, which was hers to begin with. She was far from being immoral, and it was obvious she loved her husband.

This wasn't the first time Florent had pushed a woman overboard to get at the truth. People confess everything with the sea and its waves ready to engulf them. He'd done it with Lise, and she'd finally admitted what she'd done. She had filed a complaint against him in Martinique, but it had come to nothing after he swore to the cops at Fort-de-France she fell in by accident.

He went down into the cabin and released Tempest, who had been barking for some time. She knocked Florent over, ran straight to the stern and leaped into the water. The dog truly was a "St. Bernard of the Sea." Harmony grabbed her neck She was out of breath and exhausted from struggling against the waves, and ashamed she'd had to admit to a part of her life she was not proud of, especially her fantasy concerning her brother. Right after her fiancé's death, it had gotten much worse. That's why she had taken Ben on vacation to Florida to the amusement parks. He had accompanied her everywhere until she met Max, only reappearing on that bench in St. Barts. Whenever she got mixed up in stressful events, he was there, and he did her good. But no one would ever understand that.

Florent had discovered part of her secret life, but she still hadn't told him everything. She had resisted. Not all truths are meant to be revealed, and if she hadn't notified the gendarmes about the ransom money, it was because she was afraid they would demand to know where it came from, leading to more questions, maybe even the reopening of the investigation into her fiancé's death.

She had held out all these years, so it would be idiotic to crack now.

She would be home in two days, and could forget this miserable vacation. And Max would be returned to her.

# Chapter Forty

"The worst thing about finally putting together a puzzle is finding there are missing pieces. He came back and left nothing behind but a message: 'Come find me,' and I will. There are no secrets in life, just hidden truths that lie beneath the surface."
*Dexter, Season 1 quote*

January 6, 2017. A warm, gentle sea breeze was coming in through the jalousies and circulating throughout the apartment Yves and his wife rented. A St. Barts couple had renovated it into a cozy dwelling for their son, who had churlishly fled to Guadeloupe to escape them. This suited Yves and Nadia just fine, as they were housed like kings. Procuring a three-bedroom apartment on this island was a real exploit, especially since Nadia had not wanted to live with the other families in the homes near the fort.

Maya was down for her long afternoon nap, and Nadia had rushed out so she wouldn't be late again for her aqua-gym class. The perfect chance to reflect on all the questions torturing him, such as why Sonia Marques was on the island, or if anyone was behind her death. He had scribbled down all kinds of hypotheses and juggled them this way and that in his head, but nothing fit. Pieces were missing. The autopsy results had come back from the coroner in Guadeloupe, showing Sonia Marques had indeed died from anaphylactic shock after ingesting seafood. They had even gotten hold of an old medical file from a hospital in Valenciennes where she had received care until adolescence. The second of six children, she'd suffered from eczema, asthma and food allergies. She'd also been psychoanalyzed for behavioral problems by a child psychiatrist, who concluded she had rejected her social and family environment. She had abruptly left home when she turned eighteen.

When her mother was informed of her death, all she said was, "I knew she would end badly. So she wanted to live in the tropics? Too bad for her." And when they announced the expense for bringing her body home: "She has to annoy us to the very end, that one." A child that had not been loved when alive would not be loved when dead.

Yves had counted on the forensic analysis to arrest Cédric Deruenne and Fernando Sanchez, but as soon as they were exonerated, Sanchez took the first flight for Miami. Deruenne started spending most of his time between Florent's yacht and the Wallace villa.

No murder meant no investigation, but Yves was convinced his brother's disappearance was linked to Sonia's death and Max's disappearance. And Cédric had let slip a precious bit of information: Sonia Marques had lived in Miami and worked as a hotel receptionist. Harmony had said she and Max met in Miami. Too many coincidences rule out "coincidence."

Yves tried to worm out some info from Florent, for he was certain he played a pivotal role in the case. But Florent was evasive, and now Harmony Flynt had gone home, claiming her husband had sent her a message online.

Before leaving, she called Commander Roland, who had smirked with delight as he lectured her. "You see, Madame, we were right. Your husband left on his own behalf. Once again, the public funds of the French people spent in vain. It costs dearly to organize a search at sea in the middle of the night; plus we brought out the helicopter. The next time your husband runs away, maybe you'll wait a few days before calling the police."

Florent had confirmed that she was his client, which amounted to saying he couldn't reveal everything to Yves. Private eyes were worse than defense lawyers in that respect. If necessary, he would wipe out clues, erase anything compromising to his client. And if she was still his client, it proved the "Rousseau case" was not yet wrapped up.

Yves kept cogitating. As soon as this enigmatic Max Rousseau resurfaced, they were going to have a long talk. Did he know Sonia Marques? Did he know François?

Maybe the manuscript would offer him a clue.

A little while ago, Florent had surprised him with an email with the subject heading "For your information." In lieu of a message, he'd written: "Any resemblance to real persons, living or dead, is not always purely coincidental..." There was an attached document, which he was now printing. The first page started with four initials: M.I.T.T., evidently the title of the book Max Rousseau was writing.

The last of fifty pages clacked its way out of the printer, and after checking on Maya, Yves settled down to read them in the hammock he'd set up on the terrace, a gift from Christine, Jérôme's wife. It was hand-made by an Amazonian tribe in French Guiana. Yves felt another twinge of disgust for his colleague. The pretty street-vendor had come back to the station to announce she'd found her identity card, and she was with a handsome stallion of a man, a surfer type many girls fell for: long, sun-bleached hair, chocolate brown skin, flashing smile, and Jérôme had been forced to abandon his dream, but not without recriminations.

He went back to reading. The chapters were short, rhythmic, and even though he hardly ever read fiction, he couldn't tear his eyes from the pages. Two hours flew by. He didn't even hear his daughter Maya whimpering, but when she started to scream, he came to. In his haste, he got tangled up in the hammock, and as he struggled to extricate himself from, he tumbled to the ground. He ran to her room.

"I'm sorry, little darling. Papa didn't hear you."

She held out her arms, her cheeks wet with tears. He lifted her from her crib and hugged her. As he walked to the door, he stepped on a toy and flinched with pain. Maya had tossed her toy teacups, plates and spoons all over the wood floor – her newest game. Suddenly, Yves stopped. The dinette, Maya's miniature kitchen, Max Rousseau's book, the missing diploma, the phobia about test-taking. His brain worked like a food-processor, and he finally had all the ingredients.

The missing puzzle pieces. Or so he thought.

He had listened to authors talking about their first novels, and the common factor was they often contained autobiographical elements hidden among the fictional parts; getting back at family members or friends, revealing a secret, lamenting an early love affair, admitting faults.

The chapters he'd just devoured narrated the arrival of three friends in Indonesia: two men and one woman. Lionel and Benoit were both orphans and had studied at the same school in Paris, "Sciences Po." Lionel had earned his degree, and already signed a contract with an international firm in Hong Kong. Benoit, although brilliant, more gifted than his best friend, had flunked out. His irrational fear of taking tests had prevented him from graduating. He would have to do his last year of school all over.

The female character, Clara, was Lionel's girlfriend. They had known each other since high school. The kind of couple who walk a tightrope between two skyscrapers, making the reader wonder which one would fall first, and whether they would pull the other down with them. An up and down relationship if ever there was one.

At the end of a night-long party at a bar, one of those disreputable dumps that Western tourists feel obliged to visit at least once during a trip to Indonesia, the lovers get into a fight. The party comes to a screeching halt and they leave, angry with each other. They walk a long time on a deserted dirt road and get lost. Old mattresses, broken stoves, construction debris and trash of all kinds line the road, and not being able to find their way, Clara and Lionel get even angrier with each other, trading worse and worse insults until they start hitting each other. Benoit gets in between them, and the woman takes advantage of this to push her boyfriend one last time. Normally, a push like that would have no consequence, but he loses his balance and falls backwards, in the worst possible spot. An iron picket wedged into the ground pierces his thorax.

They apply pressure, they call for help, but no one is around, and there are wounds that simply can't be treated with pressure and pressure alone. Lionel stops moving, then stops breathing, stops reacting to their shouts or the pain. The implacable domino effect had caught up with them. If the couple hadn't gotten into an argument, if they hadn't gotten lost, if Benoit hadn't interposed, if that piece of iron had been only a few inches to the left or right, none of this would have happened.

Filled with panic, Clara persuades Benoit to help her hide the body. They're in Indonesia and they had been drinking, and she is sure the authorities, known to be severe, will not believe their story. Benoit hesitates, but she trots out her sob story: she was a "poor Cinderella who never had any luck," with no father, an obese, unemployed mother with six kids, of whom she was the least beloved, who'd had to work since she was sixteen. He gives in.

They take the corpse and bury it on an idyllic islet, the kind where, in bright sunshine, the incredibly clear, turquoise water contrasts so greatly with their terrible drama.

Yves had been interrupted at the crucial moment, when Clara and Benoit decide to declare that Benoit was missing, not Lionel. That was the most immoral act. Benoit took up Lionel's identity, he took up Lionel's life, his diplomas, his future job. All with Clara's collusion.

"Lionel" was dead and buried on a tropical island, but "Benoit" was reported missing in Indonesia. Benoit, Lionel…missing in the tropics.

So M.I.T.T. meant "Missing in the Tropics."

Everything seemed clear, and shivers ran up and down his spine. Did these three characters represent Sonia, Olivier Rousseau and his brother François? and was Indonesia actually Tortola? Could Olivier Rousseau be the character Benoit? If so, then François was dead. Unless it was François who had taken the role of Benoit – yes, that may have happened. If so, François was involved in the crime. Was he living under the name of Olivier Rousseau? And what about Max Rousseau?

Now nothing seemed clear. How was he to unravel all this?

And how many more people were to go missing in the tropics?

# Chapter Forty-One

"Your time is limited, so don't waste it living someone else's life. Don't be trapped by dogma – which is living with the results of other people's thinking. Don't let the noise of others' opinions drown out your own inner voice. And most important, have the courage to follow your heart and intuition. Everything else is secondary."
Steve Jobs


After returning to Milwaukee from St. Barts, Harmony anxiously waited for Max to come home, or at least to contact her. But nothing happened – no phone call, no email. After a week of nail-biting, she got desperate and called Florent, begging him to keep working for her.

He had read Max's manuscript, M.I.T.T., and shared his personal version of the facts: her husband was an imposter, and he had clearly explained it in fictional form, in his novel. And that wasn't all. Cédric Deruenne had moved onto his boat after Sonia Marques' death, and was still there, licking his wounds. He couldn't get over it; he cried every time her name was mentioned or if a song on the radio included the word "Miami."

Cédric had also confessed his guilt about dumping poor Brigitte, and one drunken evening, a whole pack of confessions had come out.

Florent explained in detail everything Cédric had said about Sonia's plot: coming to St. Martin with Fernando, her Colombian accomplice; missing the ferry and hiring a fisherman to bring them to St. Barts; getting Cédric to help in exchange for her "love." All he had to do was pick up a man at the Gustavia lighthouse and bring him to the Wallace villa, and ask no questions or let anyone know about the man's presence. And in a few days, she would be rich, without having to do anything or hurt anyone! The man was not a prisoner, but she locked him up in a bedroom so he wouldn't be tempted to speak to anyone, and risk compromising the operation. She merely had to send a video of the visitor and then a load of cold, clean cash would fall from the sky.

Cédric had accompanied her to St. Martin the day she picked up a cardboard box a blonde woman left on a Hope Estate sidewalk. Everything went like clockwork. The mysterious lodger, after having taken his part of the stash, a cool fifty grand, had informed them he wanted to leave the island right away, and Sonia had merely replied, "If I need money someday, I'm going to count on you – don't forget it."

She then had to figure out how to get all that money to Miami without getting caught at customs. On that terrible Thursday, the man she called Stéphane had left for the airport to take a private plane to Punta Canta. Sonia had just ordered some cod accras from a take-out restaurant – she loved those crispy fritters – and she had been careful to mention they absolutely must not contain any shellfish. But Sonia spoke English with a strong French accent and the Haitian cook taking the order spoke English with a Creole accent. The Tower of Babel. That must be why shellfish accras were delivered instead of regular cod accras.

Cédric had gone to the post office, and Fernando went with him, as he'd run out of cigarettes and like most smokers, had to get some that very hour. When they came back, Sonia was lying on the couch, her face swollen, and everyone knows what followed.

Cédric had made a composite sketch of this "Stéphane," who had vanished with the money. His physical description and the clothes he was wearing left no doubts as to his identity – Max Rousseau was the third man in the Wallace villa. Florent remembered the square jaw, the dark skin, the blue eyes. And Cédric had taken him to the villa, where he recognized the room where the video was made. The taupe wall with the sunrise painting you caught a glimpse of in the video.

So Max's initial disappearance was a set-up staged with Sonia Marques. If her autopsy had suggested the slightest suspicion of murder, Florent would have had to reveal all this to the gendarmes. As a precaution, he sent the M.I.T.T. manuscript to Duchâteau, who could use it as he wished. But if Rousseau had usurped someone else's identity, who was he really? And what happened to the other man exactly? Accidental death, like in the novel, or was that a softened version of a real murder?

Florent had told Harmony all of this, without reserve. According to his theory, Max had stolen the money from his wife, and deducing from his novel, there was a good chance he was also an imposter. That explained his reticence in having his photo taken.

Harmony refused to file a complaint against Max. No complaint, no victim, no guilty party.

And the lone element that could have helped them was the video with the ransom demand, which, unfortunately, she had deleted, as the supposed kidnappers demanded.

After learning all this, Harmony had spent a couple of sleepless nights turning the matter over. It all held together, especially with the resurgence of that name Sonia.

But she had to find out for herself.

# Chapter Forty-Two

"I solemnly swear that I will tell the truth, the whole truth, and nothing but the truth."
Witness Oath

A few weeks later, she realized she had been walking right past a hidden message from Max.

One day, as she was straightening out his desk, she started looking at the post cards he'd pinned on the wall. All were from old colleagues or clients from the hotel in Miami, except one, from the Baie des Sirènes resort in Grand-Béréby, a beach in Africa. On the back, someone named Arnaud had written, "If you want to change your life one day, I'm ready to welcome you in San Pedro. Just come to my little restaurant 'Sous l'ombre du baobab.' Not too fancy, but you'll enjoy the sweet life. Diplomas aren't everything."

It was postmarked 7/7/2004, from Côte d'Ivoire, and it was addressed to Stéphane Cordier.

She remembered their last conversation on Shell Beach, when he'd claimed he wanted to spend his last years in Sweden, and then those strange words he'd asked her to repeat: "Appearances are often misleading. Sometimes you have to imagine the other person in the exactly opposite situation." He had written those same words in his notebook, along with these: "Injustice, birth, rebirth. Why do some of us succeed and others do not? Must a person be born under a lucky star? And for that, does he simply have to change his skies and find the one star that will bring him luck? Under a star of Western Africa?"

Ivory Coast was opposite Sweden, and it was in Western Africa. That old post card had been kept like a precious relic, a buoy to grab in order to start a new life. She could imagine Max living the rest of his life there. And there were other messages in his notebook that seemed written directly to her:

"Can love be sincere if it's built on secrets?"

257

"Will you be the one who throws the first stone, you who also hide a terrible secret? But I love you anyway."

The French restaurant *Sous l'ombre du Baobab* was situated on a splendid beach of San Pedro, which had the most beautiful beaches in the Republic of Côte d'Ivoire. She called, pretending to be a vacationer looking for a good French restaurant, and asked about the menu. The enthusiastic restaurant hostess woman had gone over the entire list of items, and even without her asking, told about how they'd hired a new French chef in January.

The following day, Harmony scheduled her vacation days for early February and bought her plane ticket, destination: Ivory Coast. She had landed the night before, and spent the night in a noisy hotel in downtown Abidjan.

The next morning, she was on a bus to San Pedro. She was astonished at how comfortable it was: air-conditioned, with wide seats that seemed new, a television in front to while away the time, even though the view of the passing countryside was amply sufficient. This road linking Abidjan with San Pedro was nothing like the many decaying roads in the United States, with their endless potholes attesting the lack of maintenance. It was shameful for a country that liked to consider itself *numero uno* of the entire globe. But it was too many trillions in debt.

The bus entered San Pedro. The frontier with Liberia was close to here. A lot of people animated the roads and plazas, lending it unsurpassed human warmth. She liked watching the African women with their curious dresses in bright, elegant fabrics. A few kids were running after the bus as it maneuvered into a parking space, making Harmony gasp, because the driver didn't seem aware of them. The bus stopped. Her heart was pounding; she was almost there. But one last effort was required of her – she hailed a taxi for Grand-Béréby, an hour's drive from San Pedro, and climbed in.

258

She had undertaken this lengthy journey to prove that Florent was wrong. Even if Max's identity was false, she was convinced their feelings for each other were sincere, and always had been. He couldn't have abandoned her like that, so brutally, just to get money out of her. He couldn't be like that. But it would be a foolish journey, even idiotic, if she didn't find what she was looking for. She may have mistaken the destination, but Harmony would follow her intuition and her heart. She had become a true adventurer – so different from when she'd started out on her dream Caribbean vacation.

Two hours later, Harmony was sitting on the terrace of "Sous l'ombre du baobab." However, there was no baobab, just coconut palms. In front of her, the ocean whispered calmness – no raging waves or heavy winds, and she could not remember ever having seen a sky with such myriads of stars.

Old Blondie hits played one after another, making her want to dance, even though she was a pathetic dancer. She kept hearing the sound of a spark close to her, at irregular intervals, then realized it was a contraption that attracted mosquitoes with its UV light, then electrocuted them when they hit the grill.

She had arrived in time for dinner. She had just finished dessert and the server, a sculpturesque Ivorian with long braids, was clearing the table. Harmony asked her to send her complements to the chef, to tell him the tiramisu was the best in the world, even better than the tiramisu in Miami.

Her heart started beating painfully, and her blood raced. Then she saw Max approaching her table, wearing a green apron and a chef's hat. She was struck at how thin he was, but his eyes were the same deep blue.

A few seconds later, the server was astonished to see the new chef passionately kissing the newly arrived American tourist. Frenchmen living in Africa had the reputation of being hot-blooded, but not to that point.

He released her and held her at arm's length, gazing into her face.

"So you understood the messages."

259

"I almost didn't. Who are you, Max?"

"I'll explain everything, down to the last detail, after my shift."

"Promise me one thing – you're not an assassin?"

"No, Harmony! Just an imposter, the victim of a blackmailer, Sonia Marques."

"Did you know she's dead?"

"Of course. I always read any news about St. Barts on the internet."

"Then why didn't you ever contact me? With her dead, your problem was solved."

"I preferred to wait here to find out what your reaction would be. Either you'd come or you'd denounce me."

"But you committed no crime."

"Identity fraud is punishable by several years in prison. Would you want to spend the rest of your life with that hanging over your head? Not to mention my helping that woman hide a body."

"I want to live the rest of my life with you. And I'll support you, and help you turn the page, for both of us. You do know about my first fiancé, don't you?"

"Yes. You remember when we first met? You were drunk. That night, you told me you discovered he was cheating on you, with your friend. Like anyone, you wanted them dead, but then it really happened. Jonathan Clark paid your neighbor to provide a solid alibi for you. Seeing how vulnerable you were back then, the cops or the insurance company could have incriminated you. Judicial errors are so easy to make, especially when you end up with a life insurance payment of two hundred and fifty thousand dollars."

"And do you think I'm guilty?"

"No, bad people are sometimes punished by something other than human justice. I know you're incapable of doing harm, except to yourself."

He looked at her fondly, then kissed her again.

"I have to get back to the kitchen. Wait for me, and we'll get together when I finish? I swear to tell you the whole truth, nothing but the truth."

# Chapter Forty-Three

"Maybe it's not blood bonds that make us a family. Perhaps it's the people that know us and love us anyway. So we can finally be ourselves."

*Cecily von Ziegesar, Season 5, Gossip Girl, television series based on the novel series of the same name.*

"What are you calling me for?" Carolina said gruffly.

"I want to ask you out to dinner. Are you free tomorrow?"

"No! Don't you remember the other day scolding me for mixing business with emotions? But thanks anyway, and stop by Casa Rosa sometime – if you pay, you can still get your little striptease."

Florent hung up. Carolina had won that round, a decisive KO. He would try again the next day and the day after that if she kept up the defense, but if her feelings toward him were at all genuine, she would end up accepting his invitation. He would take her to a classy restaurant.

He climbed out of his old Chevrolet, allowing Tempest to follow him. She hated being left alone, especially if there was a chance to see new territory.

It was time to make a visit to Brandon Lake and his girlfriend Tania, who lived in a Creole cottage in the Salines neighborhood.

Harmony had been communicating frequently with Florent ever since she'd left for Africa, explaining how she had tracked Max down, and gotten the whole story from him. She had entrusted him with the truth, and a new mission: to eliminate anything that could lead to the discovery of the truth and to her husband's arrest for identity theft, and to buy Brandon and Tania's silence.

True to her secretive nature, she was keeping her husband unaware of all her actions.

Harmony and Florent now knew the truth, that Olivier Rousseau, whose middle name was Max, was indeed dead, buried in the sands of a deserted beach on an islet in the Virgin Islands six years earlier.

Brandon and Tania had been in the Virgin Islands at the same period, working at the Bomba'shack, a local bar built of sheet iron and colorful planks on a Tortola beach. They'd witnessed something there, probably the fight between Sonia and Olivier, which had ended in his death. Harmony felt sure of it. Brandon hadn't been checking her out on the ferry; it was her husband he was observing, and that was also why Tania had been staring at them when they had lunch at Côté Port in Gustavia. She had done an impeccable job waiting on them, but on reflection, she realized Tania had stared at them too often, and far too long.

Yves Duchâteau had told Florent he'd seen Brandon and Tania the night before to show them a photo of his brother François, and ask whether his face looked familiar. Yves said they had both seemed more surprised than worried, and had assured him they'd never seen him before.

This assured Florent that the first step of their plan was working: make sure Brandon and Tania never said anything to the cops.

The second step was for Florent to buy their silence. He knocked on the door, whose white paint was dry and peeling away.

Brandon was on his guard during Florent's visit – he hadn't forgotten the strange way Florent had come back to the convenience store window to stare straight into his eyes. Still, he didn't regret confiding in him. He'd heard rumors about the private eye's methods, and he wasn't surprised when Florent signed a check, then paused a few seconds before entering the amount.

"How much to make sure you and Tania never talk about what you saw in Tortola?"

A little later, Florent was back on chemin de Corossol, heading to the beach where his dinghy awaited. The sea was smooth, but on climbing aboard, he found Yves Duchâteau, as impatient as a future daddy in the maternity ward, waiting to share his theory of the Rousseau case with Florent. He had unraveled the story, or so he thought.

The gendarme started out by declaring he was violating the law by shielding his brother François from legal proceedings, but hadn't he paid enough? An alcoholic mother, an absent father, a series of foster families, and much more. But François had come out if it, or almost. The day he'd failed his high school exams, the vicious circle had sucked him back in. He had left for the Caribbean with his friend Oliver Rousseau anyway, to try their luck in those old pirate territories where diplomas weren't as important as in France. Olivier and François resembled each other, like many young French from the South, with dark skin, and both had blue eyes. They also shared the same kind of difficult childhood, but Rousseau was an orphan.

Florent listened, without speaking a word. The gendarme continued in a monotone:

Sonia and Olivier had fought; Olivier had been drinking and had tried to take advantage of her, and when she pushed him, he fell, landed wrong, and died on the spot. François should never have accepted Sonia's proposition to make away with Olivier's body, but he was rewarded by being able to take on the other's identity and profit from his diplomas. But to call himself Olivier would have been too much for him, so François adopted the other man's middle name, Max.

If only he'd requested the birth certificate from Montpellier, as he had intended, he could have made sense of the story long ago.

During the six years since Olivier's death, Sonia had blackmailed François again and again. She had quickly learned he held a job as head chef in a prestigious Miami hotel, and she started milking him for money by saying she couldn't make ends meet. When her milk cow disappeared, she had found him again, married and living in Milwaukee. But this time she demanded far more. She knew how much money Harmony had gotten from her fiancé's life insurance because Max had told her, by a twist of luck, the night he met his future wife. Bad luck! But now Sonia was gone.

What did he risk by not opening an investigation into Olivier's death and Max's whereabouts? This question had tortured him night after night. But there was a risk, that of pinning the murder on his own brother, especially now that Sonia was no longer there to testify in his behalf, and explain the accident.

So Yves had chosen to reveal nothing. François, his only remaining family, had been lost to him all these years, and he didn't want to lose him again.

Florent interrupted Yves' monologue to announce he had a photo on his computer of his brother, if Max was indeed his brother. After all these years, Yves was finally going to see François again, still alive, and going by the name of Max Rousseau.

When the picture on the computer screen became sharp, he saw a man with a rather square head, blue eyes and dark skin. Similar, yes, but it couldn't fool him; it was not his brother. His heart sank.

Then he remembered there had been a third man in the bar with them that fateful night, the French tourist. Could he be involved? And the third man in the Wallace villa – he'd taken that for a ruse, but perhaps it was one and the same man. He was disappointed, but he would plod on until he got to the truth.

That's what being a brother was all about.

# Chapter Forty-Four

"We're all fakes on this whole world, we're all pretending to be something we're not."
Richard Bach, *Illusions*

"Harmony! Harmony, I know you're there. Why do you run away? You're not scared of me, I hope. Show yourself, so we can talk. We can start over from zero, without ever lying to each other again. You know we're made for each other, and what counts is not who I am, but what I am for you and what you are for me."

Max could no longer see her, but she couldn't be far, probably hiding behind a tree.

"Stop hiding!" he shouted. "You're being ridiculous!"

The road, deserted at the approach of dusk, was very close. He'd been following his wife over an hour but only lost sight of her some ten minutes earlier, and he was getting worried. He had to persuade her to come back to him. They would pack their bags and go somewhere else, where they could start again with new identities. He'd usurped so many already it had almost become a game, although it would be sad for him to give up the Rousseau personage. That was the sticking point. But she only knew the version he'd given her, so why had she run off?

She couldn't know the whole truth, that François Duchâteau and Olivier Max Rousseau were both buried on a deserted islet in the Virgin Islands.

François had buried his friend Olivier, whom he believed was killed accidentally through a bad fall caused by Sonia. She had claimed that Olivier was molesting her, and in pushing him away, he'd fallen and been impaled by an iron rod. François was infatuated with her, so he had believed her. This version did have some truth to it. The accident had been real, but the cause of the fight was different. Olivier had caught Sonia in the act of stealing his passport and diploma.

He had followed François, and found him digging Olivier's grave. When François went down into it to straighten out the body, he had approached and knocked him unconscious with the shovel, then knifed him. When he was dead, he laid him in the same hole and filled it with dirt.

It was all horribly simple. Could he have avoided killing the man? Maybe, but as usual, he had opted for the easiest solution. François knew too much and could have gone back on his word.

He'd first met Olivier and François in a bar, where the two friends were bragging about being former wards of the state, without real attachments or family. Such naïve young men with profiles like that were a gift fallen from the sky. Sonia had charmed François to get access to his identity papers and diploma, but François didn't have that magic piece of paper, a chef's diploma, which he so desired. So Sonia had improvised, and gone into Olivier's room to search for it. But he came in earlier than expected, and the fatal argument began.

Max knew he had all the competence required to be an excellent chef, but his phobia for test-taking had put a halt to his progress. A vicious circle. He failed because of the damn fainting attacks caused by his fear of failure. But with Olivier's diploma, he was able to realize his dream to escape from these islands and work in a chic Miami hotel.

But after six years of good and loyal service, he started to get bored. He realized he wanted to be a writer. And Sonia was demanding ever larger cuts of his salary. He wasn't a monster, and he'd never for a second considered eliminating her. He would never kill a woman, on principle. His own mother died under his father's terrible fist.

And then Harmony entered his life, and along with her, true love, marriage, a new start. Then Sonia had located him, furious at having been tricked, and demanding a lot more money. That's why he helped her plan his fake disappearance and the ransom demand. He had been subjected to her distrust, to the point she had locked him in a bedroom, but what Sonia didn't know was that he'd prepared an escape so clever she would never find him again. But now his accomplice was dead, a stupid error in a take-out delivery. Luck was on his side. True, he had given it a little push – he had called the restaurant a few minutes after Sonia and gotten the poor Haitian cook thoroughly confused about her accras order. And shellfish accras had been delivered. He hadn't expected her to die from it, but for once, what he'd so often wished had taken place. His conscience was clear; he'd committed no crime. It was the fire department's fault for taking so long to get there. He learned of her death only the following day, but he stuck to his original plan. He didn't want to go back to Milwaukee. He had to start from scratch once again.

He had kept that post card from his friend on the Ivory Coast as a provision. The ideal retreat, especially for a writer on the lam. He'd left a trail of crumbs for his wife to follow and rejoin him. His only error was in leaving the name of the addressee on the card: Stéphane Cordier. And the evening before, Harmony had asked him who Stéphane was. He knew he hadn't been very convincing when he explained it was a card he'd found on the ground. She seemed aware of what had transpired in the Wallace villa, and how Cédric had let slip to the cops that Sonia called the mysterious lodger "Stéphane." Afterwards, she hadn't shown much desire for him in bed, and this morning at breakfast, she avoided looking him in the eye, which wasn't normal.

Just before he had to start his shift, he'd gone to their small apartment to cuddle with her a bit. They lived right above the kitchen, as that was practical for him. As usual, he clattered noisily up the wood staircase, and opened the door with a smile ready for her, but she wasn't there. The French doors opening to the deck were wide open, the wind making the thin curtains dance. He saw that her purse wasn't in its normal spot on the stand next to the TV, and she'd dropped her phone on the rug in front of the leather sofa.

He had picked it up and found that a certain Florent Van Steerteghem had texted her: "I showed the photo to the gendarme. Your husband is neither the real Olivier, Max Rousseau, nor François Duchâteau, the gendarme's missing brother. Get out ASAP. He may be dangerous."

He had searched through her SMS history. She was in frequent contact with this Florent, and she had never told him about it. Plus, she had disobeyed him. She had sent a photo of him to this man, probably having taken a shot of his passport, as he had no others. He had run out on the terrace and scrutinized the surroundings as far as he could see. The access gate to the emergency stairwell was open, and figuring she'd run off that way, he searched all around the village. Luckily for him, a white woman couldn't pass unnoticed here. Léon, the cigarette-seller, had seen her heading toward the forest, most likely taking a shortcut to get to the main road, which led to San Pedro. He'd almost caught her, but now she was hiding.

"Harmony! Let me explain. Why are you doing this? You're a criminal too, you know. Wasn't it your fault that Steven Reardon and Megan Sutton died? We're the same, you and I."

Some instinct made him stop searching and run to the road, and when he stepped onto the asphalt, he could just make out her figure. Her blond hair shone out of the obscurity. She was sitting in a bush-taxi, packed in with a lot of other people.

He fell to his knees and started sobbing. She was the love of his life. Since the start, he'd believed they shared the same nature. Two suffering beings who just wanted peace.

Why would she reject him now, so close to being completely happy? Hadn't she killed her first fiancé and her best friend by fishtailing her car right in front of theirs? She had admitted the whole story the first night they met. Maybe it was an accident, her skidding, but the consequences had been fatal to the unlucky couple. The courts had judged it involuntary manslaughter.

Without Harmony, he didn't think he had the strength to take on a new persona. What identity was he to choose? Who should he be, and what should he do with his life? And would he have to commit another murder to attain it?

His quiet little garden and the hothouse he'd loved to putter in back in Milwaukee seemed a million miles away. And he would never have the children he and his wife had so longed for.

# Epilogue

Harmony dove under the sailboat, and was amazed to see a man dressed like a pilot and a blonde woman wearing a white nightie. Around their necks were ropes, hooked to the anchor chain. Their bodies hung in the water, gently moving to the rhythm of the current and swell.

She climbed the ladder back to the deck of Bísó na bísó. She didn't know who was the crazier of the two of them. She had her Ben, but Florent had "drowned' these plastic mannequins to fulfill his revenge fantasies about his ex, Lise, and her lover. Oh well, just another shock therapy, and if it helped him...

She wrapped up in a yellow towel warmed by the Caribbean sun. Tempest trotted up to get petted. Three plates were set on the table. One for her, one for Florent and one for her little brother.

She had to consider her future. Should she unburden her conscience by confessing everything to the American police? Explain how, in 2006, she had followed her ex-fiancé and her best friend, how she'd passed them on a straightaway, not seeing the oncoming trailer truck, and then had to cut back in so sharply it made her car fishtail and cause the fatal accident?

Florent broke into her somber thoughts. "Eat up, or the salmon pasta will be cold. Should I serve some to Ben?"

"Yes, but not too much," she said, still self-conscious about him supporting her fantasy.

Seeming to read her thoughts, he said, "And stop torturing yourself – you're innocent. If I were you, I wouldn't say anything to the cops. Plus, you have to consider your poor neighbors, the Peterson family. They took money to falsify the facts, so they risk getting into real trouble. And with your bad luck, you risk getting twenty years behind bars, or more. Better check if they have the death penalty there! Anyway, you've paid your debt to society. A brother who lives only through your imagination, a disabled mother, a bogus husband. I think that suffices."

"But not confessing is immoral."

"What the law of men doesn't judge, others will take charge of – you can be sure of it."

"What others?"

"Call it what you will – destiny, luck, misfortune, God, a goddess, your ancestors. But you were right to quit your job and spend a few months here to think everything through. Plus, in case you need it, there's the money."

Florent looked down at a black bag on the deck.

"It's yours."

"What? I can't believe it! Cedric handed the rest of the ransom money over to you? Of his own free will?"

"He's looking for forgiveness. And, after living in the Caribbean so long, he's like the people here, very superstitious. He feels the negative vibes coming from that bag."

"He's right. That's why I hid it away in my house. That money is cursed!"

Harmony nodded slowly, then said, "What about Yves – any news?"

"Yes. He says Stéphane Cordier was a young Frenchman who disappeared from San Juan in 2004. The very year Sonia Marques left home to go to Puerto Rico, and that's probably where their paths first crossed. Yves has traced him only as far as Liberia, and no one knows where he is now, not even you. But I can guarantee Yves won't give up hunting for him."

"How could I have been so naïve to believe a man like that loved me?"

"But he did love you, Harmony, in his fashion. That wasn't the question at all. The problem was he was an imposter, and probably a serial killer."

"I lived with a murderer, and I loved him… And to think I went looking for him without letting you know – I just wanted to protect him, at any cost. I'm sorry, Florent…"

"It's okay. You loved the person you thought he was. But the next time you get involved with a new companion, find out who his family is, otherwise you'll never truly know him."

"But he was an orphan, so how could I know more about his family?"

"So? Even an orphan has roots. He could have talked about where his parents are buried, or had you meet his childhood friends, or show you the places he lived."

"Tania and Brandon won't say anything?" she said, changing the subject.

"Nothing."

Harmony looked out over the turquoise water surrounding them, and tears came to her eyes. She wanted to forget, but how? Would she have to drown a mannequin, an effigy of her husband, so he would disappear forever from her memory?

**THE END**

Dear Readers,

Thank you for having read my story. I hope you enjoyed it. Please don't hesitate to post your comments on Amazon or write me via my author's blog:
www.valerielieko.com.

Thank you to Barbosa for encouraging me when I was full of doubt; to my children Roméo, Bélinda and Léonardo, three budding artists, always enthusiastic about their Mama; and to Angélique Bredeville and Arnaud Boucher, as well as Hélène Bernier, who offered me precious information about St. Barts.

Books by Valérie Lieko:

Romantic suspense novel:

*Hide and Seek Paris-SXM* (*Chassé-croisé Paris SXM*)

Fantasy series, four tomes:

*Black Jack Caraïbe Tome 1 La Dame de Cœur*
*Black Jack Caraïbe Tome 2 La Dame de Pique*
*Black Jack Caraïbe Tome 3 Le Roi de Carreau*
*Black Jack Caraïbe Tome 4 L'As de Trèfle*

Crime fiction:

*Mercure rouge*

Independently published
ISBN: 979 8560669737

Made in the USA
Monee, IL
07 December 2020